THE BOOK OF SAMUEL

Erik Raschke

THE BOOK OF SAMUEL

St. Martin's Griffin ⚛ New York

THE BOOK OF SAMUEL. Copyright © 2009 by Erik Raschke. All rights reserved. Printed in the United States of America. For information address St. Martin's Press, 175 Fifth Avenue, New York, N.Y. 10010.

www.stmartins.com

Design by Kathryn Parise

LIBRARY OF CONGRESS CATALOGING-IN-PUBLICATION DATA

Raschke, Erik.
    The book of Samuel / Erik Raschke. — 1st ed.
        p. cm.
    Summary: Living with his religious father, feminist mother, and racist grand-mother in Denver, Colorado, during the early 1980s, twelve-year-old Samuel Gerard relates his school adventures and deals with his own prejudices towards Mexican immigrants.
    ISBN 978-0-312-37969-8
    [1. Self-perception—Fiction.   2. Prejudices—Fiction.   3. Fathers and sons—Fiction.   4. Denver (Colo.)—History—20th century—Fiction.]   I. Title.
    PZ7.R18142Bo 2009
    [Fic]—dc22

                                                                            2009016677

First Edition: October 2009

10   9   8   7   6   5   4   3   2   1

For my mother, Lorita
(1945–2008)

Part One

On the day that I finally reached heaven, no one was watching, which is what my mom said always happened with great achievements. I pedaled over to Jonathon and Jesse. They were looking away from me, toward the far end of the bike jumps, eyebrows dipped into unibrows.

"Did you see me?" I said. "Made it to heaven. I touched the bottom branch."

"That's not heaven anymore," Jesse said over his shoulder. "Heaven's the third branch."

"I thought Ms. Universe's underpants was the third branch."

"You weren't here yesterday. Heaven now comes after Ms. Universe's underpants. The first branch isn't anything, but in order for it to count, you have to touch it and say 'Olivia Newton-John' three times. Also, both wheels have to be in the air. Then you can try for Ms. Universe's underpants."

The rules were always changing, but usually I got a vote in how. The day before, unfortunately, I had to straighten up my room, clean the bathroom, and mow the back lawn with our stupid push mower.

"Them." Jonathon nodded toward the distance. "They're why we changed the rules."

I pushed between Jonathon and Jesse and scanned the drainage gulch below. A group of Mexicans were standing on the opposite hill, on Tina Turner's Tabletop. Tina Turner's Tabletop was more of a ridge, made flat by the weight of a busted yellow bulldozer that had been there before even Tina Turner was born. It was the steepest side of the gulch, therefore the best starting point for the jumps.

Since the Mexicans were all standing in a row, the difference in their sizes and widths was more noticeable. Some were as tall as Jesse and me, and others were as short as third graders. They all had different haircuts or T-shirts and different-colored shoes or jackets but the same light brown skin.

"They were here yesterday," Jesse grumbled. "Them and their Huffys."

I couldn't think of a single white kid who would ride a Huffy within a mile of the jumps. In fact, I knew of only two white kids who owned Huffys, Orson Meyer and Carletta Mure, but no one took them seriously because they were Mormons.

"Look at 'em." Jonathon scowled, the freckles on his forehead coming together.

"They should get their own jumps," Jesse added.

"Look at 'em."

The three of us watched now as the oldest-looking Mexican crossed himself, started running, leaped on his Huffy, and plowed into the first jump. Before his front wheel even left the ground, his feet came off the pedals, and he crashed. Jonathon cupped his hands around his mouth and yelled, "Burrito bikers!"

"Stupid, stupid," Jesse muttered.

The shortest Mexican went next. He got a good start, barreled full speed into the first jump, flipped, and landed on his face. Jonathon and Jesse belted out, "HA-HA, HARDY HAR HAR HAR!"

A third Mexican attempted the jumps, but crashed so bad that he writhed around on the ground for several minutes. There was blood coming out of his knee, and we were all silent, waiting to see if he would die.

"HA-HA, HARDY HAR HAR HAR!"

That was when the Mexicans picked up rocks and sticks and started marching in our direction.

"See?" Jesse said. "They have no respect."

"Beaner bikers!"

We offered the Mexicans our middle finger and rode away.

✠

At the Dolly Madison Ice Cream Parlor they had the only double-decker, double chocolate-dipped Deuteronomy Delights in all of Denver. The owners, Gretchen and Clara, had hearing aids the size of car stereos and matching buttons that said MY BOSS IS A JEW-ISH CARPENTER. Jonathon, Jesse, and I plopped down on our regular vinyl stools as if we had just worked an eight-hour shift moving pianos.

"*Soldier of Fortune*!"

Jonathon headed toward a full rack of *Highlights* and *Rocky Mountain Hunter* magazines. Since he was skinnier than Jesse and me, he slid between the counter and the stools and reached for the magazine. Strands of his big old fluffy red hair got in my face.

"You got lice as big as mice."

We ordered three Deuteronomy Delights and went through the entire issue of *Soldier of Fortune*. Jesse and Jonathon went through it once more, just in case they had missed any hunting knives or submachine guns.

"What does this mean?" Jesse asked, studying the headline on the cover. "'S.O.F. Fires Up Russians in Afghanistan.'"

Below the headline was a photo of an American on the back of a camel. He was wearing Arabian clothes and holding an assault rifle in the air while a group of Arab-looking soldiers cheered him on.

"That guy," Jonathon said, tapping his finger against the American on the camel, "is helping those guys"—he circled his finger over the cheering Arab guys—"kill Russians."

"Cool."

"On camels."

"Cool times two."

Jonathon asked Clara, in his loudest voice, if he could have the *Soldier of Fortune* to use for a class project. She told him to be her guest. He rolled it up and stuffed it in his back pocket.

I ate my Deuteronomy Delight and said, "Nerd lichyth evol."

"Samuel's speaking pig Latin."

I pointed to the golden plaque on the wall behind me reflecting "Love Thy Children" onto the mirror behind the counter. Jonathon and Jesse began repeating "Nerd lichyth evol" until Gretchen brought us three plastic cups of water and we downed them like outlaws at a whiskey bar.

✠

People were always dumping half-full bottles of scotch, eight-track tapes, Polaroids, lottery tickets, and old televisions right behind the YMCA, which was a short ride from the Dolly Madison.

"There should be laws," Jonathon said as we rode. "No Mexicans allowed on bike jumps."

"That's why we changed the order of the branches," Jesse told me. "We made it impossible to get to heaven if you're on a Huffy."

"Heaven on a Huffy." It sounded so funny. "Heaven on a Huffy. Huffy Heaven."

When we got to the big pile of trash behind the YMCA, I found a mud-covered lighter, wiped it off, and put it in my pocket. Jesse found a cowboy boot with no heel. Jonathon found a mixing bowl.

I tried to ignite three damp bundles of old towels in the YMCA Dumpster, holding my new lighter against them until it ran out of gas. Then I held my arms out and balanced on the yellow parking lines, one foot following the other. If I fell I'd be dead.

Jonathon and Jesse started throwing lit matches at each other. When they ran out of matches, Jesse threw a rock at Jonathon. Then Jonathon threw a handful of gravel.

"Hey!"

Mr. Holland appeared from nowhere. Even parents were afraid of Mr. Holland, the YMCA manager, because he was a Korean War vet and sometimes stole tomatoes from people's gardens. A gook had shot off half his nose and now he hocked loogeys the same way Sugar Ray Leonard spit blood.

"It's craaaazzzzzy Chuck Norris!" Jonathon yelled as loudly as he could. "Run. Run. He'll slice our throats with bamboo."

We streaked like Flash Gordons. When I looked over my shoulder to see if Mr. Holland was following us, I saw flames flickering through the metal lids of the Dumpster. Mr. Holland was standing next to the Dumpster, shaking a black Wiffle ball bat in our direction.

Jonathon, Jesse, and I scaled the fence, leaped onto a dirt path, and clambered through the gulch reeds, across the water, over the bike jumps, and up onto Tina Turner's Tabletop, far on the other side of the drainage gulch. From there, we could safely see the plumes of smoke rising from the towels in the Dumpster.

"Who lit the Dumpster on fire?" Jesse asked.

"Samuel."

"Nice job."

"Thanks."

"I'm not afraid of you!" Jesse yelled at Mr. Holland, now that we were a million thousand miles away.

We sat down on two half-sunken tires and caught our breath. There were sparrows flying everywhere. They were making more noise than Mr. Holland.

After a while, Jesse pointed in the direction of the YMCA and murmured, "No . . ."

The Mexicans had appeared at the top of the hill, just behind Mr. Holland. Mr. Holland, who was now pouring buckets of water into the Dumpster, had his back to the Mexicans, so he couldn't see them waving at us.

"If they do . . ."

"What?" I asked. "What? What?"

The Mexicans leaned their Huffys against the wall of the YMCA and inspected our unlocked bikes. Jonathon whistled through his teeth.

"No, no, no . . ."

"They're gonna steal our bikes!" I said, standing.

"It's Mr. Obvious."

"Beaner bastards!"

The Mexicans started laughing. And the three of us watched as they rode away on our super-expensive, ultralight, professional BMX bikes, leaving us with three stupid Huffys.

✗

My mother said that our street, Cleaver, was named after Eldridge Cleaver, the famous black activist, while my dad claimed the name was from the Cleaver family on *Leave It to Beaver*. Our mailman, Mr. McElvoney, whose bottles of schnapps scented our bills mint and peach, said "Cleaver" was derived from the tools of a notorious Denver butcher who minced adolescent boys.

"If he's so smart," my mom said when I repeated Mr. McElvoney's Cleaver version, "why does he always mix our mail with the Bernards'?"

The Bernards were two brothers, seven houses down, who drove Datsuns that spewed flames from the tailpipes. They also owned a whole gang of Rottweilers. They were never home and the dogs were always outside.

I rode back from the YMCA, along Cleaver, on one of the Huffys the Mexicans had left behind. The rear rim had a flat spot that thumped the ground, and the handlebars were so loose that they easily flopped backward or forward, depending on which way you leaned.

I stopped in front of the Bernards' house. The Rottweilers approached.

"I'm not scared of you," I said, leaning close to the fence.

The dogs began barking and growling and foaming at the mouth. I was so close I could smell their bad breath.

"Come on!"

One of the dogs started digging at the ground, tunneling toward me. It would take him years, and by that time I'd be at home eating a granola bar. I picked up a stick and slid it between the slats of the fence. The dogs yanked and shredded it in seconds.

"That's nothing. Meet my fists and they'll do worse to you."

They growled. I growled back.

"I know where you live."

As I pedaled away on the busted Huffy, the dogs continued to bark and shake the fence. I rode slowly, just to prove I wasn't scared.

Ever since my father quit his job as a psychology professor at the University of Denver, he spent his days sitting in our canvas army tent.

When I got home I threw down the Mexican's Huffy as hard as I could, but that didn't crack the frame or break a spoke; instead, the right pedal chipped out a piece of our cement driveway. I threw open the backyard gate and marched straight into my father's tent. Even though it was designed to be big enough for two people, he took up more than half the space inside.

My dad was wearing a DÜSSELDORF! T-shirt and Wrangler jeans that were rolled up at the bottom. His Bible was open and he was writing something in my old sixth-grade notebook. I flopped down next to him so that my right eye was at the same level as his canvas belt.

"Hey," he said, messing my hair. "Hard day?"

I shrugged.

"I'm using your notebook. Mind?"

I shrugged again.

"I'm going to read you something." He tapped the Bible.

I shrugged a third time.

"*The LORD kills and brings to life.*" He paused here and scribbled in my notebook before continuing, "*The LORD makes poor and makes rich; he brings low and he also exalts. He raises up the poor from the dust; he lifts the needy from the ash heap to make them sit with princes and inherit a seat of honor.*" He glanced over at me. "It's interesting. The words. The language. The inherent understanding of democracy. Don't you think?"

My father had always had hobbies—French cooking, model trains, maps—but he usually drifted away from them after a while. And my father had always read parts of the Bible as a bedtime story, tucking me in, licking his index finger, and leafing through the thin pages until he found a particular passage that more interested him than me. However, studying the Bible night and day, like he was doing now, as if it were a map to Treasure Island, was a hobby that my mom said had been around "too uncomfortably long."

My father shifted suddenly and the tent trembled with his weight. He stretched his left leg, out past the door flaps, and touched his bare heel to the grass.

"*He raises up the poor from the dust. He lifts the needy from the ash heap to make them sit with princes and inherit a seat of honor.* I can't stop thinking about that. That line." He scratched the side of his nose. "Hannah couldn't have children. And she watched her husband's other wife just pop them out, one by one. Imagine. It's terrible. Feeling as if she didn't have a purpose. She went to the temple every day and prayed like a crazy woman. Eli said to her, '*How long will you go on being drunk?*' and shooed her away with the promise that God would give her a child." My father paused, but the gears were still rolling. "And just think about how Hannah's story would be viewed today. Think what Judith Plaskow or even"—he chuckled, the exhalation sounding *rat-atat*—"Nancy Chodorow or even those New Body Feminists your mother hung out with in college would say. A woman praying for a child?" He nodded toward the Bible in his lap. "It's Hannah. Her desolation. The emptiness she must have felt inside. That's what's real. Desperation giving birth to something remarkable."

I ran my fingernail against the canvas. My dad started writing again. I glanced at my old notebook. He had scribbled over the front and back covers and in the margins. He had even written upside down.

Hannah conceived and bore a son, and she called his name Samuel, for she said, "I have asked for him from the LORD."

It was weird to imagine that there was some bearded man thousands of years ago who had the same name as me. It was easier to see a connection with myself, Samuel Francis Gerard, to, say, the actor Gil Gerard, who played Buck Rogers.

My father's pen scratched the paper. The wrinkles on the side of his eyes deepened, and his mouth opened only enough for me to glimpse the pink sides of his tongue.

"Can anyone go to heaven? Even someone evil?"

"Hmm."

"What about Ronald Reagan? You know. Ronald Reagan. Ronald Reagan."

Ronald Reagan's name rolled off the tongue like the curl on his forehead.

"I'm aware of who our president is."

"Ronald Reagan."

My dad looked up. I had made him smile.

"I believe you are referring to how your mother feels about him. But when she says he's 'evil,' she's just being figurative. The question you should ask is, What is evil? Plenty of people tell you what evil is. Evil is Gorbachev. Evil is Arafat. Evil is Castro."

"Evel Knievel."

"There's nothing in the Bible about what really constitutes evil. Evil in the twenty-first century, eh. But"—he tapped the notebook—"that's what I've been doing the last few weeks. Putting together a guidebook using scripture from the Bible. Getting to the root of what 'evil' is."

"Did you know that in 1975, Evel Knievel once jumped fourteen Greyhound buses?"

Father clicked the point of the ballpoint pen in and out, and in and out. I turned on my side and put my head in his lap. My father took long, deep breaths, exhaling through his nose. After a while he began taking more notes. The sun went behind a cloud and the color inside the tent went from the color of cash to February gray.

I closed my eyes and imagined that I was Evel, dressed in a slick white suit, blue and red arm tassels flapping as I sped along the motorway on my motorcycle. As the ramp got closer and closer, I focused my stare, cranked the accelerator, and gritted my teeth.

✶

I woke up an hour later, head in my dad's lap, hungry enough to eat an entire Chinese buffet. He was reading. I rolled out of the tent and went inside to make some popcorn. My grandmother was watching *The Jeffersons* and shaking her head every time the canned audience laughed.

"I did laundry too," she said, nodding toward the television. "It's not difficult."

"Do you want popcorn?"

"No thank you," she said. Then she turned to the television

again. "Look at them. Look at those wretched people. Well, at least you're a good boy. Can you bring me a glass of warm water?"

I was supposed to *understand* my grandmother and why she was always so angry, but *understanding* her required knowing world history. She hid in her attic during the First World War until soldiers destroyed her house and smashed the heads of her puppies. Then her family got sick and died, and she was orphaned. She made money by nursing crippled soldiers. When Hitler became president, she predicted another war and bought a steamer ticket to America. She married my grandfather and had my aunt and my mom. Then my grandfather got emphysema and died right after my mom was born. In order to support herself and her new family, my grandmother worked sixteen-hour days sewing and tailoring, and when my mom got polio, she took on a night job cleaning offices.

"I only wish," my grandma said one night as we watched Charles Bronson blow someone's face away, "that there really were heroes like these people on television."

When my mom wasn't home I would ask my grandmother all sorts of questions, just to see how she would answer. For example, if I asked why the Chinese were short, my grandmother would say it was because they sat on mats instead of chairs. The Italians invented welfare so American taxpayers could care for all of their children. Black people and cats had the same attitude problem.

Now, as I filled up a glass with warm water from the kitchen tap for my grandma, I thought about how my mom said the Democrats put fluoride in the tap water so poor people wouldn't get cavities. My grandma said that poor people should "get off their lazy butts and brush their own teeth." I held the glass up to the window and studied the water, but all I could see were little bubbles.

The Jeffersons was ending when I returned to the living

room. I handed my grandmother the glass and her fingers briefly touched mine. They felt like rice paper.

"Some people just take and take," she said, nodding toward the television, where the credits of *The Jeffersons* trickled down the screen. "And others give as much as they can. But I always say that doesn't balance the world out." She took a sip of her water. "Instead, it just makes one side heavier than the other."

She patted the seat next to her. I sat down; she took my hand in hers. She smiled at me and I smiled back and then we watched a commercial where two women in white lab coats dipped tampons in blue liquid.

✕

When my mom got home from her job testing polluted groundwater, I brought my bowl of popcorn out to her vegetable garden. She was wearing a white sweater, and her smooth black hair made a clean stripe down the middle of her back. Next to her was a pile of dandelion corpses.

"We should grow alfalfa," I suggested.

"What for?"

"To feed horses."

"The closest horses are at Cherry Creek. I think there are only two of them."

"If we had alfalfa, then people might buy horses."

"Is your father here?"

I nodded and she did one of her sigh/laughs. For years, my mom and I had waited on the front porch when my dad came home from the university.

"I'll get him."

She waved away my offer and plucked another dandelion that was next to a yellow polka-dotted pumpkin. She had planted so many different squashes over the years that they had become all mixed up and intermarried like the British royal family. She lifted the pumpkin from the ground and held it up for inspection. It had curly brown scars on the bottom.

"Remember when I took you to the botanical garden? Rows of perfect string beans and cherry tomatoes."

The botanical garden was probably the most boringest place ever.

"When I was sick with polio," she said, "I spent a lot of time looking out the window. I would watch those wild Florida plants choke and consume one another. They were so beautiful and so merciless."

She twisted out another weed from the ground.

"Can you get me the hose?"

I set down my bowl of popcorn and went to the side of the house where the hose was coiled around an old hubcap. When my mom talked about her polio, my head got all cloudy. It was hard to imagine her at the age of twelve, the doctors snapping her spine so it'd grow one way or another.

And even though it had been so long ago, she had never fully recovered. When the weather changed or she slept without her special foam pillows, she would spend much of the day popping Tylenol. Other times she begged my father to rub her shoulders and he would grind into her spine the same way he kneaded dough.

One night, my mother tried to show me pictures from back when she had polio and was stuck in the hospital, but I told her I didn't want nightmares. She had sighed, and as much as I hated to let her down, I had had to lie. The truth was, I hardly ever got nightmares. I was just terrified of anything that could prove that, at one time, my mom had been sick and helpless.

I turned on the tap. The water was cold and clear and I drank mouthfuls. Even though I wasn't thirsty, there was nothing better than drinking from the hose. I pulled it around the side of the house. When I came up behind my mom, she was wiping her eyes.

"Here's the hose," I said.

My mom took the hose and began to spray the dry spots on the ground, her head down, her eyes staring straight through to China.

"He's writing a book," I said, after the silence became too much. "He's taking quotes from the Bible about evil and putting them all together. Maybe it will become a bestseller."

"This isn't like all those other books your father has written. You know that, right?"

My mom continued to spray the lettuce, the afternoon light hitting the mist and creating a miniature rainbow. It was beautiful, but my mom hardly noticed the green and yellow and red stripes floating midstream. I thought maybe she needed a hug, but on the other hand, hugging her sometimes made her cry. So I stood there and uncoiled the hose while my mom coated the lettuce in fluoride.

3

Jonathon had used all his birthday money to order hi-tech weapons from the back of the *Soldier of Fortune* he got at the Dolly Madison. But they would take four to six weeks to arrive, so we came up with another plan to get our bikes back from the Mexicans.

"They go to the tunnels to have sex and take drugs," Jesse said. "They have to leave their bikes somewhere."

The tunnels were where the entire drainage system of Denver emptied out into a gulch. Movie tickets, pop cans, newspaper clippings, dandelions, candy wrappers, photographs, cotton-balls, dead mice, dead birds, tennis balls came from the gutters, flowed into the tunnel, pooled at the waterfall, and eventually poured into the gulch.

We rode the Mexicans' bikes over to the gulch and left them

behind a row of bushes. Then we hid behind one of Geronimo's glass bottle piles. His real name was Henry. But to us he was just the homeless Indian we called Geronimo. He was short and wide and had a round face with eyebrows so thick they shadowed his eyes. I had never thought much about Geronimo until we started looking at pictures of the Old West and learning about Indians in school. Our textbook said that many of the Indians were lucky to become comrades in the building of such a great nation as the United States. The Indians gave us many important things: hemp to make marijuana clothes, corn to make Fritos, and gourds. And although Thanksgiving was a celebration of friendship between Indians and Americans, usually, after eating turkey and stuffing, Jonathon, Jesse, and I would find Geronimo alone in the gulch, drunk and passed out.

Today, Geronimo was leaning against the bulldozer on Tina Turner's Tabletop, scratching his bare shins. He scratched and scratched and scratched, then stopped, then scratched.

"I see my bike," I said, pointing to the waterfall.

"Our bikes must be farther in," Jesse whispered to Jonathon.

"Shhhh. I'm hunting Mexicans," Jonathon said in his best Elmer Fudd imitation.

We slunk across the gulch and into the tunnel. The tunnel was low, and Jonathon, Jesse, and I walked like Igor in Frankenstein. Above us, on the street, we could hear forklifts backing up, people shouting, manholes clanking, and jackhammers jackhammering.

"Go hide it," Jonathon said when we reached my bike.

"I'll go with you."

They both shushed me and Jesse pointed for me to take the bike out. I walked away, happy to get my bike back but uncomfortable with leaving Jesse and Jonathon behind.

It was hard pushing my bike along the mossy bottom of the tunnel because the wheels kept slipping. I listened carefully for

Jonathon and Jesse, waiting for the sound of gunfire, but once they had turned the corner, at the far end of the tunnel, all I heard was the traffic roaring above.

When I emerged into the light, I headed straight up the side of the gulch, toward Tina Turner's Tabletop, pushing my bike in front of me. I didn't want to miss Jonathon and Jesse when they came back out, and I also wanted to sound the alarm if any more Mexicans decided to show up.

When I reached Tina Turner's Tabletop, I found Geronimo in the driver's seat of the bulldozer, chomping on a mouthful of Doritos, the artificial orange powder lining his lips and finger-tips.

"Howwww," I said to him, holding out my palm in traditional Indian style.

"White bread," he growled.

This wasn't the response I had expected, although in the past, Geronimo had called me much worse.

"I said 'how' like Indians in the movies. You're supposed to understand."

"White bread, cottage cheese, and a glass of milk."

I sat down several feet away from Geronimo, feeling sulky. He grumbled and turned his back to me, finishing his Doritos in solitude.

It seemed to take hours for Jonathon and Jesse to come out, and when they did my heart sank. They didn't have their bikes, but they both had bloody lips, and Jonathon's left eye was swollen.

I ran over. Jonathon was crying.

"I'm gonna kill them so bad," he stammered.

Jesse grabbed the Mexican's bike, the one he had left with me, and threw it into the waterfall. Jonathon did the same.

"You're gonna go back to your country," he yelled in the direction of the tunnel. "I'll kill you. And your mothers! And your . . . your whole family!"

We all sat down. As soon as Jonathon stopped crying, Jesse started. But it was mad crying, and he frantically wiped away the tears. I wanted to cry too.

"My mom will sue their Mexican asses."

"My dad knows someone in the FBI."

I didn't say anything, but I knew that Jonathon's and Jesse's parents wouldn't do anything. They didn't even come to parent-teacher night to pick up report cards.

✗

Jesse had to go home and clean the gutters, so Jonathon and I walked over to Dolly Madison and bought two Deuteronomy Delights. We sat outside on the Dolly Madison bench, in the sun. The sky was a dry blue and I was sure if I looked hard enough, I could see into space. The white tops of the Rocky Mountains, which usually looked like vanilla ice cream cones licked sharp, were browned by Denver's smog. The flags lining the rows of FOR SALE automobiles at Big Todd's Auto flapped in the wind. An empty plastic cup lay in the middle of Yale Avenue, run over and over by different cars, each time the *crunchety crunch* lessening. A man sprayed water against the tinted windows of the Midland Bank, moving the stream back and forth.

"What happened back there?" I asked.

Jonathon grunted.

"Did you fight them?"

"What do you think? Huh?" He nosed his foot around the sidewalk. "God, they're stupid, Samuel. I hate them. All of them. They have crosses around their necks, you know? Little gold-plated crosses. Not even fourteen K."

"Do you think God made Mexicans?" I asked, hoping the question might make him feel better.

"Doubt it," Jonathon replied.

"What about orange soda?"

"Probably."

I could tell he liked me changing the subject.

"Aluminum?"

"Duh."

"Communists?"

He thought this one over.

"Do you think God made Olivia Newton-John?"

"Oh, yeah," Jonathon replied, and grabbed his crotch.

✕

When I got home, my dad was digging a hole in the middle of the backyard. His shirt was off and he had a bandana tied around his head. The afternoon was getting hot, but when I sat down, the moist lawn cooled the back of my legs.

Instead of asking him what he was doing, I just sat quietly and watched until he noticed me.

"I'm digging my own grave," he said finally.

"You didn't ask Mom for permission?"

He made a "Whatareyougonnado?" face and stabbed the shovel into the ground. There were moons of sweat around his neck and under his arms, and his cheeks were red from the heat.

"What do you think?" he asked.

"Is it a swimming pool?"

My father shook his head and took a sip from a can of Coors.

"You want a sip?"

I nodded and my father handed me his beer. It tasted horrible, like grass-water. I swallowed and felt it eating away at my esophagus. I immediately gave the can back.

"Where've you been?" he asked.

"At the gulch."

"What'd you do?"

"Threw rocks."

A plane was flying overhead, leaving a slug trail. I couldn't hear the plane because Bill, the bassett hound three doors down, was barking, probably at Mr. McElvoney delivering mail.

"Your mom and I set out to live the simple life in the sixties," he said. "Sometimes I start to believe that simplicity is impossible in the world we live in. Especially in this country, where everything is just 'go go go.' It's nice to hear that you and your friends can still enjoy throwing rocks."

I smiled with one corner of my mouth. He looked into the sky and, spreading his nostrils wide, inhaled half the stratosphere. Gradually, he closed his eyes and squeezed his eyelids together. Then he opened them slowly, as if he was hoping to see something different.

"Spending hours writing meaningless crap that nobody understands except your colleagues, who don't really like you anyway. Or reading meaningless dissertations by students who know more about Carl Jung than they know about themselves. The pursuit of meaninglessness."

Bill stopped barking. I looked into my dad's face. It was so heavy with disappointment.

"Jesus said you can gain everything in the world and lose your soul. How I want to go back to those days when I believed I could affect people positively, when I still had heaps of hope." Then he motioned for me to follow him. "Come on. I need your help with something."

We walked over to the garage and set up a ladder. My father clambered to the top, near the rafters, dug around where we stored all the things we never used but didn't throw away, and handed me two thick railroad ties. We carried them out of the garage and set them by the hole.

Carefully, he positioned one tie on top of the other, took two pieces of thick rope, and fastened the wood pieces together. Then we slid the cross into the hole. He shoveled dirt around the base and tested its sturdiness by giving the cross a wiggle.

"Let's hope the tectonic plates don't shift," he said, "or we'll have to do it all over again. Can you go get me another Coors?"

I went inside and brought my father a fresh Coors, and he

drank it as if it was the best thing ever. He set down his beer and hoisted me on his shoulders, and we strung up Christmas lights. Afterward, we sat on the lawn and admired our gigantic cross.

"The symbol of a cross is so simple," he said. "But it has so much meaning."

I nodded. He nodded to my nod, licked his teeth, and said, "Before you were born, and I was going to school in Santa Barbara, your mother and I used to camp on the beach. She would wander up into the hills and gather wild plants and herbs, then cook them with vegetables from our small garden. I would gather mussels off the rocks and boil them over a fire. And I remember being on the beach and listening to the waves and the seagulls and your mom saying, 'You don't need God when you have nature.' Even though I loved the beach and the simplicity and the beauty, well, nature, to me, has none of the beauty of God. I told her so." He smiled like a new student realizing he's walked into the wrong classroom. "We never worked that one out. Your mom and I. We haven't talked about it for years. I guess that will change today when she gets home."

My dad lay down and exhaled. I lay down next to him and looked up at the cross. From the vantage point of an ant, it seemed enormous.

✕

My mom came home around six and sat in our Ford Fiesta for several minutes, staring at the cross.

"You've been busy."

"We made it without any power tools," I replied. "Like the Romans."

"Hmm. I see. Samuel, can you go inside and defrost the peas?"

It felt as if my mom and dad were always sending me into the house to do something. I turned my back and marched off. The minute I closed the screen door, they started talking.

I took the peas out of the freezer and set them on the counter. That was when I heard my mother shout something. I crept back to the windows. She was pointing angrily at the cross and saying, "What is this, Mark? I give you space to find yourself. Are you just so unhappy?"

"My kingdom is not of this world . . ."

"See the wedding ring on your finger? Your kingdom most certainly *is* here."

My mom swallowed and studied my father. Then she took his hands in hers. She whispered something. Suddenly my father acted as if my mom's hands were as hot as fire. He pulled his hands away and put them behind his head. Then he made two half-spins away from her.

"I turn on the television and I see what's going on. . . . Selling guns to fraudulent governments and turning away while they slaughter their own people. Keeping brutal dictators in power for our own interests. This country is being built on blood. When it could be so good. So beautiful. And I don't do anything. I sit here and enjoy the fruits of evil. With health insurance and an electric shaver and five different flavors of pie to choose from at the grocery store."

He was nervous. Cornered.

"How would Jesus handle the negligence here in Denver? Right in our own neighborhood. Look at Henry, for God's sake! Living in a gulch. Me, you, your mom . . . we live in a bubble. Cleaver Street is a bubble. And for Samuel that's good. That's what we wanted until he got older. But for me . . . I can't sit by and watch anymore."

"You're Mark Gerard, not Jesus."

With his free arm, my dad punched his waist, once, twice, and a third time. Then he closed his eyes, took a few deep breaths, and slowly reopened them.

"Once, I told you how important God was to me. You didn't

accept what I said. At least not in your heart. You just hoped it would go away. But it didn't. In fact, my feelings, my need to connect to something higher, have grown."

"That's not right, Mark."

"I was . . . I've always been embarrassed of my faith around you."

He let go of the cross, stepped forward, and met her eyes.

"God speaks to me," he said. "Ever since I was sixteen, God has been speaking to me. Even now I hear him. God has been speaking to me and giving me advice. He convinced me to go to college, to marry you, to be a father to Samuel. Everything I've done right is because I've listened to Him. Maybe I have psychosis. Maybe I'm bipolar and see the world in grandiloquent terms. But what if, just what if, God really is speaking to me?"

My mom winced. My dad stepped forward again and, this time, took her hands in his.

"If you love me, then believe in me. Believe that I'm not crazy. Believe that there is a possibility, however small, that God is speaking to me. That soon I will be able to decipher His message and begin to do what I need to do. Understand me. Trust a little. You and Samuel will do fine by yourselves."

My mom wiped her eyes and didn't say anything for a minute. Eventually she pointed to the fresh earth around the cross and said so quietly that I had to read her lips: "You dug up my string beans."

The next day, I was on fire.

We played basketball the whole afternoon and I made one free throw after another. Jonathon and Jesse tried to stop me, but it was impossible.

"How'd you get so good?"

"Pure talent."

"You usually suck at basketball."

I ignored this last comment and sunk a three-pointer. Jonathon and Jesse were sore from fighting the Mexicans, and ordinarily I would have pitied them like fools, Mr. T style, but I was having too much fun winning.

"You get in trouble?" Jonathon asked Jesse. "Not having your bike and all."

"Naw. You?"

"My dad hasn't noticed anything. He was supposed to go on a date with my mom. They got into a big ol' fight."

Jonathon's parents had been divorced for two years, but had recently started dating each other, as if they were teenagers all over again. The only problem was that Jonathon's mother was also dating a Russian who sold painted spoons in the Albertsons supermarket parking lot.

"He's miserable again," Jonathon said. "My mom and dad hate each other more than when they were married. All they do is fight over the fact that she's got another boyfriend."

"I wish my mom would start dating again." Jesse sighed. "Then I could have the house all to myself." He looked over at me. I was dribbling between my legs. "Can we take a time-out?"

I lifted, shot, and dropped another basket.

"You got something in you, Samuel."

"I'm gonna take on Alex English next."

Alex English played for the Nuggets and was the best center in the whole NBA. He drove a BMW and lived in a gated community five blocks away. We had once seen him through the window of T-Rex's Steak and Grill, making out with a *Playboy* Playmate.

"I want to go home," Jonathon said.

"One more game," I said.

"I don't feel like it."

"I'll give you guys a four-point advantage."

"You'll probably still win."

He was right. I was the best.

⚹

My dad didn't join us for dinner. He read and ate a tuna fish sandwich in his tent. In fact, I wasn't sure he had even stepped foot in the house since last night, when, cured by my mom's silent treatment, he had taken down the cross, pouting as he crossed the lawn with the lumber over his shoulder.

While the three of us ate linguini, Grandma started complaining about black people.

"And that clear plastic they wear on their heads," Grandma said. "All the time. Full of grease. 'You got Jiffy Pop in there?' I asked one of them. He gave me the finger. His big black fin—"

"We've been testing groundwater out at Rocky Flats," my mom interrupted, "where they make nuclear missiles. You know the water is saturated with pollutants."

"You're going to grow a third eye," I said. "Like the fish out there."

She aimed her fork in my direction. "I'll look exactly like I always have. So will everyone I work with."

"And you'll grow nine feet tall."

My grandma was struggling to hold her glass of water. My mom helped her steady her hand and said to me: "Then you'll really have to listen to me, young man. Nine feet tall. Wouldn't that be something?"

My grandma drank carefully, but a few droplets of water leaked from the side of her mouth.

"Finally," my mom said, taking a bite of food, "real work. My work . . ." She checked our eyes. "Let's just hope that over the next year our evil president doesn't take the money from our contract and put it into making more ICBM's."

Last year a military man from the air force base in Colorado Springs had visited our Social Studies class. After school he had a special "boys only" meeting. We asked him questions for hours and he distributed different sheets of important military information. One sheet spelled out the most important acronyms: NUCINT, Nuclear Intelligence; AWSCOM, Advanced Weapons Support Command; LCPK, Low Cost Precision Kill.

"ICBM," I sang now. "ICBM. ICBM. Intercontinental ballistic missile. Ronald Reagan. Ronald Reagan. Intercontinental ballistic missile. Reagan Ronald. Ronald—"

"Children should be seen, not heard," my grandma said, covering her ears.

My mom waved for me to stop.

"Intercontinental Ronald!"

It was hard to shut my mouth because the words were building up in my cheeks.

"You know what I heard on the radio driving home from work today?" my mom said. "The Russians and the Americans have enough nuclear missiles to blow up the world six times over! It's amazing, the energy and money we put into destroying one another. Six times over."

"Cool!"

"It is *not* cool. I can't believe you'd say such a thing."

I picked at my food. I could never say anything right. So I whispered: "Intercontinental ballistic missile. Intercontinental ballistic missile. Ronald Reagan. Ronald—"

✗

My mom ordered me to take a bath, which was fine, because the only other option was to sit next to my grandmother and listen to German opera.

I filled up the tub, stripped, and, making sure the window curtains were closed and none of my friends could have the slightest chance of discovering my secret, opened the sink cabinet and took my box of plastic boats from behind the cleaning products. Soon I was completely surrounded by destroyers, battleships, and aircraft carriers.

I was about twenty minutes into a full naval rout of German U-boats by American destroyers when my father walked in, lifted the toilet seat, and peed.

"How's the bath coming along?"

"Fine."

"Who's winning?"

"Us."

"Who's 'us' fighting?"

"Them."

"That's the way it should be," my father said, nodding his approval. "You know those moccasins we have hanging in the living room? The story behind them kind of goes back to what we were talking about in the tent. About evil and how it's perceived. Have I ever told you about my grandfather?"

My father's caterpillar eyebrows bent in concentration. He wiggled his penis, zipped, flushed, rinsed and dried his hands.

"Your great-grandfather was a sculptor and a philosopher. You know, quite a few men in our family have been artists and thinkers. And I guess that's common in Bohemia, where the word 'Bohemian' comes from. Rich in arts. Philosophy. Science. Learn this in Social Studies? Czechoslovakia. That whole part of the Hapsburg Empire. That's our roots." My father lowered the toilet seat and sat.

"Grandma says your family is godless."

"Your grandma's knowledge of history is very narrow. A few relatives are, were, atheists. Now, Czechoslovakia is supposed to be Communist. Well, Socialist. Not believing in God is the norm in that kind of society."

"Grandma says that Czechoslovakians are too dumb to be Protestant and too poor to be Catholic, so that's why they worship manual labor."

"Do you want to hear about your great-grandfather? About the moccasins?"

"Okay."

My dad steadied himself into the story. "When your great-grandfather immigrated to America, he joined the army. They gave him a uniform and shipped him out to the Dakotas to serve under General Custer. Every day he had to get up early and scout for Indians. It was miserable work, and his regiment hardly had any food to eat. But he liked being outdoors. He said in the afternoons he would find a nice quiet place, far from the other troops, and read or jot down his thoughts. He had so many plans here in America. He wanted to start a farm and have a big family and work together with his neighbors to create a real community, like his village back in Bohemia. He would sit by himself, mapping out his dream community, a communal farm, constructing a philosophy where everyone could live equally. His dream was to create a utopia. But a perfect society and the killing of natives don't mix. One afternoon, while your great-grandfather was out by himself, he accidentally bumped into a young Sioux boy who was trapping rabbits." He paused.

"And? What happened?"

"He pinned the boy down and covered his mouth. If he let the boy go, he'd call out to the Sioux warriors who were passing below. They would kill your great-grandfather. Thus no future. No me. No you. No utopia." My father paused, resuming in a quieter tone. "He slit the Indian boy's throat and held him as he bled to death. And according to your great-grandfather, who admitted that his grasp of the Sioux language was lacking, the boy's last words were 'White devil.'"

My father studied me to see if I was still listening. I docked two destroyers against my belly but kept my eyes on him.

"Your great-grandfather told me that as he watched the boy die he was so distraught, so horrified by what he had done, that he left his notebook, his plans for a perfect society, behind and, instead, removed the boy's moccasins. He said that he no longer wanted to create a utopian community. Instead, he spent the rest of his life wearing those moccasins on his own feet. He went around the country telling people about the violence Americans were perpetrating against the Indians." My father pinched the tip of his beard. "If you are aware that violence exists, and you do nothing about it, nothing to stop it, then that's almost as bad as actively participating." He paused, wincing, as if my great-grandfather's advice were a hunger pain. "A message like your great-grandfather's didn't go over so well in Manifest Destiny–era America. A soldier returning from the front and condemning his own army. It was especially bad in some of the areas that had a history of fighting the Indians. Wyoming. Kansas. He was run out of a few towns. The irony is that he was also called the 'devil' by those people, pioneers who had lost family to the Indians."

My father inspected the bath mat for almost an eon.

"Did you know that one of the top five greatest American battles was the Alamo?" I said, breaking the silence. "One hundred eighty-seven Americans killed more than two thousand Mexicans in eleven days."

My father looked up, stunned. "Did you learn this in school?"

I started to nod proudly, but stopped under the weight of his disappointed stare. My father gazed at the American and German warships that had taken a break in their battle for Samuel Island.

"Well, keep on the good fight," he said, nodding to my boats. "*I do not ask that you take them out of the world, but that you keep them from the evil one.*"

As he left, lost in thought, closing the door quietly behind him, I wished I had said something else besides a quote from my Social Studies textbook. I inhaled and slid my butt down along the tub until my chin touched the water. I didn't know what my father wanted me to say when he talked about the Bible and evil. I don't even think *he* knew what he wanted me to say. Saying something to my father, as I had done about the Alamo, in the end, meant nothing, while saying nothing probably would have meant everything.

As the morning sun was rising, I heard my father talking. I rubbed my face and threw off the covers. The sun was resting on top of the Salvation Army building. Birds were chirping like in the jungle movies. Outside, my father was kneeling in prayer.

When I was younger, I often fell asleep on my father's chest. He would read and I would wake up and fall back asleep and wake up. Lying there, I felt safer than I had in my whole life. But that was when he was a professor with a wine belly. This morning, stretching under the morning sun, he no longer looked soft. He was more like a boxer or a running back for the Broncos.

I opened the window and the wood against wood screeched. "How long have you been there?" he asked, turning.

"What are you doing?"

He motioned for me to come near him. He helped me climb

out the window. Then he put his arm around me, bit his bottom lip, and pointed at the orange horizon.

"It's amazing," he said. "There's no human in the world who could replicate such a masterpiece. We can only sit on our little planet and gaze up at it."

"I heard that every day one baby in the Sahara goes blind from all the sun."

He sat down and then I sat down. The grass was wet and the water soaked through my pajamas, but the warm August morning sun felt perfect against my face.

"When you were born, you had the umbilical cord wrapped around your neck. Twice. And you didn't want to come out. The doctors said that your oxygen level was low and if something wasn't done you could have brain damage. They stuck a suction cup to your head and tried to pull you out, but you were stuck. I prayed for the first time in years. I prayed that my child would come out and live a happy and full life. I even told God that I would do whatever He wanted if He just let you live. The crazy thing was that just after I finished that prayer, your mom pushed. I mean, she was delirious, but she had just enough energy to give that final push. You popped right out. For the longest time I refused to believe that it was because I prayed. I was just so happy to hold you. This little purple thing with big alien eyes."

The morning was becoming louder with birds and airplanes and cars. It smelled like grass and thin mountain air. Time inched along. A traffic helicopter hovered briefly in the distance, over I-25. Bill the bassett hound let out a few early-morning barks.

Suddenly there was a huge explosion. I thought it was an earthquake or a nuclear missile. My dad stood and looked around. I stood too. I was covered in goose bumps.

"What was that?"

"Shhhh," he said, putting his finger to his lips.

A gray puff formed in the sky. My father took my hand and I followed him down the alley. As we walked we could hear the screaming bullhorn from the firehouse, then the fire trucks honking their way onto Colorado Boulevard.

Two blocks later we reached a burning house. All the windows were shattered and the heat was making the curtains blow outward until they, too, caught fire.

My father and I sat down on an adjacent lawn while ash snowed everywhere. The firemen coated the house in foamy water.

The firemen began shouting and preparing to enter the house. We watched them break down the front door and head straight into the belly of the blaze.

More and more neighbors were coming out of their houses, standing around in bathrobes and whispering to one another. A few even came over to us and asked if we knew anything.

After several minutes, the firemen brought out the body of the woman who had been inside. I had seen her before. She used to sunbathe on her front lawn and once paid me a whole fifteen bucks to shovel the snow from her sidewalk. She was a short woman with long brown hair, weight-lifter legs, and enormous breasts. Now, under the sheet, there was hardly anything left.

The firemen came, huddled with my father and a few other neighbors and explained what had happened. I inspected at least seventy-three dials on the fire trucks. Later, as we headed back up the alley, my father put his arm around my shoulders. He had an amused expression on his face, as if the fire and the firemen had confirmed some idea in his head.

We stopped by the Bernards'. The Rottweilers were lying close to their house, all five of them keeping one eye on us and one eye on the smoke a few houses away. The explosion had been loud even where we lived. I couldn't imagine what it must have sounded like to them.

"In the Old Testament," my dad said, looking over at the dogs, "there were long periods where the prophets would be waiting for a sign from God. They had one ear to heaven. Their crops, their lives, depended on how God felt."

The O'Shanys were sitting out on their porch, sipping coffee. They waved, and my father and I waved back. They asked about the explosion, and my father summarized what had happened. Then, as we started walking home again, he said, "This morning we awoke to God's sunrise. But our existence is so fragile. The pilot light in that woman's water heater gets blown out. The basement fills with gas—"

"That wouldn't really happen to us?"

"We live with an angry God."

"What is He angry about?"

My dad leaned his head back, closed his eyes, but didn't answer.

"I don't understand," I insisted. "Why would God put out a pilot light?"

"He's sending us all a message, Samuel."

✖

When we got home, my mom was waiting for me. She hardly let my father finish his explanation of the morning's events before she said to me: "Go get dressed. I've only got this day free, and I'm checking things off my list. First is school clothes."

"Noooo."

"We're going to JCPenney."

"No. Please. No."

"Get dressed!"

I skulked away, taking my sweet time to get to my room. I tried to change out of my pajamas, but they wouldn't come off. The fire had welded them to my skin. I would have to wear them forever and I relayed this to my mom.

"I don't have all day, Samuel!"

When I came back out I could tell she and my father had argued again. She was nervous and distracted. He was in his tent.

In the Fiesta, I told my mother what I had seen at the fire, playing up how badly it had scared me. I suggested that I should probably stay in bed for the rest of the day and maybe miss the first few weeks of school, but she only turned up National Public Radio, pretending to be interested in a story about endangered flamingos. I didn't say how I knew that she was driving the long way to the mall so we wouldn't pass the burned house.

Unfortunately, my mom found a parking spot right in front of the mall, so even walking ten feet behind her bought me only one or two minutes.

I hated JCPenney, with all the old women in polyester pants with zippers in the back and name brands that no one had heard of endorsed by actors no one knew. The only good thing about JCPenney was a wooden escalator whose slick railing you could slide down twice as fast as on a banister without burning your butt. But when we went, every year, my mom always bought me the most boring, tasteless clothes that looked exactly like the clothes from the year before. Occasionally, she would sew on an Izod alligator or a Le Tigre tiger, but somehow it never looked right. The kids at school called me Izod Dorkwad.

"You're paying for the brand," my mom said once we had arrived and she had gone straight to the clearance racks.

"I know. That's the point."

"The point is it's thievery."

"That's not a point."

"In my book it is."

"You have a book?"

"I'm not going to continue this conversation, Samuel Francis Gerard."

After my mom selected the usual creased slacks, flannel shirts, and colored socks, turning me into a business casual lumberjack, she tugged me over to the register, frowning and shaking her head.

"I don't get how you guys live with yourselves," my mom

lectured the salesclerk. "I mean, not you specifically, because you're just a clerk and make what? Two or three dollars an hour? I really mean those guys at the top. They rip off the little old Nicaraguans on one end and the cost-conscious consumer on the other. I'm just trying to buy some school clothes for my son and it's liable to put me on the welfare rolls."

And a few minutes later: "Look at that total. That's a mortgage in itself."

My mom loaded me with bags of clothes that had been fashionable during the pioneer days. As we walked toward our car, everyone in the world was laughing behind my back, even the security guard, who winked as we passed through the antitheft detectors.

✖

Since I couldn't jet pack or teleport myself away from my mom and my JCPenney clothes, I settled for taking my bike. But even then, first I had to help dry thirteen dishes, take my grandmother's sewing kit down from a top shelf, sweep the porch, straighten my desk, and then, then, "Oh, one more thing, Samuel: the garbage," before I was granted permission to launch. When I peeled away, heading straight toward Jesse's house, I was going so fast that by the time I turned onto Iliff, the asphalt under my wheels instantly melted into oil.

I dropped my bike on Jesse's front lawn and strolled inside. Jesse's mom was asleep on the couch, a torn carton of cigarettes and an empty jug of wine on the end table and Peter Berg arguing about Israel on the radio. Jesse's mom had been drinking heavily, ever since last year when her now ex-husband, Jesse's father, began an affair with pageant winner Miss La Plata County.

Jesse and Jonathon were playing Frogger and didn't even notice as I jumped, stair-to-stair, into the basement.

"I read that NASA uses Ataris to launch rockets," Jesse was saying.

"They don't use Ataris to launch rockets," Jonathon said.

"I read it."

"You don't know how to read."

I said hello and sunk into an eight-ball beanbag.

"I read about NASA using Ataris in the newspaper."

"They don't tell you that stuff in the newspaper. They talk about terrorists and the Broncos. Besides, haven't you ever seen the big pictures of NASA? They have rooms full of big computers. They don't have Ataris."

"He's right," I said.

"Shut up. How do you think they steer the space shuttle into space?"

"Not with a joystick."

Jesse's mom stocked a mini-fridge with Pepsis. I took one out and opened it. I could drink three in one sitting.

"Stupid frog!"

Jesse threw his joystick onto the carpet. He always lost at Frogger. I picked up the joystick and Jonathon flipped Restart.

"They use an Atari to steer the space shuttle too," Jesse said, opening his own Pepsi.

"Give it up," Jonathon said.

"Everyone knows they use Ataris on the space shuttle. It's a national secret."

Jonathon hit Pause. "You're stupid. They don't use Ataris on the NASA launch pad, in the space shuttle, or anywhere except in your imagination."

"You want to fight over it?" Jesse asked. "Just like you fought those Mexicans."

Jonathon stood up, and then Jesse did.

"I couldn't see anything. I didn't know there were three of them on you."

"Sure you couldn't. You were scared."

Jonathon pushed Jesse. Jesse pushed Jonathon.

"I'll never get your back," Jesse said. "Ever."

"You can't fight anyway."

"At least I try."

Jonathon threw the first punch. Jesse threw Jonathon into the wall. Jonathon hurled the Atari at Jesse. Then they started grabbing everything they could—paperweights, forks, the vacuum cleaner, the toilet plunger. When there was nothing left to throw, they grabbed each other like wrestlers. Jonathon pinned Jesse and started choking him. That was when I pulled them apart.

"Stupid frogs!" Jonathon snapped, shaking loose. "Stupid Atari. Stupid NASA. Stupid Mexicans."

As he paced around, Jesse stood up and watched him warily. I ordered them to shake hands. Instead they hugged.

✖

My dad spent the day and the evening praying in front of the burned house. Later, as we were watching the ten o'clock news, the back gate opened. Clutching his Bible, my father went straight into his tent and zipped the flaps. My mother was about to cry, but didn't want to do it in front of Grandma, so she excused herself. She walked into her bedroom and closed the door.

Grandma changed the channel to Johnny Carson, who had a boa constrictor around his neck. She laughed and laughed and laughed.

"Them Papists," she said, wiping her eyes.

Around midnight I heard my mom crying. This kind of crying, the crying that sounded as if it were pounding down the walls, was the kind that was more pain than anything else.

I tossed and turned in my bed, shoving pencil erasers in my ears and taking them out. It was hopeless, frustrating, like seeing a kitten being tortured by a circle of older, tougher kids.

Twice in my life I had heard this kind of crying from my mom. The first time was when we were returning home from the grocery store and our trunk was filled with bags of food. We saw what looked like a Navajo family sitting on a median on Colorado Boulevard. The mother of the family had placed her little daughter out nearest the cars. The girl was propped up with metal crutches that clasped to her skinny biceps.

$ FOR DR., their cardboard sign read. And my mom had pulled over and dug frantically in her purse for change, but she had used her last nickel for the gumball machine, for me. Although they barely spoke English, my mom leaned out the window and apologized to the family, giving a list of excuses and promising to come back, until a car behind us honked. And then another. When she returned later in the day, they were gone.

The second time my mother had cried like this was when my father first set up his tent.

"How long is this going to last?" my mom had asked. "Your job. Your responsibilities. Mark? Your family? You can't just throw everything up in the air and hide in a tent."

And my father had just pounded in the tent stakes, the right corner, the left, and grunted simple answers. My mom had collapsed right there on our back lawn and cried, until my father silently picked her up and carried her to bed.

Around midnight, I climbed out my window and sat next to my father's tent. I could hear him snoring. After a while I unzipped the flaps and peered in. He was lying on his side, fully dressed, his toes twitching in his sandals. His Bible was under his arm, but I pulled it out as smoothly as a jewel thief.

I tiptoed across the alley, found a quiet place under our neighbors', the Wallacks,' elm, and using the matches that my mother kept under the fireplace, I lit Genesis, Exodus, Leviticus . . . The thin pages vaporized into a black ring, barely giving up a fight. But it was the sheer number of pages that made the task difficult. It took me almost an hour to burn the entire Bible.

I was hunched over as I did this. Hunched so that my back was to the sky. I was sure that I would feel the hand of God smacking me on the back of my head. But during those perfectly peaceful two hours nothing happened. Nothing. The only sensations I experienced were the warmth of the fire, the wonderful smell of burning paper, and the hope that my dad would give up his "hobby" and come back home for good.

X

The next day I slept until one. I would have slept longer, but my grandma kept barging in and complaining that Jesse wouldn't stop calling.

"You have to get over to Washington Park," Jesse said when I called him back.

"Why?"

"Our neighbor saw your dad. By the lake. He's gone totally nutso."

I hung up, dressed, slurped down a glass of orange juice, and rode as fast as I could over to Washington Park. It seemed as if I hit every red light, and every street that had once been downhill was now suddenly uphill.

When I finally reached the park I rode around the lake twice, eventually finding my dad on the bandstand, dressed in army clothes but not wearing any shoes. He looked terrible, his eyes dazed, a white crust lining his lips, his hair flat in the back and messy in the front.

"At first God came to me in a powerful explosion," my dad was shouting from his podium. "It was to wake me up from my slumber. To open my eyes to the world."

People in the park walked by, but no one made eye contact. Once they were a good distance away, however, they started to whisper. A bearded man on a three-wheeled bicycle told my dad to put "a sock in it."

"Last night God took my Bible. At first I was confused and asked why He had forsaken me. Then I realized that He did not want me to speak from scripture, but from the heart. And this is what I want to say. . . ."

A group of white boys, T-shirts hugging their bodies, sleeves cut off so that their tattoos were exposed, passed by.

"Stick it up your ass!" one of them yelled.

"Satan rules!" yelled another.

"We as citizens of this great country have allowed our eyes to be blinded to the rest of the world. Here, in a day where all we have to do is turn on the television to see suffering in Africa, war in the Middle East, and brutality in Southeast Asia, we still choose to do little or nothing about it. We, a proud Christian nation, shrug at the peasants being slaughtered in El Salvador with American-made guns. We say, 'There is nothing we can do.' How can we carry the words of Jesus in our hearts yet turn away those who ask us for help? How can we make weapons that we know will bring harm to others? Why can we not set an example for the world?"

The boys were all singing: "Duh Duh, shout! Duh Duh, shout! Shout at the devil!"

"I am here to speak the Gospel. My interpretation. The Gospel according to Mark Gerard. I am for peace. I plan to go forth into the world, naked, vulnerable, and human, just as Jesus came to us."

One of the boys, wearing a Judas Priest T-shirt, picked up a chunk of cement, wound up, and threw it as hard as he could. It hit my dad right in the forehead, leaving a long red gash. They laughed and started pelting my father with more rocks. I couldn't bear it anymore. I rushed over and screamed for them to stop. And they did. For a brief second. Before all three turned and put me in a neck hold. The boy in the Judas Priest shirt grabbed me by the legs and began pulling me around.

I screamed for my dad. I screamed and screamed and suddenly the boys let go. I covered my eyes and heard what sounded like punches. A few seconds later, my father was lying on top of me.

And as I lay there, my face buried in my father's neck, I heard the thud of their boots against his body. People in the park began yelling; there were sirens, and slowly the kicking stopped. The boys cursed and spit on my father. As they went away, my father prayed: "*Father, forgive them, for they do not know what they do.*"

After a few minutes, a group of people descended upon us. They asked over and over if we were all right. A policeman went to his car and got a first-aid kit. Blood was running from my father's nose, his right eye was swelling shut, and his lip was turning purple. Someone gave him an ice pack.

"Go home," my father said to me when the policeman was out of earshot.

"Aren't you coming too?"

"God is warning me. I must get moving."

"Dad?"

"Go home and pray for me. Today, God was saying I must do this alone."

He kissed my forehead. "Pray for me. Pray real hard. Pray God will let me come back so we can be a family again."

"I don't want to!"

"Go!"

"No."

He gave me a soft push.

"If you don't leave . . ."

I refused to hear the end of the sentence. "No. No. No."

I walked backward, away from him, almost tripping over a tree's roots. I grabbed my bike and rode across the grass.

"No," I repeated, when the park was no longer in sight.

✕

My mom made me repeat what had happened at Washington Park. And each time, at the end, she shook her head in disbelief, telling me to start over again. Then, when she couldn't hear the story anymore, she told me to take a bath and spent the next several hours calling friends and hospitals. But I knew, no matter whom she called, she would never find my dad.

I unleashed my American and German destroyers and sank under the water, submerging myself in the stillness of the tub, alone with my thoughts, leaving the boys' abuse floating alongside my plastic battleships.

What my father had done at Washington Park wasn't like opening a jar or screwing a loose bolt, nor was it like Jan Pieter's father, who lived only blocks away, kicking a soccer ball into infinity. It wasn't like Richard Berrit's father sawing logs in competitions or Les Lowenstein's father hang-gliding over Red Rocks or Harris Bolden's father swimming once a year in Lake Dillon, under the ice, wearing nothing but a tiny Speedo. What my father had done today, by laying on top of me, had been equal in worth to Erik Estrada's pulling a woman from a burning gas tanker in *CHIPS* or William Shatner's risking his and the *Star Trek* crew's lives by using the *Starship Enterprise* to block a powerful death ray. He had stuck to his beliefs. He had revealed his inner strength, the same kind of strength that separated Superman, Aquaman, Batman, and Green Lantern from the rest of us.

✗

My mom ordered a pizza for my grandma and me and spent the rest of the day in her room. My grandma tucked me into bed and hummed a German song until I pretended to fall asleep.

Around midnight I heard my mother crying. I got out of bed, padded across the cold floorboards, and slipped into her room. There were only shadows, dark and darker areas where the light from the street lamp cast a wide stripe across the floor. My mother was huddled under a mass of sheets and blankets, the curves of her body distorted so that, at first, I thought she was upside down.

"Mom?" I whispered.

I shook her lightly and she dropped a photo. I picked it up. In the photo, she held up the hem of her wedding dress as white rice sprinkled all around, smiling as if caught in a rainstorm on a hot day.

I nudged my mother and she moved to the right side of the bed. I climbed under the covers and joined her in her pocket of warmth.

"I'm just looking for answers. But these pictures, they don't offer anything substantial. They just get me all emotional."

I handed her a tissue.

"Your grandmother cleaned houses, sewed people's clothes seventeen, eighteen hours a day. Barely covered my surgeries and medication. And when I needed braces, she took on another job and another and another. What have I done?"

"You help me with my homework."

My mom blew her nose and set the tissue on the nightstand.

"On my thirteenth birthday, your grandmother took me to go see the great Reverend Fred Roberts. It cost fifteen dollars a ticket back then. Three days' wages for her."

She hesitated.

"And when we went inside, the men at the doors saw the braces on my legs and escorted me to the front row. Reverend Roberts gave a sermon and then waded through the crowd, healing people. When he came to us, he asked my mother to support me while he performed a miracle. His two assistants raised my braces into the air and broke them apart for the whole crowd to see. Reverend Roberts put his hand on my head and prayed. That voice. Like a bullhorn right in my face. Praying so that even the audience in the balcony could hear. Praying that God would give me physical strength."

I offered her another tissue and she wiped her eyes. During movies my mom would cry, especially if someone died at the end.

"I was so young," she said. "I didn't know what to do. I prayed with Reverend Roberts. I prayed harder than I had ever prayed in my life. And as we finished praying, the men who had taken off my braces lifted me to my feet and Reverend Roberts announced that I had been healed." She shook her head. "But I wasn't. As everyone cheered or prayed and the reverend walked on to the next sick child, I yelled for him to come back. I begged him not to leave, but his two assistants pushed me back. There was praying and screaming and . . . your grandma took me straight outside. She didn't say a word. Her face was completely blank. She never mentioned Reverend Roberts or how she managed to buy a new pair of braces for me. They just appeared two days later."

I gave my mom the wedding photo and she held it under a band of light from the street lamp.

"The night before last, your father came into my room and asked me to pray. He wanted me to pray for us. For our happiness. I prayed, Samuel. I really did. I prayed as hard as I did that day with Reverend Roberts."

Part Two

The next morning, I tried to watch as much television as I could. I started with the nine o'clock cartoons, hardly moving from the screen, but by eleven it was all soap operas. So for two hours I sat in my dad's tent. The sun had warmed the inside, bringing out all his smells. Since he had left his clothes in a perfect pile by the entrance, I tried on a pair of his pants. I looked like an "after" photo in a weight-loss commercial.

At noon I watched *The Andy Griffith Show* with my grandma. She gummed lima beans until *Bewitched* came on. Then she fell asleep. At two, during *Sanford and Son*, the phone rang.

"Guess who just called me?" Jonathon said before I could even finish "Hello."

"I'll give you three tries."

"Rod Stewart?" I said.

"Seriously."

"The pope?"

"Fine. Cynthia and Christine. They talked business."

Cynthia and Christine were the two most popular people in school. Jonathon and I barely made the top hundred.

"They're conducting a survey," he said. "They want to know who the best kisser in the whole school is. They want us to go to Cynthia's house tomorrow."

"They were probably joking."

"I called William and Clyde," he said. "They participated in the survey yesterday. Said it was fantastic."

"What about Jesse?"

"What about him?"

I thought it was strange that Jesse hadn't been invited, but I was also excited to be included in such a prestigious survey. Asking too many questions might hurt my chances of making out with Cynthia and Christine.

"So what did you say?"

"What do you think? I said you were super gay, but I would come alone to help with their survey."

"You did not! Did you? You said I was gay? You better not've."

"I'll swing by on my way over there tomorrow," he said. "We have to be there by three. Wear something nice. Don't be 'Izod Dorkwad.' "

When I hung up with Jonathon I watched *Diff'rent Strokes*. Then I watched *Three's Company, The Dick Van Dyke Show, All in the Family, Silver Spoons, I Love Lucy, The Honeymooners,* and *The Addams Family.* After that, my mom came home and I helped her with dinner. But during that whole time I couldn't stop thinking about kissing.

✠

It wasn't hard to find Cynthia's house in the Cherry Hills neighborhood. It was a pillared mansion just like in *Gone With the*

Wind, but she had a three-car garage, a basketball hoop, and a satellite dish on the roof.

Since Jonathon had thrown the Mexicans' bike in the gulch, I gave him a lift on my handlebars. It was three o'clock and thirty seconds when we arrived. Thirty seconds too late.

Jonathon rang the bell. We looked at each other, at the sidewalk, at the crocheted door hanging, at our feet, at anything besides the peephole.

"Hey," Christine said, opening the door. She was wearing a short ivory skirt, a turquoise halter top, and a sweatband that pulled back her long blond hair. She could have been a model or the hottest professional tennis player ever.

"Hey," Jonathon and I said at the same time.

"You guys rode your bikes all the way over here? You must be hot. Come cool off."

The house was something out of *Dynasty*. In the entryway a huge crystal chandelier hung like a cloud of glass. All the rooms were carpeted white, most of the furniture was white, and everyone in the family photos was white.

"Thanks for helping us out with our survey," Christine said. "You guys are the last on our list."

In the kitchen, Cynthia's parents had a juicer, a microwave, a six-slot toaster, a food processor, a trash compacter, a three-door refrigerator with a separate ice maker, a gas and electric stove, a million cooking utensils, an ice-cream machine, and enough food to feed Jonathon and me for weeks.

"Is your house like this too?" Jonathon asked Christine.

"A little smaller, but we have a condo in Vail."

Cynthia appeared wearing an orange summer skirt that stopped right above her knees. Her blond curly hair hung over her shoulders. She was even more beautiful than when she assisted Mrs. Warner in Home Economics class.

Cynthia waved to us and said, "Let's go to the living room."

The living room was gigantic, but all Jonathon and I noticed was the projector television. When Cynthia switched it on for a demonstration, we studied it like a magic trick.

"If I lived here you would never see me again," Jonathon whispered. "Ever."

Christine brought everyone Cokes. The leather couch crinkled and crunched as we sat down. Cynthia and Christine were both wearing the same red sparkly nail polish. In six years of school, I had never been this close to anyone so popular.

"To break the ice," Christine said, "we thought we'd play Truth or Dare."

Before Jonathon or I could agree, Cynthia said, "Jonathon and I dare Christine and Samuel."

"We do?" Jonathon asked.

"Dare us to do what?" Christine responded.

"Go French-kiss in the closet for ten minutes."

"Samuel and I accept your dare."

It was obvious that Christine and Cynthia had rehearsed this part many times. I looked to Jonathon for support, but he just gave me the thumbs-up.

"Ready?"

As Christine pulled me away, I stepped on her heel, then tripped on the carpet edging, but I managed to get inside the make-out closet.

"Okay?" she asked, shutting us in darkness. "I'm a little nervous."

"You are?"

"I don't like a lot of the boys at our school, but I've always thought you were cute."

"You did?"

"Not so much last year. But now you look better."

She leaned in and kissed me. It was slow, soft, and magnificent.

"I can tell you've French-kissed before," Christine pulled back. "It's obvious a lot of the boys haven't."

"How—"

She kissed me again. Christine smelled like potpourri, and her mouth tasted like ginger ale. As we were kissing, she put my hand on her breast.

"That feels sooooo good," she whispered in my ear.

I lifted her shirt and put my hand on her bra. Sometimes my mom made me hang out her bras after she had washed them. When I touched them then, it was gross. Touching Christine's was amazing.

"You're the first boy ever to touch me," she whispered.

We continued kissing until drool ran down our cheeks. I used every bit of tongue strength. After a while we stopped to catch our breath.

"Why didn't you try and have sex with me?" she said, her tone deepening.

"Do you want me to?"

"I would have said no. Of course." She pulled her shirt down. "You're a good kisser, but obviously gay."

"I swear I'm not."

When Christine and I came out of the closet, Jonathon and Cynthia were waiting for us by the front door. Jonathon looked as if he had just pooped his pants and Cynthia looked as if she was pretending not to smell it.

Cynthia announced that Jonathon and I had to leave before her parents got home. They didn't even let us finish our Cokes.

"Thanks for having—"

Cynthia closed the door. The sun and the sudden end left Jonathon and me dazed. We picked up my bike and looked at the front door one more time before he hopped on my handlebars and we rode away.

"That was weird," Jonathon said as we coasted past all the

mansions. "When you guys went in the closet we started kissing. After a few seconds, she put my hand under her shirt, but then said I was being too aggressive. Then she pushed me away. She said if I was going to treat her 'like a slut,' then it was time to leave." He shook his head. "I wonder how I rate compared to the other boys."

It was my turn. "Christine said I was a good kisser, but that I was gay."

"You *are* gay."

"I'm not. Do you think we did better than the other boys?"

"There's no doubt," Jonathon said, but he didn't sound convinced.

✗

As we came into my neighborhood, we saw at least fifteen Mexicans standing on the sidewalk. I knew they all lived in the same house, but I had never seen them together at the same time.

"You filth," my grandma hissed. "Look at all this trash in your front yard. Some of us work hard. We clean. What's your problem?"

They all started yelling. I apologized and took my grandma's arm. This time she shook me off.

"You lazy good-for-nothings. Breeding like rabbits!"

There was another flurry of Spanish. My grandma kept pointing to their house and yelling. They yelled louder. Compared to all the other houses in the neighborhood, the Mexicans' house looked bad. Their bushes were brown, the lawn was bare, and there were piles of unused metal objects scattered around the yard. But I remembered the college students who had lived there before. They always had kegs and beer bottles in the front yard.

"This country wasn't built so you could mess it up. Go back!"

Spanish came out of fifteen mouths at once. Even the little

kids on pogo sticks joined in. I noticed Jonathon's and Jesse's bikes leaning against the side of the house.

"White *puta* probably lived off her husband her whole life," a teenager said to the group. "Now she's on Medicare."

"I deserve everything I've gotten."

I looked at Jonathon and nodded toward the bikes. It took him a second to catch my hint. Then he snuck away.

"I'm really sorry," I said.

"Next time I see her here . . . I don't care how old she is."

"Dirty spics."

"Dirty whore."

Jonathon was wheeling the two bikes behind the Mexican family. Even though she resisted, I tugged my grandma toward our house. The Mexicans were still yelling when we turned the corner.

"That was awesome," Jonathon said, catching up to us with the two bikes. "They didn't even notice."

My grandma muttered, "Stinking bean eaters. Goddamn—"

I put my hand over my grandma's mouth, but she still muttered curses all the way home.

When my mom came home from work, she flipped through the bills and disappeared into her room. Her jacket, gloves, and lunch bag were piled on the recliner evenly, as if she had simply melted through them and onto the pillows.

I took out the trash, dusted the shelves, and hung the laundry, checking off everything on my chores list three days before the deadline. But I could still hear my mom crying in her room.

When she emerged, her face was pale and a few strands of hair were stuck to her forehead. I wrapped my arms around her and squeezed. Although she was weak, and her hands were full of used tissue, she returned my squeeze.

"I needed that," she said.

We went into the kitchen to make cheese wontons. I prepared a salad while my mother rolled the wonton dough. We had a peeler in the shape of Ronald Reagan; the shavings came out his mouth. On the side it said: "Stop Peeling Back Public Programs."

"Samuel, clean the carrots minus the vomit sounds. Please."

Outside the kitchen window two squirrels were chasing each other along the wooden fence. The squirrel in back caught the squirrel in front and they humped while running half speed. When I asked my mother if I could take a photo of them, she said she would just pretend I had never asked such a question. I told her she didn't have to pretend, that I really had asked it. My mother put her index finger lightly against my lips.

That night we watched an investigative show and I learned that celery prevents cancer and only certain cigarettes cause it. Also, there was a homeless man in Las Vegas who held kids hostage while he robbed and raped their single mothers. My mom said she couldn't watch anymore "televised hysteria" and went to bed. I didn't know what "hysteria" meant, but after the show I made sure every window and door in our house was locked.

✄

Since my mom was preparing a birthday party for me, she sent me away after our Saturday morning breakfast. I met Jonathon and Jesse at the bike jumps. It was great, all of us jumping on our bikes again.

Jonathon started off the jumping while Jesse and I watched from Tina Turner's Tabletop.

"What do you think you'll get?" Jesse asked me. "For a present."

"Probably something useful."

Jonathon screamed "Olivia Newton-John" three times and landed his first jump. On his second jump he easily touched Ms. Universe's underpants.

Jesse shook his head. "Birthday presents are always useful. I hate useful."

"Useful sucks."

On his third jump Jonathon almost reached heaven. On his fourth attempt he made it. He could have never accomplished such a feat on a Huffy.

Later, we went to the gulch and stuck our feet in the water. I never wanted to leave the trees, the birds, the sun.

"This time next week we'll be sitting in class," I said.

"Not me," Jesse said. "I'm running away."

"Really?"

"I wish. Can't afford it. My mom refused to give me my allowance until I start taking more responsibility around the house."

"Responsibility sucks."

On the opposite side of the gulch, Saula Sobinski appeared in the tall grass. She was catching grasshoppers and squishing them between her palms.

"Is that a Rocky Mountain hippo?" Jonathon whispered.

"She doubled in size," Jesse added in an equally low tone.

"Weights."

"That's fat."

"Sumo Sobinski."

We laughed, but not loud enough for her to hear.

✗

Ever since first grade, Saula had won the spelling bees, the booka-thons, the academic achievement awards, the free trips to gifted and talented camp, and the annual math challenge. By fifth grade, most kids stopped contending when they heard Saula was participating.

Saula had always been the biggest girl in our class. Her face was soft, pretty, but she was never pretty like the more popular girls. Short skirts made her thighs seem bigger and heeled shoes made her too tall. Therefore Saula always wore jeans and Keds.

The summer before sixth grade, Saula's father moved back to Poland, where he had a whole extra family. Because Saula's mom worked late at a cafeteria, she made Saula join a bunch of after-school athletic teams. It seemed like every day Saula was competing in a soccer tournament, a field hockey match, or a basketball game. Although she was big for her age, she got bigger and more muscular with all the exercise, and by the end of sixth grade, Saula's boobs stuck out farther than most of our teachers'.

Also, because Saula was out every afternoon, she went from being the best kid in class to being someone like me, who knew just what it took to pass. Before, if you had copied Saula's homework, your grade would be perfect. But once she started playing sports, Saula copied from Jamie Peters or Lawrence Bimburger, who usually got one or two answers wrong.

Last January, Saula's mother married an actor from Wichita. He had kids of his own and didn't want any more. So Saula's mom moved to Wichita and gave her guardianship to Saula's sister. Saula's sister lived with her ex-con boyfriend, who, according to our classmate Lisa Hardgraves, smoked banana peels and sold bootleg porn from the back of his Volkswagen Rabbit.

After her mom left for Wichita, Saula began hanging out after classes with the high school kids. She smoked cigarettes, and once Jonathon and I caught her drinking whiskey in the gulch with Geronimo. She dropped all her sports and cut school, sometimes for an entire day. The school district psychologist knew it was time to get involved when Saula was caught making out with a Mexican in the woodshop storage room.

Even though she was regularly dismissed from class to go draw pictures or watch movies with the district psychologist, by May Saula had been suspended seventeen times, a school record. Most of the suspensions were for fighting, but a few were for insulting teachers. I had witnessed one such incident when our Chinese gym teacher, Mr. Manchu, whom we all called Mr. Man, told Saula she had to do jumping jacks with all the kids. Saula threw a basketball at him and said, "Stick your Mao B.S. up your ass!"

Later I told my mom about the gym incident and asked what "Mao B.S." was. After my mom finished laughing, she became all sad. "It's horrible what happened to that child," she said. "So smart. Such potential. Some people just shouldn't be allowed to be parents." Then, for the next half hour, my mom rambled on about Mao and what he did to China. If I had known that my question would come with a history lesson, I would have kept my mouth shut.

On the final day of school last year, someone pulled the fire alarm. After the firemen completed a thorough inspection and drove away, whirring their sirens just for us, Mr. Roosevelt, our principal, checked each student's hands for permanent ink from the alarm handle. Saula's palms were stained bright purple, she said from making borscht with her sister. Still, she was escorted to the office, where, according to Evan Daniels, who happened to be turning in his vaccination card at the time, she lifted her shirt and exposed her boobies to Mr. Roosevelt. After that, no one was really sure what happened, but the stories went from the district psychologist's putting Saula into a straitjacket to Saula's getting pregnant with Mr. Roosevelt's baby. In each story, it was made clear that Saula didn't wear a bra, which, according to Sarah Becks, whose mother had once lived in New York City and was a "people person," meant that Saula would probably become either a hooker, a tarot-card reader, or a yoga instructor.

Over the summer the reports about Saula kept coming in. Jeffrey Logales heard that Saula had sex with eight Mexicans in one night. Marty Gulzar's brother saw Saula break a pool stick over someone's head in a bar fight. Jonsey Williams read in the newspaper that Saula shot a Hell's Angel in the balls, in self-defense.

No one was quite sure what to make of these stories, but, because they got better and better, we continued to pass them around as truth.

¤

"I heard that Saula tears the heads from puppies and drinks their blood," Jesse said now.

We were watching Saula as she crept through the tall grass, carefully hunting six-legged prey. Her hair was pulled into pigtails, high on her head, so that from afar, she looked like an Arapahoe warrior.

"That's Ozzy Osbourne," Jonathon snapped at Jesse. "He tears off the heads of puppies. Everyone knows that."

"Okay. Well, I heard from Olivas Srinvas that Saula gets all the Mexicans to spit in a cup and then she drinks it."

"God, you're stupid. That's Ozzy Osbourne too. He does that at concerts. And not just with Mexicans."

"Everything I said is true," Jesse protested. "You don't know. You don't know anything about Saula or Ozzy Osbourne. You're the one who's stupid."

Saula heard us and looked up. With her left hand, she shielded her eyes from the sun, and with her right she kept on squeezing grasshoppers.

"Hey, jerk-offs," she yelled. "You staring 'cause you wanna buy something?"

We all shook our heads. Then we looked in different directions, all away from her, while she continued on through the grass.

"Let's go to Albertsons and eat bulk gummy bears," Jonathon suggested.

This was a fine idea, but as we pulled our legs out of the gulch, both Jesse and I almost fainted. We had leeches on our calves.

"Don't tear them off," Jonathon said as we started panicking. "You have to use salt."

We rode to Jesse's house with the leeches on our legs. I almost started crying because I knew they were sucking all the blood from my body.

"Slow down," Jonathon yelled. "They're bouncing all over the place."

When we got to Jesse's house, his mom threw wine on the leeches, but that didn't do anything except stain the carpet. Jesse and I shuffled into the bathtub and Jonathon used a whole carton of Morton's salt.

"When it rains, it pours," his mother said, rubbing her forehead.

Slowly the leeches started to bubble and fall. Blood was streaming down our legs. Jesse passed out and we had to carry him to the couch.

✴

When I got home, my mom put me in the shower and then put Band-Aids on my legs. There was nothing better than sitting on the toilet while my mom fixed me up.

"Come have a piece of cake," she said when she was finished.

"Isn't it for my birthday party?"

"Lucky for us, I had enough batter for two."

Grandma joined us, dentureless, gumming each forkful as if chewing cud. She and my mom had decorated the whole backyard with streamers and balloons.

"I'm going to give you your present now," my mom said, taking our plates into the kitchen.

When she came back, she had a small box tucked under her arm. I was glad it wasn't shaped like a book.

"It's not much," she said. "I spent most of the money on your party."

I shredded the wrapping paper, tore apart the box, and from the mess pulled out a bike chain and a padlock.

"Did you get me a new bike?"

"Don't say that." My mom frowned.

I gave her a semi-convincing hug. "This is . . . useful. Thank you."

✳

I wasn't as popular as Cynthia and Christine, but Jonathon and Jesse and most of the kids from my neighborhood—the Rogers twins, Lisa Obermann, Bill Franklin, and Alex Brown—all showed up with presents for me. Everyone was polite enough not to ask about my dad.

"Warm muesli bars!" my mom announced, bringing out the billionth tray of snacks.

We all got water guns and kazoos and chased each other for hours. My mom hired a hippie who made Nepalese tigers, Siberian wild hares, and exotic fruit out of balloons.

"He told me this was a boysenberry," Jonathon said, holding a knot of balloons. "But to me it looks more like a dingleberry."

After the hippie left, a magician magically appeared from behind our crabapple tree. He cut off Bill Franklin's arm and reattached it. Later, Alex Brown blindfolded the magician while Lisa Obermann chose the three of spades. The magician then removed his blindfold and pulled another three of spades from behind Lisa's ear. When he pulled twenty handkerchiefs, tied end to end, out of his pants pocket, Jesse laughed.

"He had 'em in his butt."

"Shhhh," Jonathon said. "He's amazing."

Right after the magician took a break, I was ambushed by a dozen water guns. I returned fire, and by the time cake was served, we were all soaked.

At one point, I heard the phone ringing in the house. I didn't see my mom or my grandma anywhere, so I went inside, answered, and accepted a collect call from Mark Gerard.

"Happy birthday, son."

"Hi, Dad."

I could hear shouting and music in the background.

"I can't talk long, but I wanted to wish you all the best."

"When are you coming back?"

"Having a party? I can hear it. I hope you invited lots of people."

"I wish you were here."

"Wish I was too. Your mom around?"

"Dunno."

I opened the shade and saw her on the front porch, sitting close to the magician.

"Doesn't matter," he said. "Could you do me a favor? Don't let her know I called."

"Sure. But you called collect. She'll ask."

"It's loud here. Can you talk louder?"

"Never mind!"

"I want you to know things are going well. God's giving me signs every day. I am doing right."

"Uh-huh."

I peeked through the shades again. The magician took a sip of my mom's Pepsi and whispered something in her ear.

"I'm connecting people to Jesus," my dad said. "I'm really doing it. I might be making a difference."

"That's great. When can you come home?"

"What?"

"Can you come home?"

"Not just yet. Look, I have to go. I'm running out of quarters. We'll talk soon, okay?"

I wanted to remind him once more that it was a collect call, but instead I just hung up without saying good-bye. I stood there for a minute, staring at the phone.

I looked out the window again. The magician was moving his arm behind my mom's back. I opened the front door and leaned out.

"Dad just called."

Their postures stiffened. My mom looked over her shoulder. The magician stood and announced: "I'm going to hide some balls under cups."

He trudged around the side of the house, the gravel walkway crunching under his feet. Once we couldn't hear him anymore, my mom asked, "Why'd you do that?"

"I was just saying."

"It's been so long since I flirted with a man."

"What about my party?"

"I've been working all morning," she said, taking my hand. "Our magician's an easy distraction."

Tears formed in her eyes. I had hoped my mom would feel guilty, not sad.

"Sometimes I just think you and Dad are being selfish."

"Maybe, but only one of us is really getting what they want. Him. Your father." She kissed my forehead. "Where was he?"

"Didn't say."

"But your dad does win the prize, doesn't he?" My mom said in a deep voice: "You have won the selfish prize, a giant, golden Bible."

We both laughed at this, although like most parents' jokes, it wasn't that funny.

✴

After cleaning up the backyard, my mom, my grandma, and I were so tired we were in bed before the ten o'clock news.

That night I heard noises in the backyard, but I couldn't tell if they were real or in my dreams. The next morning Jonathon and Jesse called. Their bikes had been stolen.

"In the middle of the night," Jesse said.

"They can't do that," Jonathon added later. "Sneaking around in the dark. Mexicans. They can't do that. There's laws."

When I looked out my window, I saw that my bike was still safely locked to our picnic bench with my new, useful lock.

After breakfast I really wanted to go to the jumps, but since Jesse's and Jonathon's bikes had been stolen, I had to go cruising alone.

"I'm going for a bike ride by myself," I told my grandma as I left.

"That's the spirit," she replied, patching a pair of my pants. "No depending on others."

I rode slowly at first, sucking in the fresh Sunday morning air, but by the time I got to the university, I was pedaling full speed. It felt good to be on my bike, alone. I didn't have to talk or make conversation and I could go wherever I wanted, making sharp turns unexpectedly and without warning.

I rode past the Sanderson Prosthetics Outlet, Dana's Lingerie Boutique, and JCPenney. Past Double Donuts, where cooks dropped their cigarette ashes in the batter; past Garment World, where shirts were more expensive than our Ford Fiesta; and past Albertsons, where my classmates Brad Tolbert and Frank O'Malley got paid for bringing shopping carts in from the parking lot. I sailed by the Happy Mountain Chinese restaurant, Wrangler Liquors, Kate's Boutique, Bill's Gun and Pawn, Mile-High Fried Chicken, Simply Suds Cleaners, and Big Todd's Auto.

On my way home, I took the downhill route, through the two blocks of rental homes where the Mexicans lived. Since it was early, and I was one of the only people in the world awake, I figured it would be safe.

As I turned the corner, it appeared as if the whole police precinct was parked on the Mexicans' block. Most of the police cars were parked in the middle of the street, but others were parked on the Mexicans' lawn. As I rode through the maze of people, I saw Jonathon standing by his dad.

"Hey," I said.

"Hey."

If the Mexicans had just stolen Jonathon's bike they might have gotten away with it, Jonathon explained, but they also took his father's Weedwacker.

"They'll be paying for any damages," Jonathon's father, his round face reddened and his small hands clenched into fists, informed a bored police officer.

"Seen the inside of their house?" the officer responded. "Don't think you'll be getting much."

"I don't care! They'll work it off."

The police led a shirtless boy, who was younger than me, into a patrol car. As Jonathon loaded the Weedwacker and two bikes into their station wagon, his father asked if the Mexicans had stolen anything of mine. I shook my head.

"You cannot let these kinds of people get away with murder. Believe me. I know from experience."

Several of the Mexican fathers approached the police. I had

been raised to respect the police, no matter what, but the Mexican fathers had no problem raising their voices.

"You have one boy's word against another's," a father said.

"And for that you bring in your whole cavalry," a second father added.

"How did the Weedwacker get in your garage?" the police officer asked.

"Boys will be boys," a third father replied. "And I say 'boys,' not 'men,' on purpose. And you know you wouldn't be going through all this if my boys were white."

"So you're saying your son *did* steal the bicycles and the Weedwacker?"

"See? Guilty before proven innocent. What a country."

"Take responsibility," Jonathon's father hissed at them. "If not for yourself, then for your children's actions."

"You're an evil man," the first father replied to Jonathon's father. "You and your white posse."

The arrest went on and on and it only made me sad. I said good-bye, and as I rode home, three Mexican boys whom I'd never seen before and one whom I'd seen at the jumps followed me on their bikes. I started riding as fast as I could, but they kept up with me. I cut behind University Hills mall, through the loading docks, and into the gulch. When I looked back they were gone.

✗

I stopped off behind Albertsons. Sometimes the butcher would throw away entire boxes of old meat. Today, I found a dozen pieces of prime rotting pork chops in a bag.

I rode back toward my house, straight to the Rottweilers. When they saw me coming they started barking and growling. I unwrapped the package and tossed in the meat. The dogs were suspicious at first, but after one of them took a bite, they all followed. After they chomped and chewed and finished every last bite, they waited for more. I held out the empty bag, but their expressions stayed the same. As I got on my bike to leave, they began barking.

✕

That night my job was to make the pasta. I held a bag of noodles and stared at the pot of water on the stove. If I never looked away, I could prove that a watched pot did boil.

My mom was slicing zucchini and humming along with Joni Mitchell. It was a song with one guitar and one flute, and no matter how hard I clapped my hands or screamed, it was still terrible.

"Are Mexicans evil?" I asked as casually as possible.

My mom stopped humming. I couldn't look away from the pot of water to tell if she was looking at me or not.

"How can you ask such a question?"

She appeared in my line of vision, dumping the zucchini slices into a frying pan, pouring in olive oil, and igniting the burner.

"If you're beginning to think things like that, I'm definitely taking away the television."

My mom always said I could ask her anything. Because of this, Jonathon, Jesse, and I voted her "most normal mom." But now I wasn't so sure. Especially when she threatened to punish me for no reason.

"You're serious?" she asked, noticing my frown.

I was afraid to nod. She left my line of vision and started chopping something else.

"You can't just apply evil to an entire group. Our president will say that the Soviet Union is an 'evil empire,' but I don't personally think every single person living in the Soviet Union is evil. Maybe a few . . . like that awful Ukrainian man who always lets his terrier poop on our lawn." The chopping became faster. "There's Soviet television. Supposedly they have programs devoted to convincing their citizens that the United States is evil.

We say the Soviet Union oppresses their people because they don't allow freedom of speech. They say we oppress immigrants and blacks. So instead of finding some sort of common ground to move forward from, to collaborate and correct our mistakes, we build more nuclear missiles and aim 'em at each other."

"Okay. So how do you decide who's good and who's bad?"

"Well," she said, "if I say you're bad and you say you're good, who's right?"

"Me."

"Why?"

"Because I know I'm good."

She smiled. "But I could say that you, Samuel, are bad, and since I'm your mother, what I say goes."

"No you can't."

"It's my house."

I spun around, taking my eyes from the pot. "That's not fair."

"Calling someone 'evil,' I think, is a way people misplace the blame for their own unhappiness. It's a way to judge. Judging takes a lot less time than really understanding someone." My mom shrugged. "But in the end, *evil* is just a word. Its power is equal to that of the person who uses it."

The phone rang. Since it was exactly seven, the call was most likely from my aunt Virginia in Florida. She and my mom would talk for at least an hour.

I wanted to tell my mom that what she had just said was close to how my dad had described evil. That maybe everything he was preaching wasn't so bad, that maybe she wouldn't be so upset by why he had left if she knew exactly *what* he had left for.

I turned back to the stove. The pot of water had begun to boil.

※

As I set the plates of food on the table, my grandma scowled. Then she shook her head and sighed.

"I tried to feed you properly as a child, but you were so picky."

My mom looked at me and rolled her eyes. We sat down and dug in. I hadn't eaten in so long that my stomach was bloated and extended.

"Samuel," my mom said. "No one wants to see your belly."

My grandma took a few bites and set her fork loudly on the plate.

"I can't eat this."

"Oh no."

"Here you are," my grandma said, "grown up, your life in ruins, and you're still sticking to your stubborn eating habits. I don't know what you're trying to prove. Tofu. Squash. Whole wheat pasta? Making me eat this stuff when there's plenty of good butchers. Thousands of ranches with cows and pigs. Did you know that there are more cows in Wyoming than—"

"It's healthy."

"Do I look like I need healthy? When all I want to do is enjoy my remaining bit of time, I get 'healthy.' The least you can do, after all I did for you as a child, is feed me right."

"Mom, shut it."

"Now you tell me to shut it. Disrespect me and starve me at the same time. Not only mean as a mule, but stubborn as well. With an evil streak. I'm sure that's why you got polio."

"Make me feel guilty for getting polio. It was all my fault."

"You've probably forgotten. Your sister and I killed ourselves keeping the house together. We nursed you through your sickness, took you to doctor appointments, helped you with all the rehabilitation. And after taking care of you, we went and worked sixteen, seventeen hours. I was just waiting for the knock from Social Services. And even with that, even with poverty just on the horizon, I fed you good. Wurst. Chicken legs. Pork chops."

My mom leaned forward on her elbows and looked straight into Grandma's eyes.

"I remember how we ate. You've never given me the chance to forget. What I want to know is, why are you bringing this up now?"

"Because you need to know," my grandma said. "You need to know how you've hurt us. Made us suffer from your stubbornness. And you need to know that what happened with your husband is just as much your fault as it is his."

"What was I supposed to do? Chain the man to a chair?"

"You shouldn't have married him in the first place. I told you. I warned you. Him and his soft hands. And when you told me about his ideas, that hippie stuff, I said no over and over. And what did you do? Looked at me like I was a backward old woman. Said Mark helped you find freedom. Freedom from your oppressive life with your sister and me. You left, just like that, to do your own thing. Without so much as a thank-you. Freedom, huh? Sleeping in a car. Going to concerts and dancing in mud."

"Mark saved me from your rules and regulations," my mom replied with force. "Your constant view of the world in black-and-white terms."

"And what would we have had without my rules and regulations? Tell me. We were living day to day, always just a stone's throw from homelessness. Listen to me when I say this. Listen for once. We would have had chaos. Just like *your* family has now!"

My mom rose to her feet, slammed her chair under the table, and fled to her room. I stared at Grandma. The millions of wrinkles, the shaking hands, the watery eyes . . .

"If my mom hadn't married my dad, I wouldn't be here," I said.

"And that probably would have been better for you," she replied. "A boy growing up without a father. There should be laws."

I picked up my plate and went into the kitchen. I could hear my mom crying and my grandma chewing while I leaned against the counter and finished my pasta. Through the window I could see Mr. Wallack giving his wife a neck massage.

✠

After the dishes were washed, my mom took the television into her room so that Grandma couldn't join us. Lying in her bed, we watched a Hallmark movie where an angel helps a young orphan boy get a good family. My mom kept complaining that the movie was "sentimental garbage," but at the end, when the angel went back to heaven and the orphan and the family were all waving good-bye, we both had tears in our eyes.

Around midnight I snuck into my grandma's room. I could see myself in her mirror; a lurking shadow in G.I. Joe pajamas. I stood right inside the door, listening to the antique clock ticking by her bed. Through her thin white hair I could see brown spots dotting her scalp like ink stains. Where her hair ended, the wrinkles began, branching like the forks of the Platte River. Flesh and skin slid away from her bones. For someone whose presence was always everywhere, her body reminded me of a dried columbine.

I closed the door behind me and inched closer to my grandma's bed. Everything was clean and every object had a certain place . . . except me. If I left now, she would discover the footprints on the carpet, the turned doorknob, the stirred air.

I hovered over my grandma for a minute.

"You can't be mean anymore," I whispered.

I could see the tips of her worn, yellow teeth pushing up the edge of her lips. I could almost see her dreams.

Suddenly, she opened her eyes, reached for her hearing aid, and adjusted the volume.

"What?" she said sleepily.

I pulled back a little, but kept quiet. The clock ticked. I gathered up as much strength as I could.

"I want you to be nice to my mom," I said. "Just because you had a bad life doesn't mean you need to make hers bad too."

"She's done that to herself."

"No, she hasn't.

"Good night, Samuel."

My grandmother took out her hearing aid and turned on her side.

I shook her shoulder.

"Promise!"

"Go away!"

"Promise!"

"Damn you!" she said loudly, unable to judge her own volume.

I shook her and shook her and shook her. My grandmother sat up and fumbled to put in her hearing aid for a second time. There was no caring, no concern as she huffed and groaned, clearing her head of sleep; there was just an anger in her eyes that I had never seen before; a speck of light surrounded by a bottomless black pool.

"You . . . child. This sheltered world of yours with macaroni and cartoons . . . you have no idea." She fluffed her pillow and shoved it behind her back. "I left Germany and came to America to protect my children from what is out there. What's been expected of me to survive. Men and their violence." She paused and lowered her voice to a hiss. "You. Little American boy. You with soft scented toilet paper and LEGOs. Tell me to be 'nice.' *Nice*. What a word! Your father is the same way . . . thinking he can give up his job and teach the world to be 'nice.' "

I could only make out my grandma's nose and eyes in the darkness.

"Your suffering becomes invisible to others. You need to learn that, and your mother needs to get used to it. We are alone, child. Me. You. Alone. And it will always be that way."

I backed away. My grandma took out her hearing aid and set it next to her bed. When she closed her eyes, I waited for a minute. When her breathing became deep, scratchy, I knelt down and prayed.

⚹

As I lay in bed, I could still feel my grandmother's hatred sticking to me, as if a metal spider were crawling along my spine. I closed my eyes. I opened my eyes. I closed them. I turned on my stomach and buried my face in the pillow. I was shivering. I flipped back and stared at the ceiling.

Finally, after what seemed like hours, I started to drift off into that strange grayness that connects a dark bedroom to the misty light of dreams. But somewhere, somewhere floating in that velvety space, my mother screamed: "Samuel! Samuel, wake up! Call an ambulance!"

⚹

In the hospital, Dr. Rashmi set the photos of Grandma's brain against a wall of fluorescent boxes and the three of us sat on swivel stools. Dr. Rashmi had huge biceps, wore three gold rings, and spoke like Gandhi.

"Your mother's been having mini-strokes over the past few months. Tonight the fault lines finally cracked."

"Oh wow." My mom exhaled, then bit her nails. "I should have brought her in. I should have seen it. I got up to get a drink of water. I heard her talking. It's a good thing my son was in the other room."

"Her behavior is probably attributable to the damage in her brain," Dr. Rashmi went on. "We see it a lot. Rage. Anger."

"When I was growing up she was always fighting with the neighbors. Her veins would bulge"—my mom tapped her forehead—"right here."

Dr. Rashmi nodded patiently.

"Our family issues have nothing to do with you, but it has been sooooo difficult. My husband and I are having problems. My mother's blaming me. She's the most vicious when my barriers are at their lowest. And now, to finally have some clarification. The method behind the meanness."

"Your mother will be very different from the woman you knew."

"That can't be all bad."

"In terms of care, she'll need some sort of assisted living. Unless either you or your husband is prepared to take on a new full-time job, I suggest a visiting nurse, which is expensive, or a nursing home."

"Oh, I can't just send her packing."

Dr. Rashmi shrugged his cheek muscles. I couldn't stop staring at his shoes. He had shiny brown loafers with a nickel instead of a penny.

"Obviously, I can't quit my job. But a nursing home? They're all so depressing. And oh, you should see, she really doesn't do well with certain people."

Dr. Rashmi put his smooth, manicured fingers on my shoulder, but he spoke directly to my mom.

"My wife and I had to deal with this at one point too. Now we have to drive half an hour to visit my mom at the nursing center, but it is quieter in our home. We have more breathing room. We're in a better mood when we see her."

"I had polio and my mother . . ." my mom started. Her eyes

were getting wet. She took a deep breath. "She did everything to take care of me."

"Your mother isn't a child, nor is she cognizant of the world in the same way you were when you had polio. Often stroke victims do not recognize their own children." He looked at me. "Or their grandchildren. My advice—and it is just that, advice—think about what's best for the whole family and plan accordingly."

After thanking Dr. Rashmi and the nurses, my mom and I went to the hospital cafeteria to drink tea. I sat close by my mom and tried to make conversation, but she hardly said a word. Inside her ear, I saw her brain, and inside her brain I saw a billion different thoughts circling like honeybees.

✄

After breakfast the next morning, we went back to the hospital. While my mom and the social worker called nursing homes, I bought a Snickers from the vending machine and watched two guys in scrubs unload a shipment of blood.

Around lunchtime a nurse said that Grandma was awake and we could go visit. As we walked down the hall, my mom rattled on: "Next week school starts, and if you're out by three, well, then you can eat and be at the nursing home by four. Therefore, um, you can visit her. Maybe do your homework there. Make sure everything is going smoothly. That will work out. Then she won't feel just dumped off . . ."

When we got to my grandma's room, a black nurse with long braided hair was sitting on the side of the bed. She was spoon-feeding Grandma steamed vegetables.

"Look at you two," Grandma said. "My most precious children. So beautiful. So wonderful. Don't you think, Ms. D'Angelo? Ms. D'Angelo is from Ghana. Are your children as beautiful as mine?"

Ms. D'Angelo studied us with a gentle smirk and then nodded. My grandma stroked Ms. D'Angelo's face.

"D'Angelo," my grandma cooed. "The angel. Such a perfect name for such an angelic woman."

I nodded and my mom nodded, but even if someone had slapped us on the back, I doubt we would have made a single sound.

¤

On the way home our Fiesta stalled at a stop sign.

"I can't have this break down too."

After three tries, it started again and we puttered forward. As we pulled into the driveway, I couldn't hold it inside anymore and said, "Mom. I went into Grandma's room last night, before the stroke. I told her to start being nice to you. She yelled at me. She said people needed to learn to suffer."

My mom looked at me as if I had made a dirty joke.

"What are you trying to say?"

"I prayed for her. I thought maybe, just maybe, God would help out. Make Grandma be nice to you. But instead she had a stroke."

"Be nice to me?"

I stared at her, confused that she seemed confused.

"You can't make someone be nice." She met my eyes. "And as for God, there are other people much worse off that He should focus on." When we stopped at another light, she met my eyes again. "But I do think it's sweet that you thought of me."

"I prayed, 'Father, forgive *her,* for she knows not what *she* does.' I think my prayer worked too well. Didn't Dr. Rashmi say that she might really have no idea what was she was doing?"

My mom chuckled but didn't say anything.

"So you think God really did it? I mean, you saw. With Ms. D'Angelo."

"There can be plenty of other explanations."

"But it's possible," I replied.

"That God did it?"

"Yeah."

"I don't like this talk. It's too much your father."

"Can I have Grandma's room?"

My mom frowned.

"I'll pray for her room if you say no."

"No."

"No?"

"No."

I clasped my hands together and closed my eyes. "Dear God—"

"That's enough," my mom said, giving my left ear a hard tug and swallowing a smile.

I spent the last week of summer vacation helping my mother settle Grandma in the nursing home. I didn't jump a single jump or get a chance to burp in Jesse's or Jonathon's face once. My mom told me I could have the last day of summer break, Sunday, free, but it was raining so hard that Denver was sinking under water. President Reagan would call in the navy, my mother and I would live on a raft, and the first day of school would be canceled because all the writing paper would be wet.

"What do you want for your last dinner before school starts?" my mom asked.

"Snails."

"We don't have snails."

"They have them in France."

"How about lasagna? That's Italian."

At exactly ten o'clock in the morning, Jonathon called. He

said we should go to Collegiate Shopping Mall and meet "hot chicks." I said that every time we went to Collegiate Shopping Mall to meet "hot chicks," I never met "hot chicks." Jonathon said that he would loan me one of the "hot chicks" he picked up, but I'd have to pay him back with interest.

Even though I had been going to the mall for years with Jonathon and Jesse, I could never tell my mom about it. She always said that the mall was no place for kids. But now, legally, I was a teenager.

I covered the phone and yelled, "Mom! Can I go to the mall?"

My mom's decision-making thoughts electrified the air. I could feel her hesitation even though there were three walls separating us.

"I guess so," came her response.

I pushed my luck. "Since it's raining, can I have a ride?"

More hesitation and then again: "I guess so."

I had hit the jackpot! I promised to meet Jonathon in twenty minutes, hung up, and jogged into the dining room.

"Okay. Let's go."

My mom said once I finished vacuuming the stairway she might consider my "proposition." I asked her what "proposition" meant. She said she was being "rhetorical." I asked her what "rhetorical" meant. She pointed to the stairway and told me to get to work, adding that the dictionary in my room wasn't just for "ambience." I wanted to ask her what "ambience" meant, but thought better of it.

"I hate vacuuming," I sang as loud as I could. "It's so boring. The vacuum is roaring . . . boooooorrrrrrriiiiiiiiiiiinnnnnnnnng-gggggg!"

When I finished vacuuming the stairway, my mom gave me a ride to the mall as promised, but she drove so slowly that we started to go backward in time.

"Don't push me, Samuel. I'm not going to speed in this rain."

When we finally arrived at the mall, Jonathon was standing out front, wearing black rubber galoshes.

"Going fly-fishing?" I said as I got out of the car.

He slapped me upside my head. I slapped him back. Then he slapped me. Then I slapped him. As my mom honked and waved good-bye, Jonathon and I strolled toward the mall entrance, ready to prowl for hot chicks, the backs of our heads sore.

We spent the next couple of hours making comments to girls who in return flipped us their middle finger like a typewriter key. We also harvested the wish pond for spare quarters and dimes, collecting a whole four bucks. Soon, however, the trip to the mall was less exciting than if we had stayed at home doing nothing.

The rain stopped just when we thought we might go crazy with boredom. Jonathon and I went outside to see if the lightning had split a tree or blown up a gas station. The clouds were pulling away from one another and big pools of water rainbowed in the sun. Since all the buildings and telephone poles were still standing, we sat down on cement benches, disappointed, and watched the water soak in through the bottom of our pants.

"Your galoshes are stupid," I said.

Jonathon hit me upside my head. Then I hit him back. Then he hit me.

✗

We left the mall and walked in the direction of Cleaver Street. Everything was wet and misty. As we walked through the gulch, rainwater flooded out of the tunnel.

We stopped at a tree that had a million spiderwebs. Each web was hanging low and sparkling with droplets. It was one of the most beautiful things I had ever seen, but I couldn't tell Jonathon. He'd just make fun.

"Do you hear that?" Jonathon asked.

There was weird singing, like an opera singer gargling. We headed off in the direction it was coming from.

"Remember how we learned last year about those naked women in Greece? They aren't real women. But they sing and sailors want to go have sex with them. Then the sailors die."

"Why do they die again?" I asked.

"The singing women kill them. For no reason."

"That's gonna be Cynthia and Christine someday."

Jonathon turned, gave me a look of serious agreement, and said, "Totally."

We cut down a trail to get to the bottom of the tunnel and found the source of the singing. Geronimo was standing under the waterfall, showering, wearing only his boots. The skin of his body was lighter than that of his face, and he had several tattoos that had become blue blobs. He also had a huge scar that started at his stomach and ended at his neck.

We stood there. After a minute Jonathon said, "He has a funny wiener."

"It's not circumscribed."

"Circumscribed?"

"Circumcised," a female voice said.

We hadn't even noticed Saula Sobinski in the shadows. She was sitting on a concrete block and coring a pinecone with a switchblade. We backed away slowly like cowboys in a rattle-snake den.

"Say it correctly!" she bellowed. Even though her hair was unwashed, her hands were filthy, and her cloths were stained, Saula's eyes flashed so brightly with anger that we both flinched. "Cir-cum-sised."

"Circumcised," we both repeated, quietly.

Then we turned and ran. Even when we were a block away, we could still hear Geronimo singing. We slowed to a walk.

"That was crazy," I whispered.

"Saula Sobinski is crazy," Jonathon replied. "This whole neighborhood is crazy. I just wish we could move."

"Me too."

"To Pasadena, or Reno, or Minneapolis."

"To Liechtenstein, or Transylvania, or Kansas City."

"Or Madagascar, or Timbuktu, or SeaWorld."

"Or to Cynthia's neighborhood."

Jonathon nodded. Then, as we walked up Cleaver, he offered me half of a fruit leather strip.

Even though it had rained buckets all morning and it was the last day before school started and I had a visitor, my mom still made me go outside and mow the front lawn with our stupid push mower. Everyone had a gas mower, including our Hungarian neighbors four houses down, who wore thick-soled shoes, canned crabapples, and spent hours warming up their car.

"I'd never even seen a push mower until I came over to your house," Jonathon said, relaxing on the back stoop. "You also don't have a microwave. Everyone has a microwave. How do you make popcorn?"

"In a pot."

"I don't understand."

"With oil. You stir it around."

"That sounds terrible."

"It is."

"Man, you should run away."

As I was mowing, four Mexicans rode by on their bicycles. They were all muscles and scars and Pat Benatar haircuts. Strangely, they were also wearing Scorpion, RATT, and Whitesnake concert T-shirts.

"I didn't know Mexicans listened to heavy metal," Jonathon whispered.

The Mexicans stopped at the edge of my sidewalk.

"Nice mower." They all laughed.

"Maybe if you picked up your trash, you'd have a lawn to mow too," Jonathon replied.

They laughed even louder, which was weird, because the joke was on them.

"We're coming for you," the shortest Mexican said, pointing at Jonathon. "When my brother gets out. He's going to get his bike back."

"It's my bike." Jonathon's tone was a whine.

As the Mexicans rode away on their Huffys, one of them threw an empty Gatorade bottle onto my lawn. When they turned the corner I looked back at Jonathon. He had lost all the color in his face.

✄

That night my mom and I ate lasagna and steamed vegetables. No comments. No fighting. No Grandma. We also couldn't stop smiling at each other.

At one point my mom set down her fork and rubbed her forehead.

"It breaks my heart," she said. "Leaving her in that home. It's not right. A daughter shouldn't do that to her mother."

But then she smiled and I smiled and I asked if I could just eat lasagna and skip the vegetables and she said, "Absolutely not."

12

On Monday morning of the first day of school, I woke up at 6:30 and pressed the snooze alarm. Then I woke up at 6:40 and pressed the snooze alarm. Then I woke up at 6— "Samuel," my mom whispered, cracking the door. "It's time."

I leaned on my side and yawned louder than a Swiss bugler.

After dressing, brushing my teeth, combing my hair, eating a bowl of granola with raisins, packing my new notebooks into my backpack, telling my mother I felt a fever coming on, and accepting her hug and guidance out the front door, I walked to the bus stop, kicking the Mexican's Gatorade bottle the entire way.

By the time the bus arrived at my stop, it was pouring rain. All the kids' talking and yelling tumbled out when the yellow doors folded open. Roger, our bus driver, who taped his thumbs because he moonlighted as a major in Drums Along the Rockies, held out his right hand.

"Back to the grind, bro."

He gave me five so hard that my right palm stung the whole ride to school.

☒

Since first grade, I had been in the same class with Randy Bogs, who was five foot seven, and Felicia O'Hare, who was four foot two; with Leticia Martinez, who braided her straight, black hair; with Lisa Hardgraves, who put her curls in wide pigtails; with Jonsey Williams, who shaved his head; with Marty Gulzar, who used Brylcreem; with Olivas Srinvas, who could beat a computer at chess; with Scotty Raines, who could dunk a basketball; with Roberto Tavares, who could do Bruce Lee flip kicks; with Sarah Becks, who could complete six cartwheels in a row; with Jeffrey Logales, who worked at Dairy Queen unloading boxes; with Laura Hale, who sold watermelons from the back of her dad's truck; and with Evan Daniels, who stole his lunch from Albertsons's deli every morning. Since first grade, I had always sat third from the back, middle row. Once, just to see what it was like, I sat in the back row and another time in the front right corner. But neither place felt like me.

☒

Mr. Roosevelt, our principal, was nine feet tall, had six tattoos, and shaved his head lightbulb smooth. He had a black belt in Tae Kwon Do, had killed a mugger once in self-defense, and could stop any fight without breaking a sweat. Kids who didn't even go to our school knew who Mr. Roosevelt was.

We were all in our homerooms, silently reading, when Mr. Roosevelt shouted, "Come back here!"

"No!"

"Now!"

In the doorway, Saula Sobinski appeared, walking backward down the hall, giving Mr. Roosevelt the middle finger.

"Get over here, young lady!"

As I leaned toward the door for a better look, Saula turned and broke into a run. Seconds later, Mr. Roosevelt stormed past, fists clenched. When Saula hit the exit doors, she yanked the fire alarm, grabbed both sides of the doorjamb, and swung herself out into the free world.

"Dude, Saula's awesome," Lawrence Bimburger, who sat right behind me, said.

As the alarms began to whir and screech, Mr. Roosevelt stood at the end of the hall, hands on his hips, head down. He whispered a few words, paused, and pulled a pack of Camel cigarettes from his shirt pocket.

✳

I had to wait until P.M. homeroom to see the list of the top twenty-five kissers in our school. I was seven and Jonathon was twenty.

"Ha-ha, you can't kiss," I said to Jonathon as we walked toward the bus.

"Christine said you're gay."

"I'm not gay, but I'd rather be gay than a bad kisser."

"Why's that?"

I didn't have an answer.

"At least you got invited," Jesse said.

I felt bad for Jesse, but not that bad.

"Ha-ha, Jonathon can't kiss."

"Look." Jesse nodded ahead. "Be careful, *compañeros*."

The Mexicans were all gathered by the front doors, blocking the exit toward the buses. Jonathon, Jesse, and I had to press past them to get to our bus. We didn't look at them and they didn't speak to us, but we were all thinking the same thing.

"My dad and I watched a documentary about the Alamo last night," Jonathon said once we were in the bus.

"My mom wants to hire a Mexican maid," Jesse announced. "My dad's going to pay for it."

"Your dad pays your mom money?" I asked.

"The judge told us he has to pay child support. But my mom's lawyer told my dad's lawyer he has to pay alimony too. My dad says alimony means 'alcohol money,' but my mom says it means 'he's-a-cheating-bastard money.' My mom told our lawyer to get us more alimony because she has headaches in the mornings and wants to hire a Mexican to clean and make breakfast."

"I want to be a lawyer," Jonathon said.

It was too warm to do nothing at home, so Jesse and I got off at Jonathon's stop. We stopped at the Mental Health Clinic because the Coke in the machine there was fifteen cents cheaper than anywhere else. We bought two each.

When we got to Jonathon's house there was a package on his front porch.

"*Soldier of Fortune*!"

We drank our Cokes and watched as Jonathon unwrapped Chinese throwing stars, a Rambo knife with a built-in compass, a hollow grenade, a pair of gloves with razor nails, three angel knives, a box of dynamite fuses, camouflage paint, a bull whip, and *The Anarchist's Cookbook*.

"What's a book doing here?" Jesse asked, scrunching his face.

"It's not a regular book," Jonathon explained. "It's a good book."

The illustrations in *The Anarchist's Cookbook* were like those of a third grader, the author called himself Jolly Roger, and the whole book was held together with a plastic spiral binder. But this particular book illustrated things like how to blow up cars with tennis balls or make a blowgun. Jonathon handed Jesse and me each an angel knife.

"Never be scared."

"These are for us?"

"Keep it in your back pocket at all times," he said. "And remember the Alamo."

I took mine and opened it. I had never owned a knife before. It was shiny, beautiful, razor sharp, and kryptonite solid.

On my bike ride home I stared at people twice my size, daring them to pick a fight with me. But no one did.

✠

After dinner my mom and I visited Grandma. When we arrived she was getting her nails painted by Jennifer, her new black nurse.

"If you were a bit older, Samuel," Grandma said, "I'd tell you to propose to Jennifer."

I blushed while Jennifer shook her head.

"Don't worry, Samuel," Jennifer said with a voice like Diana Ross's, "I like my men dark inside and out."

After Jennifer left, my grandma insisted on giving my mom and me back rubs. The most I had ever touched my grandma was when she held my hand. As my grandma buried her knuckles in my spine, I tried to pretend her hand belonged to Jennifer, but then I started to get a hard-on and had to think about something else. When it was my mom's turn for a back rub, I fled to the other side of the room and turned on *Let's Make a Deal*.

✠

My mom cried all the way to the Dolly Madison Ice Cream Parlor. She let me get as many scoops as I wanted without reminding me about cavities. I licked my double chocolate-chip pistachio and listened to her tell me how "terrible" and "irresponsible" she felt for leaving Grandma in a nursing home.

"Obviously she seems happier than she ever did living with us," my mom said. "But it's because she's not right. In the head. Right?"

I gave her a half-smile.

"Don't you find it fascinating? How she has a stroke and years and years of prejudices and hatred are just . . . they're just gone. She had an opinion on every race and ethnic group. The Hungarians did this . . . the Lithuanians did that . . . It just went on and on. And you didn't get to see the worst of it, Samuel. When I was your age she would come home red with fury. A black man had said this to her, a Jew had insinuated another thing, a Russian had cut her off. Every race riot only confirmed her stereotypes; every war proved some racial judgment. It was horrible. Horrible." My mom bit her bottom lip. "And now. Now. She's normal. She's a human being."

My mom went on for another half hour. Afterward, when I had eaten every last bit of ice cream and was licking the sides of my fingers and my mom was winding down from her list of reasons why she felt guilty, she turned and patted my head.

"You're an excellent listener," she said.

I shrugged as if it wasn't a big deal. By now I was a pro at knowing that saying nothing meant something.

13

That night I slept ten hours. In the morning, I felt as fresh as a
new stick of spearmint gum.

When I sat down for breakfast, I pounded the table with my
spoon. I would soon shrivel into dust if I didn't eat. My mom slid
a bowl of granola in my direction and I dug into it like a cheetah
with his fresh kill.

"I forgot to ask," my mom said, sipping coffee, "how was
your first day of school?"

"Boring."

"And the kids? How are all the kids?"

"Boring."

My mom frowned.

"How about your teachers?"

"Boring. Boring. Boring. Boring."

"Is there anything exciting?" she asked.

"Dismissal."

On the bus I ate nine of Jesse's Now and Laters and seven chunks of Jonathon's Bubblicious. Michelle Beard left a whole bag of Doritos on her seat, so I ate those too.

At school, I sharpened my pencil at the pencil sharpener five times, went to the bathroom every period, got up to borrow loose-leaf paper from my friends across the room, took jump shots when tossing paper in the trash, and volunteered for every errand my teacher made available.

At 10:11, a hall monitor came to my science class with a "Yellow Note." Mr. Roosevelt sent Yellow Notes if he needed to speak privately with a teacher or when there was a suspension or a parent had arrived to pick up a student.

"Samuel Gerard," Ms. Rabinoes, my science teacher, said, holding out the Yellow Note and peering over her purple-tinted glasses, "this is for you."

✂

I calculated the longest route to the office, took the back stairwell, and slid down the metal railing. I jumped off and kicked the swinging doors, emerging into the first-floor hallway. I studied the school-year calendar on the bulletin board, counting down the days until next summer.

I had wasted five minutes, so I continued toward Mr. Roosevelt's office, taking half steps. I smacked my lips and made low farting sounds. As I rounded the final corner, I walked right into Saula Sobinski.

"Get off me!"

She pushed me so hard I almost fell.

"I'm tired of seeing you everywhere," she said.

I tried to slip around her, but Saula pushed me again and I bounced off the lockers. Luckily, Mr. Roosevelt heard us, peeped out from his office, grabbed his yardstick, and headed in our direction.

"Come here, young lady."

"*You* come here," she muttered.

Suddenly, Saula pulled out a switchblade, arched her arm, and charged at Mr. Roosevelt. Mr. Roosevelt was shockproof, but this made even him blink extra. He pivoted, swung his yardstick in a circle, and struck her hand. The switchblade went twirling into the air like a flaming meteor and landed with a loud *ping*. With a second swing, Mr. Roosevelt swiped Saula's legs, and she collapsed onto the floor without even knowing what hit her.

✗

I sat on the office bench for a billion hours, which was good, because I was missing my classes.

"Butterscotch?" Mrs. Radovan, the school secretary, asked, offering the bowl on her desk.

I took a handful, which lasted me until the men from the Board of Education arrived. They all wore navy-blue suits and called each other Mr. So-and-So as if they didn't have first names.

I was taken into Mr. Roosevelt's personal office and asked by the men from the Board of Education: "Did Mr. Roosevelt assault the girl? Was Mr. Roosevelt overtly violent?"

I shook my head every time and the men appeared pleased. Then they all went to the teachers' lounge for coffee.

"More butterscotch?" Mrs. Radovan asked as I sat back down on the bench.

At one-thirty, Saula's sister entered the office. Her eyes looked over everything and nothing and her heavy body magnified her nervous movements.

"I will be reimbursed," she demanded when Mr. Roosevelt returned from his coffee break. "I had to take the bus and then walk six blocks."

Mr. Roosevelt calmly invited Saula's sister into his office. The Mr. So-and-So's from the Board of Education joined them a few minutes later.

I was called into the office again to recount what I had seen, but this time Saula and her sister listened too. After I was excused, I returned to my seat in the waiting area. Through it all, Saula sat in her chair, hands clasped, staring at the floor. When the meeting was over, Mr. Roosevelt opened the office door and everyone came pouring out. Saula's sister grabbed her arm and in front of the whole office said, "The youngest criminal in Denver. The mayor should get a look at you. Now, that would be something."

✗

At two-thirty, Mr. Roosevelt cleaned his desk and headed toward the front doors to monitor the day's dismissal. As he walked by me he asked, "Why are you still here?"

"No one gave me a pass back to class."

Mr. Roosevelt pointed to the Yellow Note in my hand and said, "What's that?"

"This is from earlier today. When you called me to your office."

Mr. Roosevelt took the Yellow Note from my hand, his eyes scanned the colored paper, and he meditated on the ceiling.

"Oh, yes. I have something for you."

I followed him back into his office and he motioned for me to sit down.

"You proved your mettle today," he said. "I needed an ally. Those men from the Board . . . they'll take a kid's word over mine nowadays."

Mr. Roosevelt reached under his desk and pulled out a framed photo of Ronald Reagan.

"This is for you," he said quietly. "The jelly-bean contest."

Last April, Ronald Reagan sponsored a nationwide contest to promote math. The glossy posters said that any student who guessed the closest amount in the Oval Office jelly-bean jar would win a prize. I had guessed 936 by calculating how many times I would have to take out the trash before I was a legal adult.

"The correct answer was nine hundred thirty-seven," Mr. Roosevelt said.

"I won?"

"At least in our school. And after your bravery today, I wish I could give you my own award." He looked through his top drawer. "I might have some ribbons from last year's field day."

When he couldn't find any ribbons, he shook my hand and escorted me out. In the hallway, I studied the photo while kids streamed around me. In the corner the president had signed his name, just for me.

¤

I carried Ronald Reagan with me all afternoon. Mr. Wallack and his wife offered to trade an apple-rhubarb pie for the photo. And Mr. McElvoney, the mailman, said he wasn't political, but gave me a free *Playboy* to keep me occupied and out of "the Young Republicans." When I went to visit Grandma, all the nursing-home attendants said I must be "the smartest boy in America" to win such an award. When I showed my grandma, she kissed Ronald Reagan's ear and offered me her applesauce. That night, however, when my mom saw the picture of Reagan on her dining room table, she almost had a heart attack.

"Jelly beans! To promote math! What planet do I live on?"

She paced between the kitchen and the dining room, scowling at the photo. I washed a few dishes and waited for her to cool down. Eventually, she came into the kitchen and hugged me.

"I'm proud of you for winning," she said, "even if that contest is a total mockery of our educational system. Maybe we should move to France. Or Holland. Someplace more progressive."

"Really?"

"We'll get packed after dinner."

"No more school?" I asked.

"I didn't say that."

But we didn't move to Europe or Tobago or anywhere. Instead, we ordered a mushroom pizza and watched *Tootsie*.

14

The next day, during algebra, when Mr. Smolsky went to the bathroom, Lawrence Bimburger kicked my calf.

"Ow."

"Heard you snitched on Saula Sobinski," he whispered.

"I didn't snitch. I just told what I saw."

"She got suspended. Suuuusssssspended. All because of what you said. You know what she did to Scott Timbleton when he got her suspended?"

"He didn't get her suspended," I said. "She beat him up in the cafeteria, in front of everyone."

"Tough luck for him, huh? She still blamed him for getting her suspended. Swore and swore revenge. And you know what finally happened? Guess. During her suspension she snuck back into school and when the teacher wasn't looking"—he reached his meaty hands outward for effect—"she grabbed him. Just like that. Pulled him right out of the classroom. Teacher didn't notice and no one said a thing. Too scared."

I didn't want to believe Lawrence. However, in all the years I had known him, he often stretched the truth, but he rarely lied.

"No one knew where he was for the whole day," Lawrence continued. "Did you hear where they found him?"

I shook my head.

"In the bathroom, holding his nuts. Mr. Roosevelt couldn't even get him to talk at first. It was like those people who see a ghost and afterward can't do anything except babble and drool. Blah. Blah. But finally he spoke. Linda Shrock was lying in the nurse's office and heard Scott and the police and everyone. I guess at first Saula tried to cut his jingle bells clean off, laughing all the way, *ha-ha-ha*." Lawrence paused, his smirk pushing his fleshy left cheek toward his puffy eye socket. "But Saula didn't go through with it. Didn't want to get blood on her clothes. So she burned him."

I searched his pimply face for a joke. He only blinked.

"His jingle bells? With matches? A lighter?"

"Dunno which, but he won't be having kids anytime soon."

"Why didn't they put her in jail?"

"That's the best part. He was too scared to testify. Zipper lips. That's why he transferred to a different school."

I remembered when Scott Timbleton had transferred. There was plenty of guessing as to the reasons why. I didn't think anyone knew for sure. But everyone had seen Saula beat him up and it had been pretty terrible.

We even had a school assembly after the incident. A Bronco lineman, who was known for always fighting during games, came and told us how violence never got anyone anywhere. After the assembly, he chose three kids to drive around the block in his new Ferrari.

"I'd start wearing a cup if I were you," Lawrence concluded. "Balls are important."

I hated Lawrence Bimburger and his stupid smirk. I hated Saula Sobinski and her stupid knife. And I hated Ronald Reagan because if I hadn't won the jelly-bean contest, I wouldn't have been in this mess.

"Give me your answer for number six," I said to him.

"Fifty-nine. You can thank me later."

Although I was still shaking a little from Lawrence Bimburger's story, when Mr. Smolsky returned and asked for volunteers, I shot my hand into the air. I answered number six on the chalkboard and got a check plus for the day.

✠

After school, the four Mexican boys who had made fun of my lawn mower, plus the young kid who had been arrested for stealing Jonathon's bike, got on our school bus. Jesse, Jonathon, and I didn't say anything, but everyone on the bus knew what was going to happen.

"You guys bring your knives?" Jonathon whispered.

Jesse and I shook our heads. I had been in such a rush in the morning that I had barely remembered my homework, much less my knife. But now I promised myself that from here on out, I would bring it every day.

"Don't worry," Jonathon said, giving us a tough stare. "I've got mine."

When we got off at Jonathon's stop, the Mexicans got off too. A dozen or so kids tagged along at a distance, eager to watch. Jonathon, Jesse, and I started walking home, hoping that the Mexicans wouldn't say anything, but one of them threw a rock. It hit me in the back.

"Do that again," Jonathon said, turning around.

The shortest Mexican picked up a bottle and threw it. We ducked and the bottle shattered behind us. Suddenly, Jonathon was attacking. Jesse and I followed. When I reached two Mexicans, I raised my fist and swung. They moved out of the way, but

I quickly turned around and swung again. I hit one of the kids in the back of the head. Two of them, one short and one chubby, tried to grab me at the same time, but I stepped out of the way. They turned and tried to grab me again. I threw another solid punch and the smaller of the two went down. The other Mexican charged at me, but I pushed him down easily. Then I jumped on top of his sweaty body, grabbed his neck, and punched his face over and over.

During that whole time, I could hear the kids cheering: "Get the Mexicans! Get the Mexicans!"

Jonathon and Jesse took on three Mexicans and, after a few good punches, sent them running. This was good for me because by that time, the little Mexican, whom I had punched in the face, was on my back and squeezing my neck. Jonathon and Jesse peeled him off, threw him to the ground, and began kicking as hard as they could. This left me free to punch the chubby Mexican.

"Who do you think you are?!"

Pow!

I broke his nose and blood started flying. But I wasn't about to stop.

"Come here!"

Smack!

It felt good. Hitting. I had wanted to punch something or someone since my father had left. But punching a wall or a door only hurt me in the end. Sitting on top of someone and punching away, hurting *him,* listening to the sounds he made, when he couldn't do anything back . . .

"Get off at our stop!" I growled.

K-blam!

"And think you can scare us!"

Biff!

"And take our jumps!"

Crunch!

At some point, the three Mexicans whom Jonathon and Jesse had been fighting returned with their bike chains. That was when Jonathon pulled out his knife. Everyone froze.

"No dirty fighting!" Jonathon yelled.

I got up off the chubby Mexican. He pushed himself to his feet and lumbered away, crying. The small Mexican that Jonathon and Jesse had been kicking also ran off. The three remaining Mexicans took one look at Jonathon's knife, then at me, and walked away in the other direction, raising their middle fingers over their heads.

"Don't forget your bikes!" Jonathon yelled.

I stood there with hardly a bruise. We were all out of breath. The kids from the bus were chanting "Go home, Mexicans! Go home, Mexicans!"

"That was so easy," Jesse said.

Jonathon was gazing disappointedly at his clean knife.

Then they both looked over at me. "Dude, you're totally covered in blood."

✕

I stood under Jonathon's shower, the droplets bouncing and water-sliding down my skin. I felt strong. *He-man* strong. But there was also a creeping sickness in my belly, as if something inside, something that made me feel, touch, smell, had suddenly shrunk into a hard little pea.

When I got out of the shower, I stared at myself in the mirror. My arms looked thicker, the avocado bumps of my biceps bigger, my calves and thighs enormous, my leg bones like two beams planting me solidly into the bath mat, and my fists—my fists were like Popeye's anvils after he ate spinach.

I wasn't sure who I was. Was I the Samuel who laid his head in my father's lap, listening to Bible stories? Or was I the Samuel who held my mother when she cried? Or was I the new Samuel, the one standing here, improved, fearless, able to defeat any enemy?

I dressed in Jonathon's clothes, although his pants were too short and his shirt sleeves too long. I tied up my bloodied clothes in a plastic sack and threw them away. I would have to invent a lie if my mom asked where they were.

"It's Samuelthon!" Jesse exclaimed as I walked into the living room.

"You know," Jonathon said, scratching his chin, "you look stylish. Here, check it out. See what Jesse and I did while you were in the shower."

Jonathon walked over and showed me his three-foot-high Elmer Fudd that he had won at Elitch Gardens amusement park last summer. Around the neck, they had hung a cardboard sign that read: SHHHH. I'M HUNTING MEXICANS.

"Isn't that hilarious?"

I nodded, but I couldn't find it in myself to laugh.

While Jonathon made ham and cheese sandwiches, the two of them talked and talked about the fight. They recounted every punch, arguing over the smallest of details. When we watched the *A-Team*, Jonathon and Jesse pointed out similarities between how we threw punches and how Murdoch and B. A. Baracus pummeled a gang of lobster trappers. Jonathon and Jesse talked about our fight with the Mexicans right up until it was time to go home.

"You know what?" Jonathon said, walking Jesse and me down the block. "We should go steal *their* bikes."

"Totally," Jesse responded. "Then they'll know what it's like."

"Let's do it right in front of their faces."

There was something in their eyes that scared me.

"We'll bring our knives and throwing stars."

With every syllable Jesse and Jonathon murmured, with every "We're gonna get them" they repeated, I felt a seed of excitement growing inside. It was that same seed that made me want to keep punching even after that Mexican boy was no longer able to fight back . . . to punch and punch. I nodded, feeling the undertow of Jonathon and Jesse's energy pulling me along. Swimming the other way would be impossible.

✖

On the way home, I cut through the gulch. I stopped and listened to the silence. The birds were flying around, noiselessly. The sun was dropping into the mountains and the sky was unscarred by clouds.

My father believed that no human could make a "masterpiece" like the sun. He thought God had His hands in everything, all the way down to the frayed elastic on your left sock or missing a three-pointer. But I was starting to believe that God was too busy to care about lost pencils or what the weather was like. It even made me mad remembering how when those boys were kicking him, my father had prayed: "*Father, forgive them, for they know not what they do.*" If God really cared, he would have stopped those boys much sooner.

I grabbed a rock and threw it up as high as I could, which wasn't very high. The rock fell back down and splashed harmlessly into the gulch.

I saw a flicker of light out of the corner of my eye. On the ground, a few feet away, a quarter was sticking out of the mud. It had a D in the bottom right corner. The D meant the quarter had been made at the mint downtown. I wiped it off, put it in my pocket.

I leaned way back and searched the deep blue sky. I half-expected to see God, sitting there on a golden throne, giving me a knowing wink.

"Snitch . . ." came a whisper.

A shadow. I heard a crunch behind me. Slowly, I turned. That was when I came face-to-face with Saula Sobinski.

It was horrible. Her face twisted. Her nose flaring. Her eyes tearing into me.

I turned to sprint, but Saula looped her arm around my

neck. Suddenly my legs were in the air as she flung me to the ground.

"Snitch! Snitch!"

Within seconds, Saula had straddled me, pinned down my arms, and shoved my face into the dirt. After making sure I was covered in mud, she flipped me over, raised her fist high in the air, and brought it down. Her knuckles landed on my jaw once, twice, and after the third time, I saw only bright little dots.

Whenever I thought there might be a chance, I tried to scramble away. But Saula was strong. She grabbed my hair, pulled my head forward, and then pounded my head into the moist ground.

"Try and run away?"

Slam!

"Didn't expect me, did ya?"

Blap!

"I'm sorry," I spit out.

"I'm sorry," she mimicked.

Saula slid upward, onto my chest, and pressed her knees into my wrists. She clasped her left hand around my neck and smirked as if unwrapping a long-awaited Christmas present.

"Get me suspended!"

She was squeezing so tightly I began to choke. My throat was collapsing. With her right fist she punched my jaw. When she cocked her fist again, I saw my blood on her knuckles.

"Come into my gulch!"

Crack!

"And say you're sorry!"

Bam!

"Get me suspended!"

Thump!

I was dazed. Everything was spinning. I wanted to cry, but I was too busy choking.

"Well, now you'll never forget me," she said. "I'll be part of you forever!"

Saula slid a ballpoint pen out of her pocket, uncapped it with her teeth, and rolled up the sleeve on my left arm. There was a sudden burning. I screamed and screamed. Out of the corner of my eye I saw her hand, red with blood, using her pen to carve into my arm. Every time the pen moved a flash of pain rolled through my body. I screamed again and again. My own warm pee crept over my thighs.

✗

When I got home, I threw up. Then I surrounded myself with battleships and warm, soapy water. The last time I had taken a bath my father told me that stupid story about the moccasins. All his stories were stupid. Even the ones from the Bible.

I inspected my left arm. My shirt had absorbed most of the blood from earlier, leaving a scab in the shape of Hawaii. But now that I was in the water, and my skin was wet, the wound was starting to reopen. There were red, maroon, and brownish bubbles floating among the white. And though the blood mixed with water on my arm, I could plainly see two red, uneven lines:

SS: "I'll be part of you forever."

I thought of my father, lying on top of me, repeating, *"Father, forgive them, for they know not what they do."* Now his words sounded different, not as if he were speaking directly to me, but as if he were speaking *about* me.

After the bath I dried off, bandaged my arm, and went into the living room. I took the glass box with the moccasins off the wall and tried them on. My toes fit snugly against the soft end, as if the shoes had been made just for me.

I wandered into my mom's room and looked into her mirror. Although the leather was gray and the beads faded, the moccasins were colorful compared to my pale body.

"White devil," I whispered.

I looked up to see if God was listening to me now. I would say it one more time. Powerful enough for my great-grandfather to hear. Powerful enough for my father to hear.

"White devil," I growled, turning each consonant into stone.

After dinner my mom and I went for a walk.

"Bad day at school?" she asked.

"No."

"You haven't said a thing. Not even at dinner. Is it because of those bruises on your face?"

I shrugged. She imitated my shrug. I shrugged again.

"Tell me."

"I got into a fight with Jonathon. It's fine now. We're friends."

She frowned and let a little *poof* escape her lips. I kicked a pebble.

"Ever since you were little. Fight, then friends. Fight, then friends. Things don't change, do they?"

She looked down at me. I shrugged.

"I bet you miss your father."

"Dunno."

"Where is he? I keep asking that. How can someone so mor- alistic just—"

She stopped herself. Then she put her arm over my shoulder and pulled me next to her. We walked like a team in a three- legged race.

"Him and his ideas. Your father. The things he said to me right after we were married. 'A woman should stay at home.' A sixties, liberated woman. What would've happened if he had changed your diapers and sat for hours sticking a spoon in your mouth while you chewed with your eight teeth? What would our life be like now if I'd gotten a job right after you were born? Why did I stay at home even though we both had college degrees?"

"Maybe you should do what Jesse's mom does," I suggested. "Get alimony."

Her face wrinkled. "Obviously I lost you somewhere."

"Jesse said they're going to have a maid."

"I didn't march for women's rights so that I could live off a man. Child support is fair. Alimony perpetuates patriarchy."

"What's perpartrirachy?"

"It's patriarchy. Pat-ri-ar-chy. And that's man confidence. Be- sides, your father is penniless."

The Rottweilers started to bark when we turned the corner. My mom made hushing sounds and let them inspect her hand. They sniffed, wagged their tails, and trotted back to their blan- kets. I stuck out my tongue. She touched her finger against my extended tongue and pressed it back in my mouth.

"I'm nice to them, but they still bark," I said.

The sun was sinking behind the Rockies, so they looked oranger than orange sherbet cones. The sky looked bluer than a raspberry Slurpee.

"Just look around," she said. "The mountains. The clear sky."

There were birds chirping, kids shouting.

"Why would your father chain himself to ideas, to a way of life that was two thousand years ago, when he could have all this? In the here and now. I don't understand. I don't know if I'll ever be able to understand. Do you?"

I shrugged.

My mom took a deep breath. I took a deep breath too. Deeper than my mom's. Then I exhaled and exhaled and exhaled until I couldn't exhale anymore.

16

On Thursday, after school, Jonathon and Jesse went to steal the Mexicans' bikes. I said I wasn't feeling good and went home.

On Friday, Jonathon and Jesse weren't in school. I passed a note around class, asking if maybe someone had heard something, but no one knew where they were.

"Saula's going to burn your balls," Lawrence Bimburger whispered during algebra.

"Why don't you shut up?"

"Burn your balls. Burn your balls."

He was really getting on my nerves. When Mr. Smolsky had his back to us, I flashed my angel blade. Lawrence looked more scared than the Mexicans.

"I'm going to cut off *your* balls."

He shook his head quickly. "No. No."

"Give me number ten."

Without taking his eyes off me, Lawrence lifted his paper and I copied number ten. When Mr. Smolsky asked for volunteers, I raised my hand and went to the chalkboard. I got the answer right and received another check plus.

✄

Mr. Vernon was six foot three and 230 pounds, and had once been on the Olympic wrestling team. Even though he was the most boringest teacher in school, everybody paid attention because he could easily rip our arms off.

" 'Let it be,' " Mr. Vernon said. "Those were Hamlet's final words of wisdom. Laertes, Polonius, and Ophelia have suffered from Hamlet's revenge. And as the protagonist is lying there on the floor, the poison seeping into his blood, he says, 'Let it be.' What does 'Let it be' mean?"

No one raised a hand. Right behind Lucy Devornay's ear was a mole in the shape of Cuba.

"Hamlet's final words. Any ideas, Rami?"

Rami Angourpy was busy sketching galactic destroyers. Since he didn't know the answer, he gazed up at Mr. Vernon like a circus sea lion waiting for a fish.

Susan Weaver appeared in the doorway with a Yellow Note. Mr. Vernon read the note and told us to study the last scene in *Hamlet*. He crossed the hall and disappeared into Mr. Roosevelt's office. Only Jamie Peters, who always did what she was told, read. The rest of the class started talking or throwing paper balls.

I put my head down. My desk smelled like dried glue.

Mark Puttazzi crumpled a piece of paper. Cerile Famout leaned back in his creaky chair.

"Let me have your Laffy Taffy," La Shanda James said.

"I kicked my brother's Nerf beyond the bleachers," Randy Bogs bragged.

"I think lettuce helps," Leticia Martinez counseled.

"Hello, class. I'm your new teacher!"

The last voice sent chills through my body. The talking immediately stopped. I lifted my head. Saula Sobinski was standing near the chalkboard.

"Let's talk about Green Eggs and Hamlet."

"I told you," Lawrence Bimburger whispered.

I lowered myself into my chair.

Saula was bigger than any kid in the room. Her shabby appearance made my skin prickle. Her hair, greasy and stringy, clung to her neck and forehead, and her clothes were spotted with oily stains. Acne had spread from her face to her bare arms. There was a thin white crust in the corner of her mouth.

"Sam I am, Green Eggs and Hamlet. Samuel?" Saula pointed at me. "What does Sam mean when he says 'I am'?"

There were nervous chuckles. Something twisted hard in my gut. My jaw clenched. There was a hot, bitter burning in my stomach. I was going to be the next Scott Timbleton.

"What does Sam mean when he says 'I am'?"

She walked over. Her smile disappeared.

"Sam? Sam I am?"

Saula pinched my cheek and squeezed.

"Who am I, Sam?"

She wrapped her hand around my arm and lifted my shirt, exposing the scab of her initials. There were a few gasps. Saula scanned the room, searching for kids who might be impressed. Most were just terrified.

"Do you love me so much, Sam I am, that you put my initials on your arm?"

Saula stank of mustard and burned plastic. Her voice was scratchy and low. I met her eyes, desperate for a real person.

"What would you like, Sam I am?" she said, in almost a whisper. "Green eggs and ham?"

I yanked my arm away from her grip and stood up slowly. My legs were rubbery and my hands trembled uncontrollably;

still I kept rising. Something dark and sugary and furious was screaming from inside.

"What? You gonna run, Sam I am?"

Silence filled the room. I pushed back my seat, stepped around my desk, and came within inches of her face.

"Ya gonna fight me?"

"*I do not ask that you take them out of the world,*" I said slowly, "*but that you keep them from the evil one.*"

All was silent. I flipped out the angel blade. The metal felt cool and unbreakable. God was with me.

In that split second, I pushed Saula with all my strength and she flipped over a desk, crashing onto the floor. I leaped over the desk, landed on her chest, and straddled her, in the same way she had done to me at the gulch.

I could hear chairs scraping and desks being pushed to the side. Kids were scattering, girls screaming and boys cheering.

I put my fingers around Saula's neck and pressed the tip of the angel blade under her chin.

"I'm going to kill you," I said so that only she could hear.

Saula was perfectly still. I pressed the knife into her soft skin. I could see my reflection in her eyes and I looked invincible.

I pressed the blade harder into her skin.

I heard my father: "*. . . it's that your great-grandfather, an atheist, a man with no interest in God or hell or even the afterlife, well, he had suddenly become a devil.*"

The knife was drawing blood. Saula was beginning to cry.

I heard my grandmother: "*Your suffering becomes invisible to others.*"

Something was stiffening deep in my chest, strengthening my grip around the angel blade, urging me to kill.

I heard my mother: "*I prayed, Samuel. I really did. I prayed as hard as I did that day with Reverend Roberts.*"

Mr. Roosevelt: "Samuel. It's not worth it. Samuel . . ."

Saula: "I'm sorry. I'm sorry."

There were eyes and faces, kids I had known since first grade, all staring at me, not understanding. They were afraid. Afraid of me. Afraid of Saula. Afraid of the violence growing between us.

"I do not ask that you take them out of the world, but that you keep them from the evil one."

My father had spent months trying to define evil, but here I had it, pinned to the floor.

"I'm so sorry," Saula muttered again.

But she wasn't sorry. Given the chance, she would get up again and cut *my* throat.

"Please" bubbled from the spit lining her lips. "Please."

Saula's hardness had cracked, and behind her eyes I saw a deep sadness. It was the same sadness that had crept into our home over the past few weeks. It was a sadness that seemed impossible to defeat, a sadness similar to my grandmother's, a sadness of total and complete loss that could cling to a person forever.

I pressed the knife harder. Saula trembled.

The edge of my blade would easily cut through her skin. And once she was dead, once she was gone . . . once I had plunged my knife into Saula's throat and heart, and listened to her scream in pain, the world would be a better place.

I looked around again. Eyes. Hundreds of eyes on me. The entire class was huddled against the wall or crowded in the doorway.

Mr. Roosevelt and Mr. Vernon were only a few feet away. Mr. Vernon was the closest. His mouth was moving. He seemed to be saying, "Let it be, Samuel. Let it be."

I stood. I took one more look around.

"Let it be . . ."

I waited for a sign from God. Anything. Anything at all.

"Something!" I screamed.

But nothing happened. Nothing. There was no sound. No breathing. No talking. Nothing except for the whimpering sound of evil that was lying on the floor beneath me, her face wet with tears.

✕

When Mr. Roosevelt called, it took my mother a while to believe what had happened. And when Mr. Roosevelt told her I was to be suspended for a week, she asked, "Are you sure it's my Samuel?"

"Unfortunately, yes," Mr. Roosevelt replied. "We're lucky Saula's sister doesn't want to press charges. Something about her probation officer and how he twists everything. Please. Just come and get your child as quickly as you can. I'll explain more."

While we waited for my mom, Mr. Roosevelt filled out papers and made a phone call to his wife. During that whole time he never asked for details about my fight with Saula or why I had brought a knife to school. It was as if he already knew the answers.

When my mom arrived, I was sent to sit next to Mrs. Radovan and helped her lick envelopes addressed to PTA members. I could see my mother through the blinds, listening to Mr. Roosevelt and wiping tears from her eyes.

After twenty minutes I was allowed back in the office. The air was warm from their bodies and salty with my mom's tears.

"I've been honest with your mother," Mr. Roosevelt said. "I've told her that I think you're a good kid. I understand why you were afraid. You're not the first with Saula. But what you did today, the way you handled this unfortunate problem, well, it was inexcusable. Violence is never solved with violence. Those who live by the sword die by the sword, eh?" He glanced at my mother for a reaction. She stared at her clenched fingers.

"Since it's Friday," Mr. Roosevelt continued, "Samuel goes home today. Stays there for a week. He can come back the following Monday. That's the longest suspension I can give. In fact, I've only done this once, seven years ago. But I think it's a decent amount of time to think over his actions. And can you do me a favor?"

He searched both our faces.

"Let's keep this to ourselves. It's big, but it doesn't need to be any bigger. Samuel, if your friends ask, just tell them . . . tell them it was a misunderstanding and leave it at that."

"He won't be seeing his friends for a while," my mom stated.

"That's between you two. But I don't think what happened today is anyone's business except for the parties involved. I'm sure I'll have a few parents calling, but I can handle my end. What I need you to do is handle yours. Discreetly. This will blow over. It will. I know I want it to." He met my eyes. "Don't you?"

I nodded.

"Good," he said, standing. He reached out his hand and we shook, his grip squeezing all the blood to my fingertips.

✠

In the Fiesta, my mom drove robotically. At the first stoplight, she said, "This thing you did? I don't understand. What did I . . . ? As your mom . . . Why would you . . . ? It's so . . . so . . . foreign."

I kept my lips zipped.

"I mean, I'm ready to go back to work. To drink my coffee. Because this didn't really happen. It's a dream. A really bad dream."

I bit my tongue.

"I never bought you plastic guns. I waited until you were eleven to let you see *Star Wars*. I've always lectured about tolerance and peace. I'm an antiwar activist, for chrissakes! The ideas, the intentions were all there. Yet, now you bring a knife to school. You almost kill a girl."

I clenched my fists.

"Even your father. He never spanked you. Never threatened to hurt you. Not physically. And now this. This act. I mean, damn it, Samuel. What? Speak. Say something! Why? DAMN IT!"

"She's evil!" I screamed. "Saula's evil!"

"Excuse me?"

"And God was behind me."

I had to make her understand.

"What about Hitler? He was evil. And America did a good thing during World War Two. Fighting evil."

"What are you saying?" she asked, hypnotized.

"I did it for us. See? I stopped Saula Sobinski for good. I scared her. Made her cry. Because she's evil. For my dad. For you. I did it . . . I did it for God! And If I just keep fighting, if I defeat evil, then he can come back. Dad can return home. You know?"

My mother stared at me. The light turned green. A pickup beeped once, twice, and on the third honk she awoke, jamming the gearshift into first. We drove in silence. Tears started coming out of her eyes and she wiped them away as if they burned. After a minute, she pulled over to the side of the road, across the street from Albertsons.

"I can't drive."

An RTD bus roared past, shaking our car.

"You did it for me?" she asked, sounding out each word.

I gave a single nod.

"And God?"

I nodded again, this time more hesitantly.

"God. God? Is this the same God who advised your father to leave us? The same God who is ripping our family apart? The same God who blew up the poor woman's house at the end of the block? Or is this the God who turned my mother into a bitter woman? Who let Reverend Roberts take my braces? Which God is it, Samuel? Which God did you almost stab a young girl for? Which God would want something like that? Because let me tell you, I will never pray to that God. Never!"

My mother closed her eyes and breathed deeply. When she emerged from her short meditation, she said, "Jesus said that when a person is confronted by evil they should not fight back, but turn the other cheek. *Love your enemies and pray for those who persecute you. Do not resist the one who is evil. Resist not evil.*"

"Well, I wish I had killed her, I should have stabbed her and—"

"Don't."

"I should have killed her."

"Samuel!"

"I hate her. I hate her so much. All those things she does to people. She's evil. I should have killed her. Cut her throat!" I slashed the air. "Like that! That's how I'd do it!"

Suddenly, my mom slapped me so hard that my head hit the window. I was floating in a planetarium of stars.

"Stop it!"

"You just hit *me*."

"You're not going to kill anyone! No one! Not as long as I'm alive!"

"Why? Huh? Why do you care about Saula Sobinski?"

"You don't kill human beings."

"They do in the Bible!"

My mom pounded the steering wheel. "This isn't the Bible, goddamn it! Why does everyone think that! This is the twentieth century. Look around. Do you see Romans? How about John the Baptist? Where is he? Oh, no. Oh, no. No. No. This isn't right. This isn't us." She tapped her finger against my forehead. "I won't let his craziness influence us. I refuse to. Have to be rational, huh? Oh, that's not it. That's not what I mean. I'm not yelling at you. I'm yelling at your dad, who put these crazy thoughts in your head." Her hair swished back and forth across her shoulders as she shook her head. "I'm going to keep working and you'll keep getting good grades. You're going to Harvard, not to a juvenile detention center. Even if I can't supervise you like I used to, you're going to Harvard. Smoke whatever and talk about Wittgenstein. Listen to the same record over and over. If your dad can't oversee your behavior now, I will. I'll find a way. Alone. Some way. Damn him. Damn him and his God and his arrogance!"

"Why are you damning him?" I asked. "At least my dad's doing something. He's making the world better. And I'm helping him. We're both doing something. Together. For God. Like when we built the cross."

"What your father is doing now is completely different."

"How? How is it?"

"He doesn't carry a knife," she said. "He's a man. You're . . . you're my son."

I lifted my sleeve and showed my mom Saula's initials.

"You think people shouldn't fight," I said. "You think we should turn the other cheek. *Resist not evil. Resist not evil*? Look at this! SS! Saula Sobinski! Her initials. I'm stuck with this for the rest of my life!"

My mom sucked in her breath. Then she grabbed my arms and inspected the scabs.

"That girl did this to you?"

"And I'm not the only one. She's hurt others. Ask Scott Timbleton. And there was this girl last year—"

"We have to tell the police."

"We can't," I reminded her. "We can't tell anyone."

Something collapsed inside my mother. She put one hand on the steering wheel to hold herself. "I'm sorry. Oh my God. This is so awful. I'm so sorry." She let go of the wheel, took my face in her hands, and kissed me over and over on my forehead.

17

On Saturday, my mom left early for work. Her boss had asked her to complete a project she was supposed to have finished yesterday. I decided that since I had the house to myself for the first time since forever, I would, after my shower, remain naked throughout the day. I ate two bowls of cereal without using a spoon, watched a gazillion Saturday morning cartoons while picking my nose, did a gazillion jumping jacks while farting loudly, and ate a gazillion peanuts by sticking my entire face straight into the container.

I played my mother's Rolling Stones, Lovin' Spoonful, and Jimi Hendrix records. I organized the towel closet, mopped the floors, cleaned the base of the toilet, and vacuumed every single carpet, including the doormats. I used only my thumbs to eat lunch.

Then I got dressed, went outside, scrubbed the inside of my father's tent, tied up the poles, and put it neatly in the back of the garage. After studying the folded tent for a while, I covered it with a black tarp and leaned my bike against it.

When I couldn't think of anything else to do, I went inside, sat at my mother's desk, and wrote on a red piece of paper:

Mom,

   I'm sorry. I'm sorry for what happened yesterday. I'm so so sorry. I want to be the best son in the world. I will resist evil from now on.

Samuel

And then I put the note under her pillow, where she would find it just before she went to bed.

⚹

Jonathon and Jesse came over around noon, walking stiffly up my front walk. I offered them each a fruit leather and we lounged on my front porch watching the Bernards lower an engine block into a Datsun.

When I asked Jonathon and Jesse why they hadn't been in school on Friday, they looked at each other.

"What's wrong? Tell me what happened."

"There's nothing to tell," Jesse grunted. "We ran into the Mexicans again."

"Did you take their bikes?"

Jonathon snorted. Then so did Jesse.

"Naw."

"Tell me."

"I said, there's nothing to tell."

I knew Jonathon was lying 'cause his eyes were sinking toward his nose. Jesse was looking deep into our pine tree.

"When we fought them at the bus stop it was easy. Defending. You knew what was ours. But Thursday sucked. Taking *their* bikes. It was different. We didn't expect . . ."

Jonathon was swinging his legs from the porch, lightly kicking the tops of our bushes.

He stopped and looked to Jesse for help. Jesse's stare remained fixed to the pine tree branches.

"Expect what?"

"We didn't expect them," Jonathon continued. "We thought the worst that could happen was that they'd fight back. A normal fight. Like the other day. But it wasn't like that."

"They hate us," Jesse interrupted. "I don't mean 'hate' like 'dislike.' I mean they really hate us."

The subject was changed. Jonathon and Jesse had heard about my suspension from Jeffrey Logales. I answered all their questions. I even went as far as telling them that while Saula was cutting me, I peed my pants.

After I was done, I was expecting a reaction from Jonathon and Jesse—something, anything, laughter or applause. But they didn't even say "Saula sucks" or "You got beat up by a girl." They just sat there, eyes lowered.

✕

On Sunday, my mom and I went for a picnic in the mountains. Every time I cranked the radio louder, my mom turned it down.

"It's noise."

Somehow I bumped into a station with John Denver Sunday.

"You can play that loud if you want."

"I would rather eat my own barf."

"The things you say."

I apologized, but kept searching for music we could agree on.

It took over an hour to reach Golden Canyon Reservoir because our Ford Fiesta was slower than Fred Flintstone's granite sedan. Even pickups loaded with steel girders passed us.

"I'll allow you to complain about my car once you're rich and can buy me a little red Jaguar convertible," my mom said when we had finally arrived. She stretched and looked out at the water.

I took off my shoes and socks, sat on a rock, and dipped my feet in the water. There were pine trees carpeting the mountains, rainbow trout flopping here and there in the reservoir, and not a single human being for miles.

My mother put on her sunglasses, took off her sweatshirt, rolled up her pants, and took the sunniest part of a giant rock. I found a pile of pebbles and tossed them into the water, one by one.

We didn't say anything for most of the afternoon, even when we ate hummus and sprout sandwiches and drank ginger ale. As the sun set and we puttered home, the mountains getting smaller and smaller behind us, I no longer cared that we were the slowest ones on the road.

✖

My mother and Mr. Roosevelt had agreed that I needed to have my head examined. Since my mom couldn't afford a real psychiatrist, she called my dad's old boss at the University of Denver, Mr. Pritchards. My mother didn't have to say much, except that things were hard since my father left. Mr. Pritchards called back in twenty minutes and said that he made all the arrangements, free of charge. I was to be seen by Wayne Carville, a psychology Ph.D. candidate.

The psychiatric center was in a mobile home. When I showed up for my appointment, the two secretaries asked me if I wanted anything to drink. When I asked for a cup of water they looked around, and realizing they had no sink, the taller secretary went across the street and bought me a Coke.

I didn't have to wait long to see Wayne. He came out of the bathroom adjusting his pants and putting his comb in his back pocket. His eyes first went to the secretaries' chests, then to their legs, then over to me.

"You look like a Samuel." He winked.

Wayne had the coolest hair of anyone I'd ever seen. When I told him I liked his hair, he said that he used only a blow dryer to make it so puffy, that people who used any sort of styling product simply lacked talent. Then one of the secretaries said that Wayne was a "blowhard" and a "pompous good-for-nothing." Wayne blew her a kiss so coolly, so casually, that I thought he must be able to have any girl he ever wanted.

We went down the hall to the back room. As we walked along, Wayne told me he was getting his graduate degree in psychology to make his parents happy. I told him the only reason I went to school was to make my mom happy. He considered my comment and shook his head, as if I had just said the saddest thing in the world. Then he turned, gave me a firm handshake, and called me "brother."

There were all sorts of toys in Psychiatric Evaluation Room #1, but most were for little kids. However, it did have an air hockey table, which Wayne and I played on for the entire hour. When our time was up, I had won seven times to his four.

"I guess you'll have to come back tomorrow," Wayne said. "Give me a chance to beat you."

"You'll never beat me."

"We'll see, bro. We'll see."

So I went back the next afternoon and we played air hockey for another hour. He put up a much harder fight, and I suspected he had been practicing. Wayne and I hardly talked, except he said that he had wanted an air hockey table ever since he was a kid. He told me his parents were very religious and that when he was my age, he couldn't wait to get out of the house. I told him that my dad spoke directly to God. Wayne nodded, as if I had said the most normal thing in the world, reset the air hockey score counter, and warned me that I was about to lose the next game.

When our hour was up, Wayne offered to drive me home. He had a polished Alfa Romeo convertible as clean and shiny as a red Christmas tree bulb. He drove faster than anyone I knew, only paused at stop signs, and took both his hands off the wheel to light cigarettes.

✗

During the week I was suspended, my mom also made me go visit my grandma every day. The nursing home was only a short bike ride away, and they gave free chocolate pudding to visitors.

"Isn't it a magnificent day?" my grandma said almost every day. On Thursday, however, it was pouring rain.

"Uh-huh."

I turned up the volume on the television. *Hawaii Five-O* was on at the same time I had Social Studies. The boat chases. The shoot-outs. The theme music. But I wasn't enjoying it like I should have.

My grandma opened the window. In the daylight, she was still my grandma, old and wrinkly, but her movements and expressions were lighter, easier.

During the first commercial, I went and sat down next to her. Outside, along the covered walkways, nurses were wheeling around all sorts of old people. Most of them looked dead. My grandmother took my hand and rubbed her fingers back and forth over my knuckles. She took deep breaths and occasionally waved at a passing nurse. Her smile would not go away.

On Friday, the last day of my suspension, Jonathon called after he got home from school. He told me I had to come over or else I'd miss "the coolest thing ever."

I could think of only two other times when Jonathon had said I should see "the coolest thing ever." The first time was when a Hell's Angel ran a red light on the corner of Colorado and Evans and hit a dump truck. Since he wasn't wearing a helmet, blood, guts, and brains were everywhere. It took them three hours to clean it all up.

The second time was when a man, five blocks away, took his whole family hostage with a shotgun. They closed off the streets for miles around, but we knew of an abandoned sewage pipe that led straight to the clearing behind his backyard. Jonathon, Jesse, and I huddled around the narrow pipe entrance, watching as Denver SWAT men kicked down the back door and stormed the house. There was yelling and screaming, but unfortunately no shooting. We even got to see it again that night, on television.

I had only two more days to go and I could return to my normal, ungrounded, unsuspended life. I had been perfect all week, cleaning and cooking, and my mom had said as much. Yet now I knew I couldn't miss "the coolest thing ever." There was no way I could stay inside. And though I hadn't even left the house, I felt guilty because I had made up my mind.

I whispered an apology to my mother, who was miles away at work, and set the receiver on the floor so the phone would be busy if anyone called. I drank a glass of milk, put on my shoes, unlocked my bike, and rode as fast as I could over to Jonathon's.

When I got there, it was suspiciously quiet. There was no television on and the front screen door was shut tight. Elmer Fudd was leaning against the garage door with the SHHHH. I'M HUNT-ING MEXICANS sign still around his neck. As I leaned my bike against the front chain-link fence, I heard noises, whispers, coming from the garage. I went over to the door and knocked once, twice, and on the third knock, I heard shuffling around inside. After several minutes, the door opened, but only a crack.

"Brothers for life?" Jesse asked, sticking his nose out.

"Brothers for life!"

Jesse allowed me to enter, then immediately slammed the door shut. Jonathon was sitting at his father's workbench.

"Brothers for life?"

"I said yes already!" Then I pointed at the workbench, at a purple towel covering something pointed. "What's that?"

"Brothers for life?"

"Yeah. Yeah. Brothers for life."

Jonathon was disappointed with my lack of enthusiasm, but he lifted the purple towel anyway. Underneath was an empty cabernet jug with a bunch of nails at the bottom.

"Wow."

"No, you don't understand."

Jesse and Jonathon took turns explaining how they were making a bomb. They had gone to Frank's Hardware, near Jesse's house, and bought a small bag of calcium carbide and beeswax. As for the jug, they had stolen it from Jonathon's neighbor, Seamus O'Dally, a high-school English teacher who spent his afternoons drinking red wine and reading poetry.

Jonathon and Jesse had already coated the layer of nails in wax and soaked a rag overnight in gasoline. They told me how they planned to fill the jug with water and calcium carbide and then glue the cap on. After that, they would light the rag on fire, wait for the reactive gasses from the water and calcium carbide to build pressure, and . . .

"Mexican salsa!" Jonathon said, clapping.

"A recipe straight from *The Anarchist's Cookbook*." Jesse giggled.

"It's gonna be like in *CHIPs* when that helicopter blew up," Jonathon said.

"Or *Starsky and Hutch* when that Camaro flipped and exploded," Jesse added.

"Or in Japan when we dropped a nuclear bomb," I contributed.

Jonathon and Jesse stared at me for a minute. They hadn't thought of that one.

"After we get the Mexicans," Jonathon said, "we should use our bombs for ransoms."

"We could get a Lamborghini," Jesse said, shivering with excitement. Ever since I had known Jesse, he had wanted a Lamborghini.

"Naw. We should start small. Maybe make our teachers give us better grades."

"Then a Lamborghini."

Jonathon ignored Jesse and began snapping out orders. I filled up the jug with water from Jonathon's backyard hose. In the meantime, Jesse got the cap ready with superglue. Once we were all set up, Jonathon poured in the calcium carbide and they sealed the jug, taping the cap over and over. As Jonathon lit the rag on fire and slid the bowl next to the jug, I got goose bumps. We stood there for a minute, unsure what to do next.

"How long do we have?"

"It doesn't say."

"What do you mean it doesn't say?"

"It doesn't say."

We studied the book. It didn't say.

"This guy Jolly Roger sure is a bad writer."

"He's not even that funny."

"So what," Jonathon said. "He doesn't have to be a good writer. Or even funny. He just has to know how to make bombs."

We slid the rag closer to the jug and went outside, closing the garage door behind us. Jonathon grabbed Elmer Fudd and we ran to the end of the driveway. Then we moved four aluminum trash cans in a row and knelt behind them.

"We should have made plastic explosives," Jonathon said.

"Plastic explosives are too hard," Jesse said.

"We could do it. We need a hydrometer. It's like two bucks."

"They're still too hard."

"That's 'cause you failed Chemistry."

"Chemistry's too hard."

I picked up a rock and tapped it against one of the trash cans, making an SOS signal. Jonathon and Jesse did the same.

"If we were on a desert island we could do whatever we wanted," Jesse said, dreamily.

"No, we couldn't because we'd be stuck on a desert island."

"Yeah, but we could still stay up all night. Pee where we wanted."

"Oooohhh."

"No parents, but no girls either."

Suddenly there was a typhoon of hot air. Pieces of glass and nails pelted the trash cans, the driveway, and the aluminum siding of Jonathon's house. The clinking and clattering went on for almost a minute. I kept my head covered, my face pressed close to the ground, and my eyes closed.

"Are you guys wounded?" Jonathon asked after a while.

Jesse and I shook our still-covered heads.

"If shrapnel pierces your spine, you might not even know you're dying. Better check yourselves."

Jesse and I looked over at Jonathon. He was John Wayne serious. So we all felt under our clothes, but the only thing I found was a stick of Juicy Fruit in my jacket pocket. We split it three ways.

"I can't wait any longer," Jonathon said, standing up from behind the trash cans.

Still, we waited another minute before making gradual steps toward the garage. Jonathon reached down to touch the handle, but quickly pulled his hand away, sucking on his fingers. He used his shirt to turn the handle. Slowly, he lifted the garage door and a plume of smoke tumbled upward.

We coughed and covered our mouths. Jonathon was the first to enter, cursing through the T-shirt that he had pulled over his nose. Jesse and I followed, stepping carefully through the debris.

Nails were everywhere. They had pierced a set of spare radials and wrapped around the metal bars of a ten-speed bicycle, an ax handle, and a NO PARKING sign. They had shattered three clay pots, shredded a volleyball net and an American flag, and mutilated a pair of work goggles.

"Amazing," I said.

"We did it." Jesse smiled.

Jonathon rushed over to the worktable, where a basketball was burning. He blew and blew and the flames fought fiercely before going out, leaving a trail of awful-smelling plastic-smoke. Jesse stomped on a bag of smoldering rags.

"What if we hadn't been able to get out?" Jesse murmured. "We would have been dead."

"I'm gonna be dead," Jonathon said. "When my dad gets home."

Jesse and I volunteered to help Jonathon clean. It was fun. Every few minutes we discovered something interesting, like a melted tennis ball or a dead mouse. By the time we were done and had completed an inventory of items destroyed, Jesse and I also had constructed the perfect lie. Jonathon would explain to his father that he had come home from school to find the Mexicans trying to burn down his garage. Needing backup, Jonathon called Jesse and me, and we came to the rescue, leaping from our bikes and fighting the Mexicans in hand-to-hand combat, right there in the smoldering garage, kicking their asses so bad they would never come back again.

"And you could say I was the one that broke this," Jesse said, holding up a busted University of Denver Pioneers hockey stick. "Over their big Mexican heads."

"Instead of being mad"—Jonathon smiled—"my dad's gonna be proud."

After I finished cleaning at Jonathon's, I went home and watched television. When my mom came back from work, she barely said a word. She didn't even ask me to help her make her eggplant parmigiana.

When we sat down to eat, I ate my vegetables first and spent the rest of dinner cutting and recutting the grayish slab in order to buy time.

"You smell like smoke," she said after a while.

"Geronimo's cardboard and newspaper piles were on fire."

"So you went to the gulch?"

"Um."

"You didn't go to the gulch?"

"Just to see what the fire was about."

"Grounded is grounded. I'll double your punishment if I have to." She shook her head. "I can't believe you sometimes."

I cut another piece of eggplant. Something was on my mom's mind and I was pretty sure it wasn't me. Otherwise she would have really laid into me about leaving the house.

"And this nickname," she said. "Why do you call that poor Indian Geronimo? He's not an Apache, he's a Navajo, for crying out loud. Your father and I have explained to you how insensitive you're being."

"Mrs. Thompson says that Navajos are alcoholics and bums. She also says that the real Geronimo, the Apache chief, was one of the worst terrorists in American history."

"Thankfully, you don't have her for Social Studies anymore. In any case, call him Henry. His Christian name. For me."

My mom gave Geronimo's situation a respectful moment of silence, tapped her fork against her plate, and nodded at me.

"Eat your eggplant."

"Dead people taste better."

"Samuel!"

"Why do I have to eat something that's gross?"

"You don't like it. Fine. You're an adult."

I was shocked. I had never heard such words exit my mother's mouth.

"Besides," she said, "I have something serious to talk to you about. Something that has come up recently. How would you feel about someone coming to live with us?"

✗

Fifteen years ago, my mother's cousin, Hilda, married Junior Douglas. Hilda and Junior had a hard time finding a minister in Pulaski, Florida, who would do a wedding ceremony for a racially mixed couple. Not only that, but Hilda was eight months' pregnant with my cousin, David. Finally, Hilda and Junior were married at the courthouse with my mother; Aunt Virginia; her husband, Uncle Rhoald; and their three children, Jeremy, John, and Joseph, as witnesses. Since Hilda and Junior didn't have jobs, they moved into Uncle Rhoald and Aunt Virginia's guesthouse.

Junior and Uncle Rhoald were about as different as tuna fish and peanut butter. Uncle Rhoald still believed that black kids and white kids should go to separate schools. He also thought black people should only clean, cook, play sports, dance, or sing. For that reason, he refused to give Junior a job at the concrete mixing company he owned. But even if Uncle Rhoald had given Junior a job, Junior would have turned it down because his motto was "I ain't jumping for the White Man," a motto I had heard him say dozens of times whenever encouraged to find work. So while Uncle Rhoald was off working, Junior spent a lot of time sitting in Uncle Rhoald's lounger, drinking Uncle Rhoald's beer.

The first fistfight I ever saw was when Uncle Rhoald punched Junior in the eye during a church picnic. I was only five, but I remember Uncle Rhoald then grabbing Junior and trying to drown him in a bowl of macaroni salad.

"Uncle Rhoald's a few evolutionary steps behind the rest of us," my mom said afterward. "But I don't think Junior's too far ahead."

Last Christmas, Junior went out to buy a tree and never returned. Around the New Year, Hilda began drinking until late in the evening and sleeping all day. Aunt Virginia and Uncle Rhoald made sure David did his homework, went to bed on time, and had clean clothes for school. Three months after Junior disappeared, Hilda went to get a manicure. On her way out, she took all the silverware. A week later she sent a postcard with no return address. She thanked Aunt Virginia and Uncle Rhoald for taking care of David and said she would return as soon as she got her head together. But they never heard from her again.

"Ain't never heard of a man getting a kid without getting laid first," Uncle Rhoald said, studying David distastefully.

When we visited Pulaski, I would spend hours with Jeremy, John, and Joseph, changing the oil in their three-wheeler or learning how to tie fishing flies. They would talk about Dan Marino, the Seminoles, speedboat racing, and what they would do if they found Farrah Fawcett naked in their bed. But the only time I really had fun in Pulaski was when I hung out with David. Since he was two and a half years older, he knew things I never would have thought of. He taught me how to get a candy bar out of a machine by tying floss around a quarter, and to light firecrackers under bridges, where they made the most noise, and he once modeled a vagina out of a lemon and a wet paper towel.

Once, my mom let me go to the movies alone with David. Instead, we went to the mall, tried on expensive clothes, played video games at the arcade, drank ten sodas apiece, and climbed on the roof to see the swamp where David swam regularly.

"I ain't got nothing to worry about in there," he said, nodding toward the murky waters. "Alligators only attack if they sense fear."

At the dinner table, David gave precise details about the movie that we hadn't gone to see. Everyone believed him. Even me.

Soon after Hilda left, David began getting into fights at school, fights with Jeremy, Joseph, and John, and fights with the neighbors. He started to steal from the liquor cabinet and got caught smoking marijuana. Then, last week, around the same time I was fighting Saula, David beat up Joseph so bad that Joseph had to go to the hospital.

Last Thursday night, after I had gone to sleep, Aunt Virginia had called my mom, begging for help. Uncle Rhoald was ready to set David straight once and for all. My mother agreed to let David come and stay with us for a while, although she wasn't sure if she could handle him either.

⚹

My mom looked worried after she asked me about David moving in. Even with eggplant sitting in front of me, I thought her news was the best thing in the whole world.

"I've never had a brother before."

"I'm aware of that," she said. "But David isn't a brother. He's your third cousin."

"Still, he'll live here. With us."

Now I would have someone to talk to every day, to share my problems with. And if my mom started crying, I wouldn't have to take all the responsibility of making her feel better.

"I think it will be the best thing ever," I concluded.

"Don't get your hopes up too high. He's in a bad state. Remember what he did to Joseph?"

I didn't care that David had knocked around Joseph. Secretly, I had often wanted to do it myself, especially when Joseph gave me daily wedgies or pushed me into the toilet when I was peeing.

⚹

After throwing my dirty underwear into the hamper, I went to the kitchen, drank a glass of water, and stared at the Wallacks' dark house. I could almost picture them in bed, their chubby bodies pressed against each other, Mr. Wallack snoring into Mrs. Wallack's ear.

After I finished drinking my water, I returned to my room, closed the door behind me, knelt down on the floor, and prayed. I thanked God for sending David. I told God I wanted everyone in the whole world to feel as good, as electrified, as I felt now.

It took me almost forty-five minutes to also pray for happiness for my mother, my father, my grandmother, and Jonathon and Jesse. And after that forty-five minutes, I was pretty sure God had listened. Even if He hadn't protected me from Saula Sobinski, even if He was upset with me for something, I was sure He'd listened to my prayer for others. Because just like in the Book of Samuel, God wasn't crazy or irrational, but instead was more like Grandma. You just had to know what to say and when to say it.

19

David arrived on Sunday. To pick him up, we had to go to Stapleton Airport. Stapleton was in Five Points, one of the poorest parts of Denver. When Jonathon, Jesse, and I threw rocks at cars and someone chased us, we ran. But when the kids in Five Points threw rocks, and someone stopped, they threw more rocks.

When I was in fourth, fifth, and sixth grade, all the kids in my neighborhood were bussed to Columbus School, which was in the middle of Five Points. Most of the kids who lived in the neighborhood were black. But I hardly saw the black kids in Columbus except in gym class, where the girls jumped rope at dizzying speeds and the boys performed perfect layups.

During parent-teacher conferences, most of the parents who came to visit the teachers were white. I once asked my mom why none of the black kids' parents came to parent-teacher conferences when they lived so close, while all the white parents came when they lived so far. My mom started talking about her life in Pulaski and how the schools were segregated and how understanding the importance of education is an education in itself, but soon got so frustrated just trying to give me a simple answer that we went to Video Saloon, rented *Roots,* ordered falafel, and stayed up all night watching episode after episode.

Now, as we passed Columbus on our way to Stapleton, I pointed and said, "I miss that place." Then I did my best Mom imitation. "Ah, to be young again."

"Well, you didn't get suspended there."

"I was a perfect student."

"I wouldn't go that far. But you *were* on the honor roll every year."

"Honor roll's a joke," I said. "Almost all the kids in my class were on it. And most of the kids on my bus too."

"What about the black students?"

I tried to remember if there were any black kids on the honor roll.

"Daniel Jackson," I said finally.

"Wasn't he on your bus?"

"Yeah, but he was black."

"But he didn't live in Five Points. And as I recall his dad was a big city engineer."

"But he was still black," I insisted.

"That he was." My mom nodded as if she was forced to agree with me.

✖

My mom decided to leave the car on a side street about fifty million miles away from Stapleton because the airport lots charged "scandalous rates."

"We won't save any money if we get robbed," I said.

"Just because we're in a poor neighborhood doesn't mean we'll get robbed."

"The chances are higher."

"You are indulging in a paranoia developed from years of stereotyping. Not all black people rob and steal."

"Poor ones do," I said. "Besides, Channel Four says that eighty percent of the robberies in Denver happen in Five Points. Ask Grandma. She knows the statistics."

My mom had the same annoyed expression Ms. Rabinoes had when Becky Delonging pointed out a mistake in the textbook.

"I'll bet all the money in my purse we won't get robbed," she said.

"Sure. If we bet and you get robbed, then you won't be able to pay."

My mother didn't respond, but I caught her smirking.

The best part about Stapleton Airport was the moving walkways. If you ran really fast while on the walkway, then jumped right before it ended, it was almost impossible to land on the solid ground with two feet together. I tried three times, running by my mother and bounding high into the air.

"This is the age when the testosterone kicks in," I overheard my mother say to a security guard.

We had learned about testosterone the week before, but I had spent much of the class imagining Lucy Devornay naked. Besides, my mom could make all the jokes she wanted as long as she didn't force me to stop jumping.

"Geeerrrrrroooooooonnnnnnnniiiiiiiiiiiimmmmmmmmooooooooo!!!!!"

We arrived at the gate half an hour early. My mother and I shared a pretzel with the money she claimed she saved by parking on the street. We sat in plastic orange chairs, watching one plane after another appear from blue sky and land on the runway.

✕

It seemed to take forever for David's plane to land, and when it did, it seemed to take forever for it to pull up to the gate, and then it seemed to take forever to unload.

People of different heights and weights wearing different kinds of clothes came down the airplane ramp. Everyone had a different expression; some people were nervous, some excited, and some tired. But they all looked as if they were surfacing for air.

Surrounded by the white passengers, David seemed darker. His arms were thicker than I remembered, his jaw rounder, and his shoulders wider. He strolled, almost strutted, out of the walkway. Two airport security guards monitored David with tough frowns, the same way the lunch ladies did whenever Jonathon and I threw Hail Marys with milk cartons.

"He's a man already," my mom whispered.

David walked over to us not so much smiling but as if he had discovered an ant and was going to burn it with a magnifying glass. He hugged my mom, hugged me, and stepped away.

"Welcome," my mom said.

David nodded but didn't say anything. He just stared at us, his eyes sharp, his hair gelled.

✕

On the drive home, David was silent. I pointed out everything interesting that I could think of, although there wasn't much between Stapleton and my house except an air force base and a restaurant where they had a pizza-eating contest every year.

"How was your flight?" my mom asked.

David shrugged.

"Did everything go smoothly?"

David shrugged again.

"So you don't want to tell me how the flight was?"

"It was gay," David said, gazing out the window.

"Gay?"

"Gay."

"Were the homosexuals in coach or first class?"

I giggled.

"What?" David frowned. "When I say 'gay,' I mean 'stupid.'"

"Are you correlating homosexuality with stupidity?"

"In Pulaski 'gay' means 'stupid.'"

"That's pretty offensive."

"I didn't say *you* were gay." David shrugged. He studied my mother and then sneered. "The plane trip sucked ass. Better?"

My mom smiled as if she was gardening on a warm spring day. I counted to eighty-three before anything more was said.

"It's been a while since we saw you, David. When was the last time?"

"I don't remember."

"A year ago? That sounds about right. Do you think Samuel is any different now?"

David turned and looked at me in the backseat. I felt awkward, but acted as old as I could.

"He's a little fatter."

"I'm not fat."

"We do need to cut back on the ice cream," my mom said.

"I'm not fat."

David winked at me, as if he had let me in on a secret. It was the first glimmer of the old cousin who often tickled me until I peed in my pants. David turned back around and tapped the window, pointing at the Rocky Mountains in the distance.

"Do you see those every day?"

"Usually."

"How many miles is it from here to Florida?"

"Maybe one or two thousand."

David's dimples went deep into his cheeks.

¤

When we got home, I took David on a tour. Although our house was smaller than his in Florida, he said he liked it more because it was wood, not stucco. He asked where the air-conditioning was. I told him that the only places in Denver that had air-conditioning were the banks and the nursing homes.

"Colorado's gay," he concluded.

David was going to sleep in a spare room, in the basement, because, my mom said, there he could have "all the privacy" he needed.

"Well," he said, "that's fine and all. But I'm not doing tons of chores. So tell your mom not to be *too* nice."

I was just glad I hadn't been moved out of my room. I hated the basement. Mr. Wallack once told me that the people who lived in our house before us performed voodoo and drank stews made of human body parts there.

"The devil rocks," David said when I repeated the rumor.

Then he started cackling like Linda Blair in *The Exorcist.* I thought it was funny and terrifying at the same time. Although I was laughing, I told him to stop . . . so he kept doing it louder and faster. I threatened to leave if he didn't stop, but I think he knew I never would. I liked being with him too much.

¤

David, my mother, and I all sat at our small dinner table eating tofu burgers and steamed carrots. David prodded his food slowly.

"Can I have something else?" he asked. "This tastes funny."

"Of course," my mom replied. "There's lentil soup and tempeh in the refrigerator."

"Why don't you eat regular food?"

"Because 'regular food' is packed with pesticides and hormones."

"Virginia eats 'regular food.'"

"Yes, she does."

"I can't eat this."

"You can buy your own food," my mom said. "The stores will be open tomorrow."

"With what money?"

"I'll be giving you an allowance. You can use that."

My mom took a bite of her food and raised her eyebrows. David pursed his lips and looked away, as if holding in a burp.

"I don't want to use my allowance," he said, throwing down his fork. "I don't want to eat tofu burgers. I don't want to eat tempeh. I want to eat what I ate in Pulaski. I want to eat what Virginia made for us. I want to eat what everyone else in this world eats. Roast beef, fried chicken, and a big, medium-rare hamburger. I want real food. This fake food doesn't make any sense."

My mom listened patiently, with very little expression on her face. She let David sit with his words for a minute before leaning forward.

"Your return plane ticket is in the kitchen, top right-hand drawer."

There was no response from David. The only sound was my mother's fork hitting her plate as she stabbed carrot slices. Tofu burgers always made a boring day special, but now, with everyone upset, I could just as well have been eating spinach.

"You and Samuel could make dinner tomorrow."

David slid his plate away and looked my mother dead in the eyes. "Your food is gay."

Then he stood up, kicked his chair to the side, and went down into the basement. We listened as he descended the creaky stairs.

"A return ticket?" I asked.

My mom finished her carrots, set down her fork, patted my hand, and winked exactly how David had earlier in the car.

20

David didn't say anything when I came downstairs and knocked. His door was ajar, so I asked, through the crack, if I could come in. He grunted something like "I don't care" or "I could care less," so I entered cautiously, closing the door after me.

His room reeked of cologne. Not the good kind of cologne made by men with four names, but the kind they sold at Thrifty Nick's Pharmacy, next to the condoms. It had been the same in Pulaski. David's and my three cousins' hair was always neatly combed, their collars stiff, their socks stretched to mid-calf, and their teeth shining from whitening toothpaste, as if they were forever ready for a date. Sometimes when I went to Florida, I spent hours in the bathroom, trying to mousse my hair, trim my eyebrows, or polish my teeth like them, but I wound up looking like a boiled tomato.

David was lying on his back when I entered, his arms behind his head and his legs dangling off the mattress.

"Hey," I said.

He didn't respond.

Looking around, I noticed that David had moved the dresser to the middle of the room and put a framed photo of his mother on top. Hilda's long, black hair was in a bun and she was wearing a tight, gold disco dress. She was standing against a brick building, holding a bouquet of small sunflowers, and looking jittery, as if someone had demanded that she smile for the camera.

"That was taken before she had me," David grunted. "Happier times."

"Do you ever talk to her?"

"That's funny."

I lay next to David and he offered me part of his Kit Kat bar.

"When she stole the silverware and didn't even say good-bye, my cousins gave me the silent treatment. What was I going to say? 'Sorry'? Sorry for my mom?"

He chewed slowly and swallowed.

"She might be all depressed, but at least you got your mom to talk to. I only had myself. I would go out to the swamps and sit there and talk to whatever insect would listen. There're lots of insects there, but they don't say anything back. Makes you feel alone. Then you squash them."

"Cool."

He glanced at me as if an insect had landed on my forehead. I waited for the smack, but it never came. Instead, he turned back to the wall.

"Rhoald had this look as if he was trying to figure out how to poison me. He would pretend he was watching football, but out of the corner of his eye . . . he would just be thinking. I could see. Those scary thoughts. Then when I stared back at him, to let him know I knew what he was thinking, he would rub his eyes or yawn as if he couldn't be bothered."

David paused.

"That look. Ugh."

"That sucks" was all I could think of to say.

"It's not all his fault. It's my father's too. God. Both of them."

"Do you think you'll go back? To Florida?"

"Wouldn't be bad if I did. Maybe Fort Lauderdale. Miami. You know, where the clubs are. Girls. I'm not going back to Rhoald, though. He calls me a 'bastard' and 'Orphan Annie,' 'Michael Jackson,' 'La Toya Jackson,' 'Jesse Jackson.' Things that make you want to punch a hole in the wall. I told him over and over that I hated those nicknames. He told me, 'Lighten up, little mulatto.'"

David rubbed his eyes with his knuckles. "I'll kill Rhoald someday. If he tries something. Just let him. Otherwise, I promised myself that I'm gonna avoid him for the rest of my life. If that's possible. He's just so damn fat. I could probably see him from space."

We both laughed, but I was louder. I had been waiting for David to break the seriousness.

"From space . . . That's hilarious."

When I stopped laughing, I almost asked David why he had gotten so mad at my mom, but I wasn't sure he knew himself. He tore open another Kit Kat bar and handed me a piece.

"What are you gonna do?"

"Me?"

"With your mom?" he said. "Virginia said she's pretty bad. Cries all the time. She said your mom loves your dad too much."

"My mom's fine," I said, not sounding too convincing. I didn't know which worked better between a husband and a wife: "loving someone too much" or sleeping in separate beds like my Aunt Virginia and Uncle Rhoald did.

"Hey, I'm sorry about that. As your cousin. I remember your dad. He's funny. Way too smart. But the Jesus thing. It's kind of . . . He's kind of . . . a weirdo."

That last word, *weirdo,* turned my stomach into a fist.

"He's not a weirdo."

"What about that cross? Heard about that. That's not normal. Even Rhoald told everyone. He and his cement-mixing friends laugh about it every day."

This made me mad. I hated thinking of my uncle laughing at my dad. Mainly because Uncle Rhoald was big, fat, and stupid and was the kind of person that didn't deserve to be saved by my father and *should* be punished by God.

"He's coming back," I said. "My dad'll have made a difference. He'll be on television. Reagan will thank him. We'll see what Uncle Rhoald does then."

"He's not coming back."

"You don't know."

"Come on."

"He will!"

"They don't." David looked at me, dead in the eyes: "Wake up. I could have said the same about my dad. But I won't. Got to toughen up, little cousin."

I didn't want to talk about our mothers or fathers anymore. So I also faced the wall and munched on the Kit Kat. We listened to the floor above us creaking as my mother moved from the kitchen to the living room and back again.

✄

My mom had already registered David at the high school, which was connected to the middle school. It was the first time I had ever been excited about going to school.

"I'll introduce you to my friends," I said to David as we ate Wheaties.

"Great. That's exactly what I need."

The rest of breakfast nobody said anything. David's face was puffy, his eyes were dark-circled, and he kept yawning so wide I could see his tonsils. We left the house a full ten minutes early.

"Your alligator's crooked," David said as we walked to the bus stop. "The one your mom sewed on your shirt."

"She didn't sew it on."

"And what's that on your arm?" He yanked up my left sleeve. "A scar. S S. Is that a gang tattoo?"

My cheeks turned red.

"Someone do that to you?"

"No. Yeah. Saula Sobinski."

"A chick?" He laughed. "She better've been your girlfriend."

I didn't say anything. He grabbed my arm.

"You're serious. What's wrong with you? A girl?"

"You don't know. She's Saula."

"No one does that to my little cousin," he said. "Especially not some slut."

David and I didn't say anything for the rest of the walk. When we got to the bus stop, four Mexicans whom I had never seen before studied David and me suspiciously.

"Staring problem?" David asked, getting right in their faces.

They shook their heads slowly. He spit right on their shoes, scowled, and turned his back.

On the bus, David found a seat in the back, put his legs up so I couldn't sit next to him, and closed his eyes. In a matter of minutes, he fell asleep.

When Jonathon and Jesse got on, they asked about David. I pointed to the back seat. They stood up and studied my cousin, peering over the four green seats that separated us from him.

"He's black," Jonathon whispered.

"He's half."

Then they both looked at me. "Are you black too?"

"Shut up."

"How is he related to you? If you're not black."

"Maybe you're an albino."

"I can see it now. Samuel's definitely black."

I leaped around the seat. Jonathon wasn't expecting me, so it was easy to get him in a headlock.

"I'm going to stop the bus!" Roger yelled.

We wrestled while Roger yelled something, like if he stopped the bus we'd be late to school and he'd be the first to tell Mr. Roosevelt exactly why. I let Jonathon go once I had shown him who was boss.

Jesse then waved us over and pointed to a magazine on his lap. Jonathon and I slid across the aisle and sat down next to him, leaning over. The picture Jesse was pointing to wasn't anything special, just an advertisement for an RCA stereo. But he was grinning big, and almost the minute we sat down, we knew why he had motioned for us to come over. He had farted, and it smelled worse than rotten lard.

✠

It was pizza day at school, but the dough was wet and the cheese crusty. Jonathon, Jesse, and I poked and prodded our lunch. Jesse nodded to his right and raised his eyebrows. Seven Mexicans, all holding trays of food, sat down across from us. Jonathon ignored them, staring at me. I met his eyes after a minute. Looked away, met his eyes again.

"I'm finished," Jesse said, breaking his fork in two. "This food makes me ill."

"They have no idea," Jonathon muttered, staring at the Mexicans.

Jesse and I looked at Jonathon and then at the Mexicans.

"They have no idea what's gonna happen to them."

"Come on," Jesse said.

"What? You think I'm wrong."

"No."

"I see it. The way you're looking now. You think I'm wrong,

but I'm trying to set some things straight. Trying to set *them* straight. They can't just act any way they want."

"I don't think you're wrong."

Jonathon frowned. "Your father thinks everyone is wrong too. All those Jesus people do. Everyone is wrong except for them, just because they've got Jesus."

"I said, I don't think you're wrong."

"Remember that blizzard two years ago?" Jonathon asked, not taking his eyes off me. "When we got out of school for three whole days? Phones were out. No electricity. My father volunteered to shovel old peoples' sidewalks. I had to go with him."

"Are you telling us a long story?" Jesse snapped. He motioned toward the Mexicans with his eyes.

"Let's go," I said.

"I'm telling you something."

"Come on."

"Yeah," Jesse said. "Come on."

Jonathon studied Jesse with an empty stare before lowering his head and returning his gaze to me. "My dad and I had barely left our block before this pickup slid through the snow and rear-ended us. It was five, six Mexicans. They had shovels in the back too. They hit us hard. Smashed our bumper and destroyed the rear axle." Jonathon finished his milk, wiping the mustache away. "Begged us not to call the cops. Said they left their insurance at home. Said we could call *them* if we needed to. When my dad tried later, their phone was 'beep, *beep, beep,* no longer in service.' After that, we learned from the police that their license plates weren't even theirs. Our insurance wasn't going to pay and since my dad had no other way of getting to work, he took a loan from our neighbor. Then he took a second job to pay back the loan. He'd be home four hours a day, but usually that was only to sleep. If he had been around more I doubt my mom would have been so unhappy." Jonathon took a slow breath and shot a look at the Mexicans across from us. "A year after my mom took off with her boyfriend, we saw those same Mexicans driving their pickup. My dad cut them off. The guy who had been driving that day, the one who hit us, offered to shake my father's hand. My dad got mad. You've seen what he's like when he's mad. Started yelling and wanting to know why the Mexicans lied. Then the driver guy shrugged and said to my dad: 'Easy come, easy go.' That's it. Just, 'Easy come, easy go.' "

Jesse had turned his Jell-O cup upside down, but the contents defied gravity, floating millimeters above his speckled plastic tray. We stared at it but said nothing.

"Tell me we don't need to make a bomb. Tell me honestly that we don't need to make a bomb. How else are they going to learn that they can't act the way they do?"

I shook my head, but I didn't know what to say.

"You weren't there the other day with Jesse and me. The day we were gonna fight them. You have no idea what they can do because nothing's happened to you. But when it does, when that time comes, watch. You'll be begging for *The Anarchist's Cookbook*."

"Hey," one of the Mexicans suddenly interjected, "you going to eat your pizza?"

Jonathon studied him blankly. Jesse and I kept our chins down but our eyes on the situation.

"You want it?"

The Mexican gave a quick nod. Jonathon snorted as loudly as possible, hocked a loogey on his pizza, and slid the tray across the table. All the Mexicans stared. The cafeteria went quiet. Slowly, the Mexican picked up the same slice that Jonathon had spit on and took a bite, chewing slowly. The unanimous expression in the cafeteria was disgust.

"Mmmmm," the Mexican murmured. "Honky is my favorite kind of pizza."

Then he spit the chewed pizza right in Jonathon's face. The Mexicans all burst out laughing. Jonathon reached in his pocket, for his knife. I jumped from my seat. Jesse and I struggled to hold

Jonathon back. We tugged him away from the Mexicans, and luckily the Mexicans, now laughing and wiping the tears from their eyes, let us leave without making any more trouble.

"He spit on me! He spit!"

On the basketball court, the three of us sat on a bench while Jonathon wiped the pizza away with his sleeve. A group of high schoolers were playing basketball. One of the boys dunked and the metal net shivered.

I looked over at Jesse and Jonathon. Jesse's skin was pale and the sun bleached it into an unhealthy white, while Jonathon's freckles blurred into shamrocks.

"Now do you see, Samuel? You can't even talk to them!"

There was a wild franticness in the way Jonathon wiped the pizza from his face.

"Come on," I said.

"Come on? Look at you. You're just scared. Scared of them. Scared of everyone."

My mouth muscles locked.

"Your whole family is the same. Everyone knows about your dad in Washington Park. Too scared to fight back."

I could've punched Jonathon.

Just then Lawrence Bimburger strolled by, munching on a Snickers.

"What's up, 'honky pizza—' "

Lawrence Bimburger might be one of the smartest kids in our class, but he was pretty stupid when it came to his own safety. Before he could even finish "pizza," Jonathon had lunged from the bench and put Lawrence in a headlock. He got in three or four punches before we pried him away.

"I'm gonna sue," Lawrence Bimburger sobbed, jogging away. "Sue! All of you!"

"See?" Jonathon growled, holding my gaze. "He's never gonna bother us again."

21

When we were dismissed for the day, I rushed outside to find my cousin. When I finally got past the trillions of kids blocking the front doors, I saw David, near a row of yellow buses, standing with a tall Mexican boy in a leather jacket. The two of them were talking as if they were the best friends in the world.

I stopped. No one seemed to notice that David was speaking to a Mexican. No one seemed to care that an invisible line of "do's and don't's" was being crossed. Still, I knew it was my duty to warn David that Mexicans couldn't be our friends.

I started walking again, hoping that maybe David would see me and come in my direction, but the Mexican was busy showing him how to light a match with his thumbnail.

"Samuel!"

There were kids everywhere. Hundreds. But that voice was all too familiar.

"Hey!"

I hadn't thought much about Saula since our fight, and now I knew why. As I turned, I caught her lumbering in my direction, her sulfur-yellow skin, the violet bags around her eyes . . . it all brought back a wave of sickness, a panic that caused every inch of my body to clench.

Something deep in my core began to growl. I wanted to rip her eyes out, grab her neck and squeeze, stick my thumbs in her throat.

I patted my pants pockets. I needed something sharp, something that would cut straight through her hide. I found a pen, tucked into the side of my backpack, and I pulled it out, gripping it the same way I would a knife.

"They're going to the preview," Robert Ochalla said, huddled in a group to my right.

"I betchya he's not finished," Lucy Devornay said, in a group to my left.

"Lova, lova, lova," La Shanda James sang, directly behind me.

No one noticed Saula approaching. No one saw me hide my pen behind my back. I was caught, the crowd surging on all sides of me.

"Logic!" Butler Catterson repeated as he headed toward his bus.

"No socks, then insoles," Lundgren Boz said to Arnold Dillin as they pushed their way through the students.

Saula burst through one group after another.

"Hey, Samuel."

She came within inches of my face.

Hee-hee. "Don't look so scared." *Hee-hee.*

She handed me a box wrapped in the *Rocky Mountain News.*

"I got you an"—*hee-hee*—"'I'm not suspended anymore' present."

I couldn't stop looking at her, trying to read her face for a joke.

"Open it."

"*Oh Mickey, you're so fine!*" Charlemagne Henry sang, skipping by and bumping my arm. Saula shot her a fiery look, but Charlemagne's body had disappeared into the mob, leaving her song drifting above. "*Watchya do Mickey!*"

I slid the pen in my back pocket, took the box from Saula, and unwrapped the newspaper. It was an empty box of poker cards with a green price tag still on the bottom. I slowly removed the lid, almost closing my eyes in preparation for a violent explosion.

"A quarter?"

"You dropped it the other day. At the gulch."

I held the coin up to the light. It had been cleaned and polished so that the D in the bottom was more visible than before.

"I wanted to go to the mint downtown and get you one of those brand-new ones. The kind so shiny Jefferson looks like a bump. They don't lock them up." *Hee-hee*. "So yeah. But I didn't have bus fare."

Before I could answer, she snatched my hand and squeezed harder than Mr. Wallack, who could crack knuckles with a simple "howdoyoudo" shake.

"We're friends now," she said.

"Us?"

"I'll get your back from now on. Like brothers."

After exactly four terrifying seconds, she turned and waved.

"Okay. See you, Samuel!"

She was gone. Still, I waved back, limply.

Although I took only a few steps, in the opposite direction, a billion thoughts invaded my brain. In the first millisecond I thought: CrazySaulastabMomcryingknifeoverherMr. RooseveltWaynedrivingcleaninghousecrazycrazySaulabecause

nowshe'scaredMr.Rooseveltcallingwifejellybeansgrasshoppers
thatlooklikeshe'llkillmelikegrasshoppers.

In the second millisecond I thought: How can my mom think
that violence doesn't solve violence?

I paused, right behind tenth grader Clay Davis and his enormous friend, a punker everyone called Granite. I tried to stand
as still as possible, closing my eyes.

The pen was in my hand, my grip tighter than ever. But I
didn't need it. I didn't need any more weapons. We were friends.
Saula and me. Friends.

I put the quarter in my pocket. It was over. It was definitely
over. God was on my side.

✳

David sat in the back of the bus, on his own. I also sat by myself,
looking out the window, while Jonathon and Jesse played tic-
tac-toe. I rolled Saula's gift through my fingers and thought of
my dad, somewhere far away. I was beginning to forget the details of his face, the smell of his skin, the roughness of his voice.

Since my mom had asked us to visit Grandma, David and I
got off at the bus stop closest to the nursing home. He kicked a
rock and I watched it roll from right to left and back.

"Who was that Mexican you were talking to?" I asked.

"Paco. Know him?"

"No. But he's a Mexican."

"He lives with his aunt. His mother took off. Doesn't even
know who his dad is." He paused. "We have two classes together."

"He's a Mexican," I repeated.

"So?"

"So, they cause all sorts of problems. You shouldn't talk to
them."

"You got your ass kicked by that girl," he smirked, nodding
to the quarter in my hand. "But I'm still talking to you."

"Did you see her?"

"Paco pointed her out. He tells me everything. He even knows who you are. His family talks about you. You and your friends. What's wrong with you."

"What's wrong with me?"

David shrugged, but didn't add anything more.

The Iranian who owned the corner store near the nursing home had three kids who never went to school but were always studying. We went in and bought CornNuts and Cokes. After paying, David and I went outside and sat down on a bench. David chomped on his CornNuts louder than a horse eating carrots.

"Man," David said, "if your mom didn't give me an allowance, I would starve to death."

He took big handfuls of CornNuts, stuffed them in his mouth, and said between bites, "You say I shouldn't talk to Mexicans. Who should I talk to? Huh? This morning I tried chatting with the dude who has the locker next to me. Big goofy white dude. You'd like him. He was all preppy with *real* Izod clothes."

David smirked. I examined the sidewalk.

"So I said, 'What's up, locker neighbor?' I was just being casual. Cool. And you know what he said? Nothing. Just looked at me, up and down. I guess he didn't like what he saw 'cause he snickered. Me saying 'What's up?' to him. Me. Vanilla-Chocolate Swirl, as Uncle Rhoald used to call me." David chuckled and crumpled his CornNuts bag. "I'm gonna kick white locker neighbor's ass. I'm gonna knock that attitude right out of him. Watch."

"There are other kids. Nice ones."

"Yeah, where? Introduce me. Like I said, no one offered to show me around today except Paco."

After David and I finished our CornNuts, we threw our trash away and continued toward the nursing home. I could say that I didn't like Mexicans because of the fight that we got in at the bus stop, but I had been in millions of fistfights with Jesse and

Jonathon and they were still my best friends. The only other ar-
guments I could make why David shouldn't hang out with the
Mexicans were because they hogged the bike jumps and stole
bikes, neither of which affected him.

Then I started thinking that maybe the only reason I didn't
like the Mexicans was because of Grandma and Jonathon and
Jesse. When I was younger, I hadn't really thought about Mexicans much. It wasn't until all the new Mexicans started moving into our neighborhood and Jonathon and Jesse and my
grandma began pointing out all the bad things that I really
started thinking—

"Check it."

David and I stopped near a gutter, where the back end of a
dead cat was sticking out from the drain. We both knelt down
for a closer look. It didn't stink, like you would expect. Its
white-and-brown-spotted fur was matted with oil and flecks of
mica and its rear leg was twisted forward.

"I don't want to go to the nursing home," David said after a
minute.

"There's free pudding."

"A swimming pool of pudding's not worth seeing her. Did
anything bad happen to her? Does she drool or limp or something?"

"She's completely opposite. So now she's nice."

A small Honda drove by and the driver honked at us, even
though we weren't in the street, that much.

"The things she used to say to my mom. Blamed everything
on her. Marrying a black man. She said that was why our family
had so many problems. She said that if my grandmother, her
sister, was alive and knew that Hilda had had a half-breed for a
child, meaning me, then she would have committed suicide. My
black dad was the worst thing in the world."

"My grandma blames my mom for everything too."

David scrunched up his face.

"And my dad too," I added. "Everything. Ev-ery-thhhiinnnnngggg. There was always a fight at dinner because my dad turned it into a game. He tried to get Grandma to say the most racist thing she could."

David snorted and shook his head. Then he found an old plastic straw in some bushes. We poked the dead cat for a good ten minutes, but David's mind was still on Grandma.

"That woman should look at herself in the mirror. She's not even my grandma. She's *your* grandma. Old hag. Making everyone feel bad so she can feel good."

We left the cat and kept walking toward the nursing home. David started swinging his backpack through the air, in a circle, and I had to duck or else he would have decapitated me.

When we arrived at the visitor's entrance of the nursing home, Jennifer was standing behind the main desk, reading a newspaper. I introduced David and she commented on how handsome he was, topping her compliment off with a wink. It was the first time I had ever seen David blush.

"Your grandma's upstairs," Jennifer said. "She's helping decorate for Hispanic Poetry Week."

David cocked his head and scratched deep in his ear.

After I signed in, I took two Dixie cups of chocolate pudding and motioned for David to follow me. We found Grandma in the second-floor TV lounge pasting pictures and biographies of Hispanic poets on the wall.

"Hi there," David said, giving her a kiss.

She held his head to her cheek. David pulled away.

"Let me admire my eldest grand-nephew and . . ."

"Samuel," I said.

"Samuel. Samuel. The naughty one. Well, be good this time and go get us some orange juice."

Although I was curious to see how David would handle my grandmother, I was also happy to be on my own for a few minutes.

I took a shortcut to the cafeteria, going down the super-crazy people's hallway. After only thirty seconds, I realized I should have taken the long way. Here, in this part of the nursing home, people were sleeping in wheelchairs, others were staring blankly at the television, and a few were walking around but going nowhere.

I walked faster. Almost jogged. There was the constant smell of pee and vomit. Someone was screaming and somebody else was crying. One woman was tied down to her bed but still managed to thrash her head around. Two men, holding hands, were marching toward me, their gums toothless, their eyes dead like Saula's.

Finally, I made it to the stairwell, where, once the security door closed, I could breathe fresh air and see trees through the long vertical windows. I sat down on the cement steps, relieved to be free. I rubbed my arms and slapped my face lightly. I was still alive, every bit of me.

"Alive!" I said, my voice echoing in the stairwell. A squirrel was loping across the lawn outside. I tapped the window to get its attention and repeated: "Alive!"

Jennifer was in the cafeteria when I walked in. She was bent over, wiping tables and humming. I brushed by Jennifer with a "Hello" and quickly filled up three cups of orange juice, my back to her so she wouldn't notice what was growing in my pants.

When I returned upstairs, my grandma and David were no longer in the television room. After wandering around, I found them alone, sitting on Grandma's bed. David was curled up with his head in her lap. He was crying and sobbing while my grandma was stroking his hair.

I quietly placed the orange juices on a table, next to the empty pudding cups, and sat in a chair by the window.

"I would have been living in a gutter if it weren't for Virginia," David muttered. "And you. You used to hate me. And Rhoald. You both hated me. For no reason."

David waited for an answer. My grandma was smiling, and her smile was so penetrating, so convincing, that it hypnotized David. She rocked back and forth and hummed and smoothed his hair. Soon his tears dried, she motioned me to sit next to her, and the three of us drank orange juice together, on the bed, in silence.

✗

When we got home at four-fifteen, I ate a carob bar and David took a nap. I was scheduled to see Wayne at four-thirty.

When I arrived at the University of Denver, Wayne was waiting in front of the mobile home, car keys in hand. I locked my bike and jumped in his Alfa Romeo, Luke Duke style. Wayne floored it straight for the highway and continued flooring it all the way to the top of the Rockies. I had to zip my jacket when we reached Georgetown, and although it was only autumn, the mountaintops were whiter than snowcapped skulls.

"O Romeo, Romeo," Wayne said, patting the dashboard, "how I love you, my sweet Alfa Romeo."

We hit the Eisenhower Tunnel at such a high speed that the daylight disappeared faster than I could blink. Wayne leaned on his horn the whole way through the tunnel. I screamed and he screamed and everyone we passed looked at us as if we were in Herbie the Love Bug instead of an expensive Italian convertible.

"We went under the Continental Divide," Wayne yelled to me as we burst out the other side of the tunnel. "Behind us all the water flows to the Atlantic and here it all flows to the Pacific. You ever been to the Pacific?"

"No."

"Maybe someday we'll drive straight to that beautiful ocean and then maybe even after that we'll keep going, right under the water. With the top down. You ever driven underwater?"

"Nope."

"Neither have I. You want to try it with me?"

"Sure!"

We stopped for hot chocolate in Breckenridge, sitting inside a small coffeehouse with dark wooden beams and a closet-sized fireplace. My face was frozen and my neck stiff from leaning back in my seat.

Outside the aspens were gold and the sky was so blue it was black. The mountains were bigger than skyscrapers, bigger than volcanoes, bigger than some planets. They were so big that I didn't really feel small in comparison, or unimportant as my mom said they sometimes made her feel. I just felt that I could begin to climb them and at some point, I would discover a whole new world with castles and lonely princesses who desired only me, a world where I could begin my life all over again, not as Samuel Gerard, but as King Samuel.

"Talk to me, little brother," Wayne said, winking at our waitress.

As I sipped my enormous cup of hot chocolate, I told Wayne about the nursing home and how the people dying there reminded me how good it was to be alive. I told him about Saula giving me the quarter and David crying on Grandma's lap. I told him how ever since my dad had left I felt like crying, but that there wasn't enough room because my mom cried for the both of us. I told Wayne that I missed my dad worse than anything, but that I didn't want him to come back if he was still unhappy because his unhappiness made my mom unhappy, which made me unhappy, and when we were all unhappy, happiness seemed as far away as the farthest planet in the universe, even farther then Yoda's home planet of Dagobah. I told Wayne how I had prayed for Grandma the night she had a stroke and how God had made her nice. And I told him I hated the Mexicans; I hated the way they bleached their rat-tails, crashed their Huffys, and tore holes in the sides of their heavy-metal T-shirts. But then I told him there were plenty of white kids who did all the same things as the Mexicans, but for some reason I didn't hate them.

When I was done telling Wayne everything I could think of, the sun was behind the mountains. Wayne had smoked a whole pack of cigarettes, but not a single word had left his mouth. Which was fine by me because, just like the times when I listened to my mom, there wasn't anything that Wayne could have said that meant more than saying nothing.

I got back just in time for dinner. David said he was going on a hunger strike. He refused to eat anything nonmeat. He sat through dinner with only a glass of water. It was fun to watch.

When my mother brought out chocolate mousse for dessert, she told David he might want to join us since we would be eating meat.

"Moooooooosssssee meat!" I said, making antlers with my fingers.

David shook his head and called us weird. He finished the mousse in seconds flat and even licked his bowl clean.

On Tuesday, we had an assembly with a black cowboy. He lassoed an empty Coke bottle. Then he lassoed Marty Gulzar. He fired blanks out of a rifle and everyone jumped. Then he told us there were lots of black cowboys in the old days. He said that many of them came out West fleeing slavery, and in Colorado they found freedom for the first time in their lives.

"This," he shouted, waving a six-shooter in the air, "was the new law!"

Black cowboys had as much right to a fair shoot-out as any white man. Since many black cowboys would have rather died than gone back to being slaves, they were feared by other cowboys because they had nothing left to lose.

✕

David slept the whole bus ride home. Everyone else crowded around Jeffrey Logales because his father had just bought him portable Pong.

"Sit down!" Roger yelled.

No one moved.

"I'll pull over the bus!"

No one cared.

"Stupid brats! I'll tell Mr. Roosevelt."

There was nothing Roger could have said or done that would have made us stay in our seats. Portable Pong was worth getting in trouble for.

✕

When I got off the bus, Saula Sobinski was sitting on the curb. Saula'd been suspended in the morning for throwing a hammer at Mr. Molinoes, the woodshop teacher. Although I hadn't seen the incident, I had heard about it in Math from Lawrence Bimburger.

"Hey, Samuel," Saula said as I stepped onto the sidewalk.

"Hi."

Although David wasn't completely awake, he managed to look down at Saula with disgust.

"How's it going?" she asked, her eyes moving from me to David and back again. "The bus ride good?" *Hee-hee.* "I don't like the bus. Do you?"

"It's okay."

I didn't really want to talk to Saula, but David spat on the ground and walked away without so much as a "See you later," leaving me completely alone with her. Saula clambered to her feet.

"I was waiting for you," she said. Then she pointed to an Albertson's bag in her hand. "After Mr. Roosevelt sent me home—you know, 'cause of what happened today"—she pulled a box out of the bag—"I went to the mint and got this quarter."

Saula grinned. Her teeth were gray with fillings. Several strands of oily hair covered her left eye, and her lips were chapped and peeling. There was also a bruise spreading over her right cheek.

"I didn't have money." She smiled nervously. "But what are they going to do?" *Hee-hee.* "They have trains filled with pennies. They're not going to miss a quarter."

Even though she seemed to want me to say "That's cool" or "Great," I was having a hard time saying anything at all. I just wanted to be with David, heading home.

"You have to see this thing," she said, handing me the box. "It's pretty awesome."

I felt uncomfortable. I didn't deserve another present, didn't want another present, especially not from Saula.

"Are you sure?" I asked.

"Sure I'm sure."

I opened the box and pulled out a layer of purple velvet wrapping. Tucked into a slot in the bottom of the box was a quarter. It was the brightest silver I had ever seen.

"Is it real?"

"See? I knew you'd be the only one who'd understand. It's more than money."

I looked up at Saula. She had the same expression a baby makes when it's curious about someone's loud laugh.

"You and I," she whispered, "we have so many things in common."

"It feels light. Lighter than most quarters."

"And it's worth a lot more than twenty-five cents."

"But if you went to McDonald's you could only get fries."

Saula snorted more than laughed and said, "I hope you let me take it sometimes." *Hee-hee.* "Quarter babysitting or something."

I nodded. She nodded back.

"I'm hungry," I said, pointing in the direction of my house. "The lunch was gross today."

"Always nasty. Lunch. Yuck."

I held up the quarter and the box. "This was really nice. Thanks."

"Come hang out. You and Jesse and Jonathon always go to the gulch. So do I. We could go there together. I was heading that direction anyway."

"I have to eat," I said. "And there's homework."

"I can wait. And later, maybe we could go to Cooper Cinemas. I have a cousin who cleans there. We could see that movie about that satanic car. *Christine*. And it'd be free. My sister isn't home either. I don't know what you're doing tonight. . . . I'm suspended. No homework. So I can do whatever."

"Yeah."

I started to back away. Saula grabbed my arm.

"Do you have cable? There's this show on tonight where—"

"My mom won't—"

"Sure. Sure."

Saula wouldn't let go. She wasn't holding my arm tightly, just firmly. She looked totally lost, like the retirees on *The Price Is Right* who had no idea how much Twinkies cost.

"We're still friends? Right?"

"Yeah. Of course. We're still friends."

" 'Cause I got your back."

"Sure."

I gave a tug, trying to free my arm from her grasp, but Saula held on, her cheeks high, her eyes narrow.

"Come with me," she whispered.

"I really can't."

"You know, Samuel. You know what it's like. My house. I know you do. Probably like yours, but different. You've never been, but . . . If I go back it'll be all dark. Ashtrays. These orange drapes that aren't even ours. But here with you, outside, is much better. We have trees, right? And grass. That's a nice smell. I know your dad stayed outside a lot. In his tent. Right?"

I felt a hand on my shoulder. I thought that somehow Saula had extended her arm without me seeing. But it wasn't her at all.

"Right before my mom left, she said to me, 'Pussy Cat'— 'cause that was her name for me. 'Pussy Cat.' Two words. She said . . ."

The hand moving me was strong, determined, even stronger than Saula's hand that was still gripping my arm.

"My mom said I should . . ."

One second I was staring straight at Saula and the next at David's back. His blue striped shirt, his crossbow shoulders, the neat line where his hair ended and the muscles of his neck began. I was surprised that he had returned, surprised that he was stepping in front of me, surprised . . . Then I saw him cock my Louisville Slugger bat high in the air, the dark lines of wood grain absorbing the sun.

I screamed, trying to grab the bat. But it all happened too fast. I could hear the Louisville Slugger whistling through the air as it came within inches of my jaw.

In that millionth of a second, I understood why Uncle Rhoald and Aunt Virginia had sent David to us. The anger, the resentment, the hurt; it had snowballed into an uncontrollable level, where David, whose mother was white and his father black, who had once been a kid like Saula and me and Jonathon, was now a body filled with a blackness as thick and cold as refrigerated syrup.

Pow!

David hit Saula right in her hip, the impact sounding as if someone had dropped a bag of laundry. She stared at me with frog eyes, there was a second of hard silence, and then she collapsed onto the sidewalk.

"David!" I grabbed the bat but couldn't wrestle it away.

"You don't talk," he said, watching me with amusement. "You act."

"Give me the bat!"

"Strength, Samuel!"

"Give me the bat!"

Even though David was holding the bat in his right hand, he managed to land a punch with his left. My nose bent to the side. I couldn't breathe, I couldn't see, and I crumpled onto the ground, next to Saula.

I focused on clearing my vision. I needed to see. I had to stop whatever David was planning next. I pushed myself to my elbows.

"Damn it, Samuel!" David shouted. "Don't you see? Don't you see what happens when you don't fight back? People do whatever they want. Someone has to stop them. And if it's not going to be you, I'll do it. Because when you're alone, no one else cares."

My head was clearing, and what I saw before me was terrifying. David's chest was pumping and his mouth bared his perfectly white teeth. He was towering over Saula, holding the bat in the air, directly over his head, just as if he were about to cut off Goliath's head.

"But I care, little cousin. This fat cow. Watch me. I care."

David kicked Saula in the butt with all his might. She rolled away, sobbing. David raised the bat again, ready to strike her with more force, but I crawled in front of Saula.

"I do not ask that you take them out of the world, but that you keep them from the evil one."

"Look at your arm!" David screamed, spittle coming from his lips. He yanked me to my feet, holding me up as I wobbled from side to side. "Scarred! Look! She did that!" He shoved the bat in my hand.

"No."

I let the bat fall from my hand, onto the ground, hearing only the solid wooden sound usually connected to a home run.

David pushed me. And with that push, a million feelings, or emotions, or sensations, that had built up ever since my father left spilled out from my insides, pouring onto the ground. They scattered everywhere, pooling around my feet as shiny pebbles of obsidian.

"Hit her!"

"I do not ask that you take them out of the world, but that you keep them from the evil one."

"Your choice."

David raised his fist. His eyes became snake-slits, his tongue flickered, his fist barreled toward me, an asteroid from the coldest corner of the universe. I knew what was coming, knew the strength of his arm, but still I didn't move.

Vooooom-crash!

When his fist met my nose, darkness briefly overcame me, and then light, and then sparkling dots. My body lost sensation. I wasn't sure if I was falling or floating. Somewhere high above, maybe seconds, maybe hours later, David growled, "You can't do this, Samuel! You have to fight back!"

Hearing the rage in his voice gave me a feeling of calm. He too was on the verge of crying.

David kicked me. He kicked Saula. Then he spit on us both, picked up the bat, and walked away.

I spent the afternoon lying in bed. David was downstairs, in his room, listening to heavy metal on a portable tape recorder, the occasional guitar chord or drumbeat shimmying through the floorboards and reminding me of his stupid existence.

The bruise on my face, just to the left of my nose, wasn't as bad as I thought it might be. In fact, the spot where David's knuckles had met my skin resembled a pair of miniature purple boobs.

I was wearing the moccasins, dangling my feet off the end of the bed, listening to the tinkling of the beads against the soft leather, and thinking about Saula. After David had left, I helped her to her feet. She almost whispered something, something about the quarter I still had in my hand, but as her lips flexed and bent to make words, she stopped and remembered that I was the boy who had once pulled a knife on her. And as she headed toward the gulch, limping, alone, I almost yelled to her. Part of me wanted to run and help, to save her from her miserable life, but another part was relieved that she would no longer want to be my friend.

No matter how hard I tried to imagine David's anger, no matter how hard I tried to understand what had happened at the bus stop, I couldn't. Even though the last few months had been hard and I had exploded with Saula and the Mexicans, I couldn't see myself reaching the same level of anger and frustration as David. He had purposely attacked someone he didn't even know, someone who had never harmed him, all because, he said, he was protecting me.

I began flipping the quarter that Saula had given me in the air. Each time I caught it in my palm and slammed it onto the back of my hand, the quarter came up heads. With each touch, the oil from my fingers dulled the shine. I flipped it again and again, higher and higher, until it almost hit the ceiling, snatching it just before it touched the bed. Heads. Heads. Heads.

At one point, I flipped the quarter too far to the left and it fell onto the carpet. I leaned down and noticed something lying under my desk, something thin and black and sprouting dust bunnies. I rolled out of bed, got down on my knees, and tried to reach for it, but the mystery object was stuck far against the wall. I grabbed my ruler, stretched my arm, and pushed it to the side. It took three tries before my old sixth-grade notebook popped out.

My father must have set it on my desk right before he left. Later I must have bumped the desk and it had fallen.

I leaned against my bed and slowly opened the notebook, remembering how he had sat in his tent, writing and writing and writing. His notes were everywhere, black ink covering page after page, long lines strung together, most, but not all of the sentences about violence, the word itself often underlined:

From the fruit of his lips a man enjoys good things,
but the un-faithful have a craving for violence.

—Proverbs 13:2

Give up your violence and oppression and do what is
just and right.

—Ezekiel 45:9

Rescue me, O LORD, from evil men; protect me from
men of violence.

—Psalm 140:1

The mouth of the righteous is a fountain of life, but
the mouth of the wicked conceal, violence.

—Proverbs 10:6

Halfway through the book the writing suddenly stopped and newspaper articles from *The Denver Post* and the *Rocky Mountain News*, articles about American naval destroyers shooting down Russian planes, Romanian spies being tortured by the CIA, and underground nuclear tests in New Mexico, were glued haphazardly to the fronts and backs of pages. There were articles about stabbings in Pueblo, muggings in Aurora, murders in Durango, rapes in Colorado Springs. Articles about United States gun sales to South America, anti-aircraft missile sales to Israel, chemical weapon sales to Iraq, and nuclear weapons contracts in Europe.

Then on the last page was a picture of a young boy, my age, lying on a porch, his skin milky and purple. Standing over the boy was a bearded man in striped pajamas, his eyes red and swollen from crying.

I knew who the boy was. Every boy in school knew who that boy was. The story had been repeated by teachers, on the local news, and by other kids, over and over, until it no longer seemed real, but more like a fable. The boy, William Kanagy, had snuck out in the middle of the night and, after hanging out with his friends until three in the morning, climbed back into his house through the living room window. His father, mistaking William for a robber, shot him six times.

Underneath the photo my father had written:

> *On the next day when they had come down from the mountain, a great crowd met him. And behold, a man from the crowd cried out, "Teacher, I beg you to look upon my son, for he is my only child. And behold, a spirit seizes him, and he suddenly cries out. It convulses him so that he foams at the mouth, and shatters him, and will hardly leave him. And I begged your disciples to cast it out, but they could not."*

Then this last part. This last sentence . . . I could almost picture my father copying it from the Bible.

> *Jesus answered, "O faithless and twisted generation, how long am I to be with you and bear with you?"*

※

That night David made spaghetti and a red sauce with bell peppers, mushrooms, onions, and carrots.

When my mom got home and finished opening the mail, she took the lids off every pot and waved the steam toward her nose.

"This is special. Special. Super special."

I stood behind my mom, a safe distance from the cook, waiting for her to notice my bruises.

"A queen has every right to relax after a hard day at work," David said. "I've been trying to tell Samuel that, but he doesn't believe me."

I glared at him.

"Samuel helps," she said, looking down at me. "What is this? What happened to your face?"

I took a deep breath, ready to unleash the truth. I would tell her how David hit Saula with a bat and punched me and how—

"His friends," David said quickly, with a fake chuckle. "Punching and fighting on the bus. They're always joking around, but it's really dangerous. The driver said they do it everyday."

"What?" I asked. "Roger said that? To you? When?"

"And that's not all he told me."

"Whatever it was"—my mom touched my face—"be careful. You and your friends. Please."

"Why don't you make yourself useful, Samuel," David suggested, sweet as pie, "and set the table."

David and I exchanged a flurry of eye contact, shooting angry thoughts at each other.

"Useful?"

"Don't be difficult. Your mom has had a hard day at work."

I threw open the drawers and cabinets and yanked out knives, forks, plates. I set the table loudly, slamming down everything twice. When we sat at the dinner table, David kept winking and smiling at me. I was forced to grip the underside of the table, swallowing my fury. He served us like a waiter in a fancy restaurant, even lighting a candle. Our huge plates of steaming pasta looked like something out of a Chef Boyardee commercial.

"Special," my mom repeated for the billionth time, taking the first bite.

I crossed my arms, the smell making my stomach growl, but pride demanding that I keep my arms crossed.

I rolled a few strands onto my fork and put it in my mouth. Although it was delicious, I scrunched up my face.

"Are we eating dog food?" I asked.

"Purina," David replied.

"It's worse than dog food."

"And what is that? What's worse? Huh?"

"Anything made by you."

"Anything? Even toast?"

My mom's eyes moved from David to me.

"Something up, gentlemen?"

David shrugged and pointed his fork at me: "He's mad because I made him finish his homework before dinner."

"I'd be mad too. Samuel usually does his homework without being asked."

"Nice try," I said to David. I picked up my fork and held it with my middle finger so only he could see.

"Let's talk about school," my mom said to David.

"School's easy. The hard part is after school. With Samuel. Setting an example."

My mom messed my hair and said, "You just work on living here in Denver. Don't worry about Samuel. He can manage on his own."

"Not according to my friend Paco. Samuel and Jonathon and Jesse steal bikes from the Mexican kids."

Although I had given in and was devouring my meal, I stopped chewing the minute Paco's name left David's mouth.

"That's not true?" my mom said/asked, glancing over at me.

"Tell your mother about the Mexicans." David smirked.

"Mexicans have Huffys. Nobody wants a Huffy."

There was an awkward silence while my mom studied us closely. I could tell she was debating over whether to push the issue or not.

"We had an assembly today," David smirked. "A guy from prison. He told us all about what it was like to live in a cell with four other guys. Some kid asked him about dropping the soap and he said that you didn't have to drop the soap in prison, that guys would just grab you anytime they wanted."

"Interesting assembly."

"It was all right."

My mom turned to me. "Did you have an assembly too?"

"We had a black cowboy."

"And?"

"And."

"And, what did you learn?"

"I learned a lot of things. I learned how people lie to cover up for the bad things they've done. I learned that some people will believe that other people are good as long as they do something nice, like make spaghetti. Oh, and you know what else I learned? I learned that David's a big fat brown piece of poo!"

"Samuel!" my mom half-shrieked.

"Samuel!" David frowned.

I got up from the table and glared at David. Then I looked at my mom.

"I thought you were smarter. You talk about Reagan and how he's an actor. Blah blah blah. But you're just the same as everyone else. All those 'stupid American voters.' You might as well be one of them." I pointed at David. "Just look at him. For you, all he has to do is make dinner and everything is fine."

I ran to my room and slammed the door as hard as I could, but it reopened. I got up and closed it a second time and then dove onto my bed. I pulled a pillow over my face and everything went dark.

✕

About twenty minutes later there was a knock. My mom stepped in and closed the door. I had burrowed deep under my pillows, deep into the bottomless caverns of Bedsylvania.

"Hey, sweetie," she said, sitting down and rubbing my leg. "Where's my little Samuel?"

I didn't answer.

"I can't help if I don't know what's going on."

I still didn't answer.

"Come on," she said. "I know David isn't easy. But I'm not here all day. I don't automatically know how he's behaving if you don't tell me."

She began to rub my back. I emerged from my hideout. Since

the day my father had left, my mom had looked haggard, as if her alarm clock was always ringing too early. But ever since David had arrived, the new challenge had been almost inspirational for her. Her cheeks were now splotched raspberry and her eyes, once again, shined.

"I want him to be nice. To treat me like a brother."

"I told you before, he can't be something he isn't. Don't try and put him in some mold you've envisioned. David's troubled. As of late, we're troubled. There's bound to be some clashes in between."

"It's not my fault. What happened to him."

"Whatever David is saying or doing isn't because of you. You know that. Everyone has abandoned him. You just happen to be in the path of his anger. Turn the other cheek. That's what separates you from him. Whatever happened, and I have no doubt something did, solve it in a loving way."

The weather outside rattled my window frame. My mother rubbed her shoulder with her hand. She had already taken four Tylenol since she came home, but I knew her bent spine still ached. It always hurt when the weather was changing.

"Why do I have to be nice to him?"

She touched the bruise on my cheek.

"I'm not asking you to be nice. I said to turn the other cheek. There's a difference. Being nice is doing something for someone. Turning the other cheek, well, it's self-explanatory. You simply aren't retaliating." She smiled. "You can do this. You are in a good place to set an example. All that strength you have."

"Strength." I blew out the word.

"You were strong enough to hold me up. After your father left."

"I didn't hold you up."

"Of course you did." She picked at something on my bedspread. "A lot of my friends had been in relationships before they married. They'd been hurt by men. Had broken hearts.

Knew what it was like to lose someone so close. But not me. 'Always a bridesmaid, never a bride,' as they say. Until I met your father, I'd never had the chance to fully give myself to someone. I'm not a looker. Not the way my polio left me. But your father, he looked through my bumps and bruises."

"Do you miss him?" I asked.

"Do you?"

"I'm not sure."

"I miss who he once was. Who we all were."

"What were we?"

My mom smiled. It was a beautiful smile; so gentle and sad and holding back a reservoir of love for me.

✄

I rehearsed my apology and jumped from stair to stair, down into the basement. I knocked on David's door and went in. He was crouched on the floor, piecing a *Playboy* centerfold together with Scotch tape.

"Miss October." David grinned. "She surfs and likes Rush."

"What's Rush?"

"Wow, you guys really are out of touch here."

I examined the naked woman, her breasts and legs so thickly oiled that they reflected the camera flash. David rolled a piece of tape across his fingers.

"My mom's going to get mad," I said.

"Like I care."

"I'm sorry," I said quickly before I couldn't say it anymore. "I'm sorry about everything."

David rolled his eyes so far back that I could see his brain.

"See? That's the problem with you. You're weak. I punched you and now *you* apologize?"

"I apologized for what I said."

He turned around. His face was twisted as if he was holding a really bad hand of cards.

"I've come up with a plan. Let's just say that if you want to come inside this house tomorrow, you're gonna have to fight your way in. Just me and you."

"I said I was sorry."

"Fight your way in," he repeated.

"No."

"No?"

"No. I won't fight you. I'm turning the other cheek."

"Then you'll stay outside," he said, pausing. "'Turn the other cheek.' What's that? You need to learn what strength is. If someone punches you with their fist, then you use a bat. They use a bat, you use a knife."

Anger was bubbling inside. The steam would soon come out my ears and my head would begin spinning round. I sidestepped to a safe corner of the room, out of David's reach.

"What about Joseph?" I said. "Remember when you sent him to the hospital? That gave Uncle Rhoald an excuse to send you here. Your fight didn't solve anything. It only made things in Pulaski worse."

"Whatever," he said, waving his hand.

"Don't say 'whatever.'"

"Whatever, whatever."

And turning his back to me, David began to tape up Miss October on the wall. I stormed out, slamming the door after me, and although it too opened again, I didn't go back to close it for him.

I kissed my mother good night, brushed my teeth, put on my pajamas, and lay in bed, following the web of cracks in our ceiling. When I got bored with that, I flipped through my dad's notebook.

"Hannah was speaking in her heart; only her lips moved, and her voice was not heard" was written in a margin, toward the front.

> *The LORD makes poor and makes rich; he brings low and he exalts. He raises up the poor from the dust; he lifts the needy from the ash heap to make them sit with princes and inherit a seat of honor.*

I removed a children's Bible from the shelf above my desk and opened it to the Book of Samuel. The first quote, about Hannah speaking without moving her lips, was on the first page of The Book of Samuel. There was a watercolor illustration of Hannah kneeling on the floor, a swaddled baby Samuel by her side, a ring of light around her head, while God, who looked like Santa Claus with bad gas, hovered above.

I closed the Bible and tossed it on the floor. I couldn't understand why my father had been so interested in Hannah. It didn't have anything to do with me, the *real* Samuel, nor did it have anything to do with my mom, who once told me she got pregnant the minute she went off the pill. Maybe it was because both my father and Hannah *needed* God to give them a purpose to their lives.

The rain was making my window shiver, hail had turned the ground white, and the wind was ripping the orange leaves from the trees. Winter was coming early, and Larry Green on Channel 4 was predicting that this would be one of the worst in Colorado history. Therefore, he said, we should stay tuned, every day.

I imagined my father sitting outside, the weather freezing his clothes, his hair clumped with ice. There was no one around for miles, no one to hear him pray, no one to hear him cry for help. "... *Her voice was not heard.*"

✠

I was still awake at one o'clock. My eyes would not close, no matter how hard I tried.

I climbed out of bed, dressed, and clambered out the window; my Levi's buttons popped against the window frame, one by one.

It was perfect weather for Jack the Ripper. A layer of clouds hung only a few feet above the ground, an evening of gray cotton candy, millions of threads of water spun together, weightless. All the sounds of Denver at night were caught up in a widow's web of fog.

I stepped carefully toward the garage, slowly opened the door, and entered. As I began to unlock my bike, something stopped me. It was a smell. An old smell, of canvas drying in the sun, of a sleeping bag.

I reached across my bike and pulled out my dad's tent. I pressed a corner of canvas against my nose, inhaling.

Feeling sad, missing my father so bad my stomach began to clench, I put the tent back, unlocked my bicycle, rolled forward, and left the garage behind. I pedaled down the driveway and onto Cleaver Street, realizing that in the fog, I couldn't see where I was going, except for the tiny strip of asphalt near my feet. Luckily I already knew every bump and dip, every curve and crossing, every pothole, every manhole cover.

I started to pedal faster, the fog getting thicker and thicker. And even though I couldn't see, I could sense that I was passing the gulch, passing the tunnel, Double Donuts, Grandma's nursing home, the YMCA, Albertsons, Dolly Madison, and Cynthia's house.

When I got to Colorado Boulevard and Evans, the fog cleared slightly. Most of the brighter neon signs, the ones that were always helpful at night, from the Kentucky Fried Chicken to the Big H Auto, were now dark, plastic shells. The yellow light of the streetlamps, the only other light besides the moon, reminded me of the Devil's Tower in *Close Encounters of the Third Kind,* right before the aliens landed.

On the I-25 overpass, I sprinted, back and forth, speeding toward one end and then turning around, heading back toward the other side. The cars beneath me were traveling thousands of times faster, unable to recognize each other beyond their two yellow headlights. If I were to slip and fall, to suddenly find myself among them, it would be too late. I would be a shadow among those cars, an insect crushed into the fender.

My lungs began to burn near Wimmer's Western Wear. My legs were filled with hot lava, and the wet air clung to my face and clogged my lungs.

"Aaaaaaaahhhhhhhhhhhhhhhhh!!!!!"

I screamed and screamed, traveling faster than the Concorde, my voice trailing miles behind because I had already broken the sound barrier twice.

My legs gave out in front of Wyatt's cafeteria. I coasted to the middle of the Colorado Plaza parking lot and collapsed onto the asphalt, sucking in deep breaths, draining all the world's oxygen out of the atmosphere.

A semi rumbled down Colorado, the twin pipes growling out exhaust. The neon lights above JCPenney buzzed. The small arm of the Midland Bank clock groaned to the right. The parking lot was empty, the stores were dark, the buildings were invisible in the night.

✠

It might have been seconds or minutes or even hours, but I awoke to a low rumbling. Although it was still dark outside, and the fog had thinned only a little, I saw something terrifying on the horizon. Two blocks away, right behind the Collegiate Shopping Mall, a huge fireball was climbing into the sky.

I sat up, gazing in shock at the glowing genie spreading out above. The flaming body stretched, yawned, and craned toward space, its white light daring the fog.

Several minutes went by before the fireball could reach no further. Gradually, it retreated, like someone who has been jolted upright by a ringing alarm but smacks the snooze button and slides slowly back into bed.

I got up, brushed myself off, and lifted my bike. I wasn't sure what to do next.

I started to ride slowly through the empty parking lot. My senses were upside-down and I was having a hard time paying attention to anything other than the darkened space where the fireball had been. I turned a corner, whipping over the JCPenney sidewalk, dodging a NO PARKING sign at the last second.

Just as I was about to cross the Yale/Colorado Boulevard intersection and the main entrance of Collegiate Shopping Mall, I leaned to the left, but with too much force. Then I hit a speed bump.

"Yuuuuuuhhhhhh!" I screamed, starting to go down.

I slid along the ground, my legs burning against the cement. When I finally stopped, I lay there for a second, deciding whether I was paralyzed or not.

"What the hell?"

"Who was that?"

The voices. I knew the voices.

"It was the police."

"That wasn't the police."

"Shut up!"

"You shut up!"

"Jonathon?" I asked the fog. "Jesse?"

"Who is that? They know us."

"It's the police!"

Two shadows appeared from the fog: Jonathon and Jesse, wearing nothing but black clothing. They stopped in front of me and hovered.

"Samuel?"

"What are you doing?"

"I couldn't see the speed bump. In the fog. But what are you doing?"

"Brothers for life?"

"Did you . . . ?"

"That fire."

"Keep your voice down."

"You keep your voice down."

I examined my leg. I had torn my pants and peeled a few inches of skin from my thigh. Then I looked up at both of them. They didn't look good either. Jittery and untrusting.

"You guys?" I asked. "You did that?"

Jesse and Jonathon blinked. Then Jesse lifted my bike.

"Can you walk? We should go."

✠

Jonathon was sitting on my handlebars and Jesse was standing on the back of my frame. We had ridden like this before, when we were younger, usually when one of us had a busted wheel or couldn't afford a new chain. But now that we were older, bigger, my calves burned as I pedaled with the three of us.

We rode to the YMCA, the highest point in our neighborhood, and climbed the fire escape to the roof.

"I heard at some prisons you can play golf," Jesse said.

"You don't know how to play golf."

"I can drive a cart."

Jesse was the first to reach the edge of the roof and his reaction told me how bad the fire was. Jesse was always fidgeting, the constant sugar he ate flowing through his blood even when he dozed through assemblies. But now his body hardened into a totem pole.

"Oh no," Jesse mumbled.

Even though I was carefully walking over the tar roof, I could see the pink and orange glow of the fire against the sky. It reminded me of the evenings after snowstorms, when the city lights reflected against the clouds and it was bright enough, even at midnight, to pinpoint enemies with snowballs.

Jonathon stepped next to Jesse. The two of them were so small against the horizon, standing on the flaming edge of hell, that I was sure the devil was going to rise up at any moment and stab them with his pitchfork.

"Samuel," Jesse said without turning.

I went to the edge. When I got there, I tried to stay calm, even though every inch of my skin prickled.

I had seen films in school where huge German bombers flew over England and carpet bombed entire cities. The Collegiate

Shopping Mall might as well have been London during World War II. If there weren't pockets of flames along the torn roof, there were hundreds of columns of smoke rising toward the sky.

The roof of Candy Cane, a shop that sold chocolate in the shape of penises, was a sinkhole. The display cases in Garment World exploded, one by one, making the same sound as lightbulbs when stepped upon. Burning pages from Nader's Booksellers floated through the air.

There were at least fifteen fire engines, dozens of police officers, and a few rubberneckers standing by their cars, watching from a distance. The sirens rotated noiselessly while the pumps spewed foamy water through coiled hoses. The firemen aimed their hoses right through the front windows of the mall. At the southern end of Colorado Boulevard, I could see engines from nearby counties arriving, while even more cars and delivery trucks pulled onto the shoulder, unable to get around the congestion of emergency vehicles.

"Remember the end of *Flash Gordon*?" Jesse whispered. "You know, when that pole goes through Ming and he dies as the entire kingdom is burning around him?"

There was the uninterrupted crackling of flames. The front of my arms and legs stung from the heat, while my back was chilled cold.

"It was just like the other day," Jonathon said. "In the garage. But we made this bomb bigger. Strong enough to kill thirty Mexicans." He wiped the sweat from his brow. "I wanted to test it behind the mall, where they have that gas pump. You know, for delivery trucks. The one that's locked up behind a cage. That was where . . . It was my idea to go there. I thought it would explode." He swallowed. "But . . ."

More engines unloaded teams of firemen. Channel 4 and Channel 9 whipped into the parking lot.

Jonathon, Jesse, and I sat down on the edge of the YMCA roof, dangling our legs over the side. Dozens of firemen sprayed foam onto the fire while others stood around chatting. The police rolled tape around the entrances, and men in bulky jackets talked on CB's. Thousands of sirens rotated noiselessly.

✗

It was nearly five o'clock when I rode home. The sun hadn't risen yet, but the purple ring at the eastern edges was busily eating away the black licorice sky. The moon, which had minutes earlier finished crossing from east to west, was just a hologram balancing on the tips of the Rockies.

Birds were chirping in stereo. There were trees stuffed with feathers and bright bluebirds replacing the empty holes where the autumn leaves had fallen.

I stopped in front of the Bernards' house. The Rottweilers were fast asleep; the only one to look over remained in his warm corner, curled tight.

"Pssst."

They didn't budge.

"Pssst."

Nothing.

"Come and get me."

I reached over the fence and unlatched the gate.

"Pssst. I'm not scared of you anymore."

Another dog opened his eyes, but didn't move. I flung the gate wide open and pedaled away as fast as I could. When I was a good three houses away, I stopped and turned. One of the dogs stood and shook his burly coat, but he was in no hurry to chase.

On Wednesday morning I could barely keep my eyes open as we walked to the bus stop.

"You see the news this morning?" David asked, nodding toward the smoke coming from the Collegiate Shopping Mall. "They think it was terrorists." He smiled enviously.

The minute we got on the bus, I fell asleep. Then I fell asleep in Social Studies. And then I fell asleep in Algebra. The worst was when I fell asleep in the locker room, right before gym.

During lunch Mike Tasher, Jeremy D'Ache, and Jason Friedman started a food fight. There were carrots, pigs in a blanket, juice boxes, apple slices, orange wedges, Fritos, bread crusts, Chocodiles, and peanuts all flying at the same time. I catapulted grape Jell-O from my plastic spoon and hit Christine right in the face. The best part was that she didn't even know it was me.

In Science we learned about the reproductive system, which

was cool because two of our vocabulary words were *penis* and *vagina*. Ms. Rabinoes drew a big diagram of a uterus and two fallopian tubes on the chalkboard that could have also been pods from *Invasion of the Body Snatchers*. I looked over at Rebecca O'Donnelly and tried to imagine the pod inside her body. She caught me staring at her, rolled her eyes, and whispered something nasty to Angela Obermeyer.

The high school had been dismissed at noon, so David took an earlier bus home. As Roger drove down Colorado Boulevard, Jonathon, Jesse, and I slept the whole way to our bus stops.

As I trudged along the sidewalk, alone, I waved to Mr. Wallack, who was sitting on his porch swing, reading *The Denver Post*. He waved back without lifting his eyes.

The Wallacks had hung two bird feeders from the rafters on the side of their house so that they dangled out over our driveway. A group of robins were picking their way through the seed and discarding the shells. I stopped to watch the way they interacted, the way they defended their food from the occasional crow or blue jay. They were determined to get as much seed as possible out of the feeder, and if any other bird got in their way, a fight would break out. The robins were banded together, a gang staking their rights to something that was intended for all.

I continued on toward the backyard, my feet as heavy as cement blocks. My heart rate was speeding up, and my brow became moist.

I unlatched the gate. Carefully, I stepped into the backyard and lifted the fake green grass doormat. The key was gone. I tried the door handle, turning it exactly how a cat burglar might. It wasn't locked and the spindle moved easily. As I cracked the door, David suddenly pulled it inward and I fell on my face.

"Hey, little cuz. Ready to rumble?"

"I'm not going to fight you," I said.

I leaped to my feet, marched forward, and tried to squeeze

past David, but he pushed me down onto the ground. I landed hard, getting grass and mud on my elbows.

"Fight!"

I stood and brushed myself off. Then I took a running start and rammed straight into him. He grabbed me by the head and although we wrestled for a good minute, he quickly gained control and threw me back onto the ground.

"I'm not going to fight!" I shouted. "This is my house!"

I leaped to my feet again, charging. I was hoping to get in through the small space between David and the doorjamb, but just as I reached the first step, his fist met my nose. I reeled backward, a light tingling spreading in seconds into a harsh stinging.

"Fight!" David screamed at me. "Fight! Come on! Get up!"

I shook my head and strained to get to my feet, but I was so dizzy that I could barely balance myself on all fours. David lifted me by my shirt collar.

"Fight!"

By now I saw the same thing in David's face that I had seen in my grandmother, in Saula, and most recently in Jonathon. It wasn't hatred, nor was it anger, but something even deeper, an expression like Ronald Reagan's when he pointed at the camera and said, "Let terrorists beware . . ."

"One punch."

"Why? Why? Why? Why?"

"You don't know what people do. The way they'll treat you. You've no idea."

"People like you," I said.

"I'm the good guy."

"No you're not. You're a horrible person. Your parents left you and Uncle Rhoald hates you and no one wants you in their home."

David pursed his lips, ground his teeth, and flexed his neck muscles. His eyes began to close in on themselves, and his hand squeezed the doorknob so tightly that his knuckles turned white.

Suddenly, he charged. I jumped up, threw my backpack at him, and sprinted off, heading straight for the back gate. I slammed the gate shut and raced down the alley. I heard David cursing as he fumbled with the latch. After several blocks, I reached Iliff Avenue, and only then did I slow down to look over my shoulder. David was hunched at the far end of the block, catching his breath.

"You can say good-bye to your stuff!" he yelled.

I gave David my middle finger. He slowly started to walk in my direction and I quickly turned the corner.

As I trudged along toward the gulch, thinking only of my pillows and comforter, I tried to count the cracks in the sidewalk. I was bored by the time I got to seven. I examined the gutters for washed-up money, but only found a red rubber band. I balanced along the edge of the sidewalk like a tightrope walker, but almost sprained my ankle when I slipped on a patch of wet cement.

I stopped and looked around. My neighborhood was silent, a ghost town where everyone would be back by five-thirty. All the houses were exactly alike; single peaks, three front windows, tar roofing, raised cement porches. My neighbors cut their lawns perpendicularly, bought their flowers from Buffalo Nursery, had the same four curtains, and placed their plastic "Welcome" doormats not to the side, not near the front steps, but directly under the door.

Two houses down and adjacent to ours, the Nemerovskys, who had emigrated from Vladivostok twenty years ago, weren't any different from, say, the Schwarzbergs from Israel or the Picolottis from Argentina. The Nemerovskys drove a Plymouth Duster, put a new coat of lavender on their house every spring, ate at Wyatt's cafeteria after church, wore orange and blue the day before a Bronco game, and smuggled in illegal fireworks from Wyoming on the Fourth of July.

I continued on, passing the Russells' house. The Russells both worked for the phone company, she as an operator and he as a repairman. The Russells had a simple front yard with a tidy lawn and a few flowers. Every summer they took a month off and drove around America in their Lincoln, snapping black-and-white photos of small towns. My mom said that Mrs. Russell had an especially good eye, and every time I talked to her, I shifted from side to side, studying her pupils, trying to figure out which one it was.

The O'Shanys' house was next. The O'Shanys wore shirts that said KISS ME, I'M IRISH or IRISH I WERE IN IRELAND. They had once admitted to my mother that they had never been to Ireland, "with the bombing and the killings in the North and whatnot . . ." But during every Notre Dame game or on Saint Patrick's Day, they turned on their green porch light, and if you happened to pass by at the right time, you could catch them singing Irish songs and cheering.

When I came to the Bernards' house, I paused. I wasn't sure if they were home, because their burgundy velvet curtains were always drawn. Their Datsuns were parked evenly in the driveway and two overturned wash buckets sat in the middle of their front lawn. The paint was peeling from the sides of the house, and the rope that held a swing a few inches from the porch had long ago frayed and snapped.

I turned the corner, trying to peek between the curtains. When I got to their backyard, I stopped in my tracks. Stomach juices washed through my guts and an undertow of guilt raked me away. The gate was still open, yet three of the five Rottweilers were lying in their muddy corner of the yard.

I imagined Bill Stuart announcing from his news anchor desk: "Rottweilers go on killing rampage while Collegiate Shopping Mall burns. Samuel Francis Gerard to blame."

I rushed forward and shut the gate. There was a ping as the steel edges touched. The lock clicked into place.

I stood there waiting for the three remaining Rottweilers to come barreling toward the fence, fangs switchbladed open. But they didn't move. Beyond the fence they could dominate an entire neighborhood, subject all cats and dogs to their rule. Yet here, in the Bernards' backyard, they slept on muddy blankets, drank from the same water bowl, ate moldy food. And, when I had presented them with a better life, with freedom, only two of them had fled. The remaining three voluntarily remained caged.

I hiked along the torn-up alleyway, keeping an eye out for a rebel Rottweiler. I half-expected to see a trail of chaos; bloated corpses, pants shredded by teeth, cat carcasses. But all I saw, at the last house before the gulch, was Mrs. Skilder's two Japanese bobtails, sitting side by side on a wooden fence, eyeing me suspiciously.

Here I was so busy thinking Jonathon was wrong for building a bomb to hurt Mexicans that I had, without giving it a second thought, committed an equally bad act. I had let two vicious dogs roam free.

Forever, or at least since the Big Bang, there has been an overturned metal tub at the gulch entrance on Cleaver Street. In the summer, by midday, the rusted tub was always too hot to sit on, but in the winter, when the sun hit it just right, it would heat up, melt the snow, and transform into a perfect place to watch any bike-jumping competition. I hopped up onto the tub, the heat of the sun-warmed metal seeping through my jeans. I looked around for people, near the tunnel, by the hollow raisin shell of the bulldozer on Tina Turner's Tabletop, and over near the chain-link fence at the top of the gulch that separated the natural world from the rusted Dumpsters in the alley behind a block of retail stores.

Standing near the entrance of the tunnel, Geronimo was bent over a shard of a mirror, combing his thin hair. He was singing, his dusty, throaty repetition of a single word gliding across the gulch, overtaking the schizophrenic wind and the lisping grass.

His singing wasn't rowdy and charged with energy like the annual rain dances the Hopi performed downtown. Geronimo's songs were heavy like mud slides.

He let out a loud whistle. It echoed through the gulch and hit my ears at such an angle that it sounded more like a chirp. As soon as his whistle evaporated, the gulch grass rustled and something short and wide headed in his direction. I leaned forward, straining my eyes, and there, bursting from the grass, their paws and underbellies coated in mud, were the two missing Rottweilers. They emerged full of enthusiasm and bounced and danced around.

I had fallen asleep for what seemed like only a few minutes, but in reality it must have been much longer. The sun was already halfway below the mountains.

I jumped down from the metal container, zipped up my sweat-shirt, and looked across the gulch to see if Geronimo and the Rottweilers were still around. There were just piles of glass, cans, clothing, tires, cassettes, busted stereos, plastic jugs, traffic signs, melted cardboard advertisements, and assorted metal hooks, plant hangers, washing machine covers, Winnebago rims, and motorcycle handlebars.

I made my way through the reeds and came to a small em-bankment, a muddy ledge where the water in the gulch had sliced a bed under a patch of wet ground held together by spruce tree roots. I almost tripped over Saula. She was lying on her back and wearing a blue cotton dress, thick stockings, and orange boots, and her hair was pulled back into two uneven pigtails.

"Hi," I said, somewhat nervous.

Saula turned and looked at me, terrified.

"Hi."

"Are you okay? I mean your hip? You know? Yesterday. Your arm? Did you . . . did he break anything?"

Saula stared at me with wide, unblinking eyes. I sat down next to her.

"It was pretty bad. Did you have to go to the hospital?"

She shook her head.

"I wish I could have stopped him."

"You couldn't."

"He won't let me in the house. He wants me to fight him. He thinks I should be tough. But I promised my mom. And it's not what my dad would do and . . . Plus I . . . I'm really sorry. I tried to take the bat. I wasn't strong enough."

Saula blinked. The wind was streaming through the grass. A frog was croaking. Three ducks quacked in unison as they paddled along.

Saula suddenly took my hand in hers and squeezed. Then she rubbed her fingers along my knuckles in the same way my grandmother did.

"You can put your initials on me," she said after a while. "I deserve it."

I shook my head.

"I wish that day at the gulch never happened."

"I wish yesterday had never happened. I wish I could take back agreeing to let David stay with us."

Saula put her head on my shoulder. I didn't know how to react so I just sat there. Her body was warm against mine, her hair light against my neck.

The sparrows began dive-bombing for bugs, an airplane slowed its engines as it prepared to land at Stapleton, and far away, a lawn mower started up.

✗

It was getting cold as I walked home. The neighborhood was quiet. A few sprinklers clicked from left to right, alone in the middle of their yard.

As I rounded the corner of Cleaver, I easily imagined David standing on our front lawn, shirtless, bullets strapped across his chest, wielding a submachine gun. But as I peeked around our spruce tree, David was nowhere in sight. It was just my mother, sitting on the porch, gazing into a cup of tea.

"There you are," she said as I appeared. "No note? No call?"

"I couldn't. Ask David."

My mom patted part of the empty stoop. When I sat next to her, she wrapped her right arm around my waist and gave me a light kiss on my forehead. She had been crying.

"Why are you sitting outside?"

"I believe someone like David is a victim of circumstance. That he just needs a little love and understanding."

My mother looked out over our front yard. I followed her gaze.

"I told him to take down that nude centerfold on his wall. He argued, of course. I was adamant. Said that this was one issue I wouldn't debate with him. And then I left and went grocery shopping, thinking he would cool off and back down."

She motioned toward the house with her thumb.

"What?"

She motioned with her thumb again, as if practicing hitch-hiking.

I stood up and peeked through the windows. All the lights were off except for in the kitchen. Pots, pans, silverware, and dishes were scattered everywhere. The television was in the sink and my mom's Altamont concert poster was smashed over the reading lamp.

I sat back down and searched her face for some trace of emotion.

"Yes, yes," she said, "I know I've been lecturing you about pacifism and 'turn the other cheek,' but I have to tell you, what David did really pisses me off."

"He destroyed everything?"

"It's not so much the physical destruction that bothers me. It's more vain than that. I'm upset that he violated my . . . my hope."

She picked at the juniper, holding a green tuft between her index finger and her thumb.

"Ideally, David was supposed to come here and I was supposed to, I don't know, save him . . . My education, my understanding of racial issues, my acceptance, that sort of thing, would make me a better mother than my sister."

I told my mother all about Saula and how David had hit her with a bat. Then I told her how I had tried to get in the house, but David wouldn't let me.

"That . . . that poor girl. I'm ready to rationalize it away. To chalk up his behavior to his poor upbringing. But on the other hand, I want you to tell me again. And maybe even one more time. Until it sticks in my stubborn head." She was breathing quickly and had to slow herself. "Look at you. A bat. These fistfights. So many problems. This is not the country your grandma emigrated to. It's more like the country she left." She sipped her tea. "The other day when you were so upset and I just told you to turn the other cheek. It was . . . it was stupid idealism."

"You were quoting Jesus."

My mom then hugged me with all her might, squeezing my guts and stomach and lungs into one big group.

✗

When my mom had finished her tea and the darkness was freezing the air and Mr. and Mrs. Wallack had turned on the television for the evening, David appeared at the street corner, shoulders hunched and head lowered. He was carrying a small bouquet of carnations wrapped in a transparent plastic holder.

"Flowers?" My mom snorted, leaning forward and squinting. "David, I'm not sixteen and we aren't dating."

"I'm sorry. I'm sorry. You don't know what it was like. In the past. In Florida."

"The past?" she snapped.

He gave a weak shrug. My mother stood with ferocity.

"Past? Past? You want to have a competition, do you, David? Being blamed your whole life as the cause of impossible medical bills . . . the focus of undeserved resentment for everything from being the first in the family to go to college to— Don't you give me that, David. Do not even try. Your past! Damn your past! I know your past. Probably better than you do. If I didn't, I never would have taken your side all those times. We're all victims of your past, and unfortunately, you got the worst of it. But that doesn't give you the right to treat us this way."

"I'm sorry," David whimpered.

"The hell you are!" my mom screamed. She stepped forward, and I was sure she would rip David to shreds. "This is my house! Mine! Ever since Samuel's father left I have kept this goddamn place from falling into disrepair. Then you come along and destroy it and all I get is 'sorry'?" She reached forward and grabbed David's collar. "If you want forgiveness, then I am going to get a lot more than 'sorry.' You're going to give me your blood and sweat and eternal soul! Do you understand?"

David nodded, terrified.

"And don't give me any of your 'past' bullshit again. I won't stand for it! There is no past anymore. There is now." She shook him violently. "Here. Got it?"

"Mom," I whispered, quietly stepping forward and holding her arm.

"Here is what you will do, David. You will begin by being the best brother anyone could ask for. I know when we were in Florida and the two of you were together, Samuel would talk afterward, for days, about the things you two did. And you will do that again. Good things. Understand? Not this fighting crap. Not *Playboy* centerfolds. Good things! And then you will find Saula and apologize and do whatever it takes to make that poor girl feel better. I don't care what it is . . . And you will also begin visiting my mother regularly, caring for her, spending at least two hours a day at her bedside."

David's eyebrows lifted. My mother's face tightened. David lowered his eyes.

"This starts now," she concluded.

Then my mother took my hand and led me into the house. When we reached the porch, she dropped my hand abruptly, went to David, snatched the flowers, and returned with a smirk on her face.

My mom and I began to pick up the house. After about twenty minutes, David came in, his eyes red, his face tear-streaked. He went into the bathroom, washed up, and then joined us in cleaning.

The three of us sorted through most of the objects David had broken. The things that belonged to my father we threw in a box and put downstairs in the storage room. The things that were big and expensive, David wrote down on a list. He would have to get a job to pay my mom back.

"If you work at McDonald's you can give me free Big Macs," I said. "Or if you work at Arby's you can give me free shakes. Or if you . . ."

"I have an idea," David said. "Why don't you shut up?" Then

he smiled and patted my head. "Or just zip your lips, my sweet little brother."

I went back to hating him, but not as much as before.

"Okay, okay," my mom said after twenty minutes. "Enough cleaning. I have an idea. I was planning on taking you guys to the mall. I read that they're open until eleven tonight."

"The mall?"

"They set out all the clothes that survived the fire in the parking lot. Why don't we go, see what they have, maybe pick up some stuff, and stop at Dairy Queen afterward? Most things are eighty and ninety percent off. Maybe we can finally afford those overpriced Izod shirts you like so much."

"Izod?"

"Izod?" David mimicked.

Suddenly I started to melt. I went from five feet to four and then to six inches. Soon, I was just a puddle on the floor.

✕

The mall reminded me of the smoker's lung that the lady from the National Heart Association brought in a jar to our school each year. Everything that wasn't gray was black. Many of the stores had caved in, and the ones still standing were only brick skeletons. The air smelled similar to when my dad and I peed on campfires.

After parking, my mother, David, and I went through the rows of clothes that had been wheeled out into the parking lot. I grabbed Polo jeans, a million Izod shirts, and a Denver Nuggets jersey two sizes too large. For the first time, my mother didn't mention labor unions or slave workers in El Salvador.

After we paid and were walking back to the car, David and I compared our loot. He had chosen lime silk pants, striped silk shirts, and a pink silk robe. I laughed at him and told him he was going to look like a drug dealer. He said that I would understand his clothing choices in a few years when I caught up with the fashion times.

Since we were all starving, we went to Dairy Queen. David and I ate chili dogs while my mom nibbled fries, and for dessert we all bought Dilly bars. I ate half of the chocolate-covered vanilla top too fast and, on the way out, got a head freeze. David showed me how if you bent upside down and let the blood rush to your head, the pain would go away. Upside down and feeling better, I told him that this was the best trick ever. David smiled, smacked the bottom of my hand, and the remaining half of my Dilly bar splattered onto the sidewalk.

Part Three

As I waited at the bus stop Thursday morning, I thought about all the places I could ride my bike so that girls could see me in my new clothes. I would start at Jeremiah's Ice Cream, where models in tight T-shirts served sundaes with tons of whipped cream; go across Lady of Sorrow's sports fields, where female students in short plaid skirts covered themselves in mud while playing field hockey; and finally stop at Tan City, where women sat around in bikinis, lathering themselves in oil and waiting for a sun bed.

"Why aren't you blabbering on like usual?" David asked.

I shrugged.

"Is this a new Samuel? Quietly thinking over the world's problems?"

"I'm not thinking about the world's problems. I'm thinking about girls."

"Well, don't stop for me. Just go right on keeping it to yourself."

When the bus arrived, I showed Roger my new clothes, but he wasn't impressed. He grumbled something about 'spoiled kids' and hit the accelerator so hard that I almost fell onto the aisle floor.

We drove for two blocks and not a single kid mentioned my new clothes. When Jonathon and Jesse got on, I stood up proudly.

"What do you think?" I asked.

"About what?" Jesse said, plopping into the seat behind me.

They both looked at me because I had a big grin. I held out my new shirt. "Real." Then I stood and showed them my pants. "Real."

"So?"

"So you can't call me Izod Dorkwad anymore."

"That nickname was like two years ago," Jesse said.

Jonathon and Jesse both lay down in their seats and pulled their hats over their eyes. It was the worst reaction that I could have ever expected. I wished I was back in my JCPenney clothes.

I moved to the rear of the bus. I wanted to be by myself. Me and my Izod alligator.

The bus shook as we went along the rough road, the tall, trembling round roof was like a cathedral during an earthquake. On the seat in front of me, scratched in black ink, someone had written: *Destiny is a slut.*

"Hey, Gerard," Roberto Tavares, who had a toupee-like haircut and a lipless mouth, said, leaning over the seat. "So no more Izod Dorkwad, okay? Wanna hear your new nickname? Gerardo Retardo."

"Sounds too much like your name," I said.

"Or how about . . . I got it, I got it. Better. Gerard the Tard."

Gerard the Tard. It was obvious the nickname would stick because the minute it left Roberto Tavares's mouth, Michelle Beard and Scott Rogers burst out laughing.

✠

The day crept by. Every assignment set before us was a test not only for my brain, but also for my willpower.

"Nice duds," Lawrence Bimburger whispered during algebra. "Izod, huh? After the lawsuit you'll be lucky to have the shirt on your back."

"I didn't do anything to you," I whispered back. "In fact, I held Jonathon back."

"You're Honkey Pizza's accomplice. You're both going to pay for what you did to me."

"You never learn," I said.

"Give me number seven."

"No way."

"Tell me now."

"No."

I turned and met his eyes. "Tell me."

"Fine. Four-point-one."

And I got a check-plus for the day.

✠

After school, I found David talking to Paco. As I got closer, they both looked over in my direction. Paco gave David a fist pound, winked at me, and joined the rest of the Mexicans by the side of the building.

David let me sit next to him on the bus.

"How was school?" he asked, brow furrowed. "Did you enjoy it?"

"Why?"

"I just want to know how your day went."

"No you don't."

David shrugged. "I'm trying to be a good brother. Or whatever I am now. Got it? So you better tell me."

He gazed at me with all the seriousness in the world.

"Well, today sucked. First, in English class our homework was the even numbers, but stupid me did the odd—"

"Yeah, yeah," David interrupted. "That's enough. I'm glad everything went well."

I wanted to go home, but David said we were visiting Grandma first. We got off at Jesse's stop, which was the closest to the nursing home, and before I could even tell Jesse I would call him later, David was tugging me down the street.

When we entered the nursing home, David and I stopped in front of the main bulletin board. There were pictures of my grandma helping out in a community gardening activity.

"I can't believe this old bat. She's got everyone in here believing that she's wonderful. Amazing how easy it is to erase an entire life and start over."

We walked on, passing Jennifer, who was delivering trays of food to the residents. She commented again on how handsome we looked, and this time, instead of blushing, David winked at her first. Jennifer returned a weak smile.

"Jennifer wants me."

When we arrived at Grandma's room, we found her sitting at a worktable with rubber wheels, gluing shiny stars to postcards for homeless children.

Grandma directed us toward a plate of pecan cookies. I took two. They were even better than the chocolate pudding.

David sat down and began to help her with the glue. I turned on the television and watched the local news. A Bronco linebacker had wrapped his Porsche around a light pole. A woman in Westminster had won two million dollars and was going to open an arboretum in Five Points. Tom Selleck had been voted

"Sexiest Man of the Year." After the local news I watched an in-depth special about fertilizer pellets.

When my mandatory hour was up, I asked David if he was ready to leave. He said he was going to stay a little longer.

✄

I hated walking. It was slow and boring. There were so many other ways to travel. Dune buggies, dogsleds, go-karts, drag-sters, hovercrafts, ATVs, jet packs, gliders, monorails, scooters, cross-country skis, Formula 1 cars, roller skates, etc., etc.

I would never make it home. Ever. Plus, I was so hungry I was ready to eat grass.

Suddenly, a red Alfa Romeo pulled up next to me.

"Got time for a ride?" Wayne asked. He waved a Mr. Good-bar in the air.

"I'm not supposed to see you until next week."

"You're holding me up."

I jumped in, and as we drove up to Boulder, heading north out of Denver, I devoured the Mr. Goodbar. Then I ate a package of trail mix that Wayne said had been sitting in his glove com-partment for a millennium.

"Candy from strangers?"

"Ouch," Wayne said. "Calling a brother a stranger."

"Sorry."

"Sorry what?"

"Sorry, brother."

As soon as the apartment complexes, tract housing, and shop-ping plazas ended, there was nothing but rolling fields and farms. Out here, horses strode around in empty pastures and people drove pickups longer than school buses. Out here, the hilltops were spotted with snow untouched by human feet and the wheat fields were mowed into golden, lollipop circles.

Wayne was driving at his usual speed, passing the other cars so fast it seemed as if they weren't even moving. When we reached Boulder, he zoomed off the turnpike and into a self-service gas station, nearly running over a man pouring oil into his VW bus engine.

"We're not breaking any records today," he said, checking his watch and vaulting over the door.

"You've driven faster?"

"I've got your safety to think about."

After filling up the tank and purchasing two Cokes, Wayne and I headed to the back of Boulder, skirting around the edge of Pearl Street Mall and downtown. We passed a small park filled with kids drinking beers, two hippie girls dozing on someone's front lawn, and a bald couple with shaved heads and dressed in robes. Soon the city was behind us and we were transformed into astronauts, ascending the mountainside switchbacks in our open-air rocket.

When we reached the top of the mountain, Wayne slowed, and parked on a gravel overlook. He turned off the car, lit a cigarette, rested his boots on the door, and gazed eastward over the plains.

The scent of pine filled our nostrils, squirrels chirped, and Romeo's engine creaked and groaned as it cooled. Miles above the rest of the world, the wind tasted like brand-new air.

"They say it's going to snow this week," Wayne said. "This is the place to see it. I used to come here all the time just to see the storms blowing in. There's something about confronting a storm at eye level."

"You lived in Boulder?"

"I was an undergraduate at the university here."

"What's undergraduate?"

Wayne shrugged and puffed on his cigarette. "Girls. Drinking."

"You can do that at a university?"

"You can't imagine."

The wind was skirting the sides of the mountains, slicking our faces with coolness. I put my shoes on the door, just like Wayne.

"My dad died two years ago today," he said. "Only fifty-four."

Wayne took out his wallet, pulled out a black-and-white photo, and handed it to me. The man in the picture looked almost exactly like Wayne, but older and balder.

"That was about ten years ago," he said. "He watched a lot of football. Worked and watched football. He'd come home in the evening and read football stats until dinner. Then he'd listen to sports radio. After he lost his job, he hardly left the house, except to go to church and donate blood."

He inhaled and held the smoke in his lungs longer than I had ever seen. When he exhaled, I exhaled too. Then he said, "I can't stop forgetting how he looked when I admitted that I'd spent much of my life trying not to be like him. I just had nothing in common with the man. Him and his La-Z-Boy."

In that brief moment, everything about Wayne—the car, the hair, the need for speed—made sense.

"But I look at myself. I catch some of the things coming out of my mouth. He's still there."

The pines scraped the wind. A crow glided inches from the giant mountain ridges.

"I saw your dad once," Wayne said. "Months ago. Before he left. He was supposed to talk to us undergrads about Jungian psychology, but instead he gave a lecture about Christianity and charity. I don't remember much. It was early. A Friday morning. I was probably hungover. But I wasn't too hungover to remember how his lecture made me feel. It was all about giving to others more than just what you don't need. He said you can only make the world a better place if you give a piece of yourself. And it might even be painful, but change, he said, even for the positive, doesn't come easy."

Wayne stubbed out his cigarette in the ashtray and lit another one.

"Ordinarily that kind of lecture would bore me silly, but your dad was so passionate, so honest. He gave examples of people who've made America great, examples of people who've tried to destroy what's great about America, and examples of people who sat by and did nothing. He said America is filled with everyone around the world, so what makes America great is our 'collective humanity' and what makes America weak is our 'collective greed.' Then he asked us to say what category we fit in. Almost everyone said they fit into the category of making America great, but when asked to give examples of what they'd done, well . . . most people came up short. I wasn't really sure where I fit in. Everyone knows the Kennedy speech, 'Ask not what your country can do . . . ,' but it's really hard. Figuring out whether you've really made a difference. Whether you *can* make a difference. So the next day, I volunteered to treat anyone who needed free psychologizing, as it were. It's either irony or fate that I got you as my patient."

"Why didn't you tell me this before?" I asked.

"I kept meaning to."

"Did you know I was his son?"

"At first I just knew your name was Samuel. I figured out the rest later."

The crow was now circling above the trees, dipping and then rising without a single flap of the wings. We sat there for a good twenty minutes not saying anything.

Then, when we both knew it was time, Wayne started the engine. In a matter of minutes we were flying down the side of the mountain. We leaned into the curves and the tires squealed. Wayne accelerated on the straightaways and I raised my hands in the air, as if on a roller coaster. When we were back on the highway, speeding toward Denver, Wayne turned up the stereo, but all I could hear was the beat.

✄

Wayne dropped me off at the corner, next to the Bernards', and as I walked home, I almost crashed into Paco and the boy I had bloodied a few weeks ago. They were riding their Huffys down Cleaver and pulled up next to me, so close, I could smell stale cigarette smoke clinging to Paco's jean jacket.

"Hey," Paco said. The other boy imitated Paco and leaned coolly against the handlebars.

"Hey."

"I need to talk to you."

I blinked once, twice.

"Tell your two little white friends that I don't want them coming down our block anymore. Especially that redheaded one. The one with the racist father. He rides by almost everyday, like he's trying to figure out something."

"I don't know if he'll listen to me," I said.

Paco was quiet. The other boy was picking at something on his rubber handlebar grips.

"You know what's funny? Your white boys got problems with us. But I bet they don't even know who 'us' is. They was riding by the other day. The two of them. My cousins, Crespin and Roman, was out front changing the oil on their Bonneville. They came from Hermosillo. You know how far that is? And at one point they looked up, wondering why these two white boys was grilling so hard. So they was like, 'What's up?' And your two friends, know what they said? 'You're gonna taste revenge.' " Paco shook his head. " 'You're gonna taste revenge'? My cousins were like, 'We don't even know you hombres.' "

"But you guys did something to them. To Jonathon and Jesse. Something so bad they won't even tell me."

" 'You guys'? One, it wasn't even all that bad. Two, it wasn't even anyone from around here. It was those bangers, the Norteños boys. They live way out. Came here one time for a barbecue. And they was just messing. Your boys was all ready to fight. Acting tough. White-boy tough. All puffed and saying they was gonna steal 'their' bikes. And the Norteños thought your friends was funny. Said they ain't never seen white boys so ready to battle. So they tied them up. Messed with 'em a little. Made 'em eat things. That's it."

I was annoyed, mad, and irritated with Paco's laid-backness. The way Paco spoke reminded me of Jonathon's "easy come, easy go" story. But I also couldn't forget how excited Jonathon and Jesse had been that day at the bus stop, when we beat the Mexicans.

I studied Paco and the other boy in the dim light. The wide lines of their noses, their saucer-sized jaws. They didn't look like the Mexicans on television, who were always drunk or carried knives and mugged blond women.

"Hey," Paco said to me now. "We should stop this. Serious. Y'know? All this fighting."

I looked over at the other boy. "What about him? Why did he get off at our bus stop that day? Why did they throw a bottle at us?"

The boy shrugged and his beady eyes twitched away from me.

"He didn't know you," Paco said. "He moved here last year. Just doing whatever his friends do."

"I gotta go."

I turned and walked away, but Paco and the boy stayed put, sitting on their bikes, watching me for almost the entire block.

When I got home, David came rushing out of the house.

"God, you're slow," he said, grabbing my wrist and dragging me inside. "We've been waiting for hours."

When I entered the house, there, sitting on the couch, drinking a Coors, was a man who was my father, who had always been my father, but was now someone so different from the father I had in my mind that he was only my father in that my heart was exploding to hug him.

We said nothing; no Bible quotes, no explanations, no "I missed you." His arms just squeezed my shoulders together and he kissed my forehead until his beard left red curlicue imprints.

✕

And how he looked. From the hole on his right shoe, where the white-socked big toe sniffed the world, to the bright purple scar just below his left eye, to the reddened crack on the side of his mouth. He was still my father.

The three of us sat at the table, snacking on salted peanuts, while my father listed all the different states he had been to, remembering all the people he had met, and explaining how he had spoken the word of Jesus to anyone willing to listen. He told us about the pollution and poverty in El Paso, the nuns who fed him fresh mushroom soup in Santa Fe, the destitution, alcoholism, and endless satellite dishes of the Southwestern reservations, the Kingman homeless shelter that transcribed his message onto a giant sheet of paper and hung it on their cafeteria wall, the Cheyenne auditorium that sold out three nights in a row with people wanting to hear him preach, the poisonous anger and resentment in Watts and Compton, the hollow belly of Las Vegas, the Moabite who slashed his face over his rightful place to sleep in the bus station, the dozens of families that gave him a clean bed to rest, the Casper evangelical minister who stayed up all night arguing with my father about his interpretation of God, and the Topeka car dealer who offered him a free, new Buick if my father would just stop saying that it was difficult for rich people to get into heaven.

"How long were you gone for?" David asked at one point. "You know? To do all you did."

"Geez, I have no idea. Samuel, how long was I gone for?"

Just as I was about to answer, down to the exact hour, my father began talking again, about the lesbians from Phoenix who wanted him to incorporate a form of heterosexual Armageddon into his message and the family from Salt Lake City who offered to drive him around Utah for a week while he preached.

At some point, however, every word that left his mouth became only a muted sound. I began looking through the beard, through the sunburned nose, through the faded clothes, through the chapped lips, through the blackened fingertips, through the words that were meant to impress David and me, and tried to understand if the man I was staring at had changed more than I had.

✗

Since my mother came home around six-thirty, my dad suggested we surprise her with a clean house and a cooked dinner.

"The kind of surprise where someone pulls your chair out from under you," David whispered.

My dad opened the refrigerator door, shook his head, and ordered me to get my shoes on. He ripped my mother's grocery list from the pad; scanned it, nodding here and there; and stuffed it into the right pocket of his shirt. David snapped on yellow rubber gloves and grabbed a rag.

"Rev your engines. David's cleaning and we're going grocery shopping."

During the walk, my father continued with his stories, and I listened quietly, jumping from crack to crack, wondering when he was going to ask what had happened to me and my mom while he had been away.

Occasionally, I would look up at him, his muscled body now stringy and beef-jerky lean. The sun had tanned straight through, leaving his skin browner than Geronimo's. And his reddish-brown beard seemed to cover his entire face except his blue eyes and the tips of his cheeks.

When we got to the grocery store, my father wasn't interested in two-for-one sales or prices per pound. Instead, he grabbed things that he hadn't tried before or that had colorful labels. Our grocery cart was full in fifteen minutes flat.

"Hop on," he said, pointing to the front of the cart.

My father revved himself up and suddenly we were off, slaloming through the deli and spinning 360's in the produce section. I gripped the sides of the cart as we flew down the detergent aisle at the speed of sound and almost fell off as we took a sharp corner into the frozen foods. When we pulled into the checkout, the cashier scolded us for being reckless. My dad didn't get upset or defensive. He just winked at her with such confidence that she blushed and accidentally rang up our cauliflower as snow peas. And then he paid, using my mother's checkbook.

⌘

As we walked home, we barely spoke. My father was lost in his thoughts. Only once did he look over at me, but he didn't say anything, didn't allow a single "I missed you" or "I love you" to come out of his mouth.

"Dad," I asked finally, "when did you get back to Denver?"

"Two days ago."

"Why didn't you come home?"

"I was invited to preach at this little church in Westminster. They also had a bed for me."

I looked up at him, sadness and pain tearing through my chest. I desperately wanted my father to meet my eyes, to apologize for not coming home immediately, but we had just turned the corner, and I realized that he was staring at our house, at my mom's car, which was now parked in the driveway.

When we walked through the front door, my mother was standing in the living room, looking as if she had lost something.

"Hello," she said.

"Hi," he replied.

"Please take off your sandals before coming into the house."

There was an awkward silence. My dad set down his grocery bags, took off his sandals, and set them by the door. My mom observed him carefully. Then, when he was finished, she turned, went to the back of the house, calmly rolled up her pants, and walked out into the garden.

Steam clouded the kitchen. Even though my father munched on half of the ingredients while he cooked, every pot was bubbling over with a delicious concoction. I cut onions and carrots while my father stirred the dinner, spicing them with oregano, curry, and cumin.

When we settled at the table, my father started off with the longest dinner prayer ever.

"And he said unto them, 'Which of you shall have a friend, and shall go unto him at midnight, and say unto him, "Friend, lend me three loaves . . ."' "

As my dad went on, my mom started grinding pepper. Then she chewed loudly on an ice cube, something I had often been scolded for doing at the table.

". . . 'or which one of you, if his son asks him for bread, will give him a stone?' "

As soon as my dad finished, I started packing food in my mouth. After thirty bites, my stomach expanded into my legs, then into my feet. My dad also plowed away, as if ending a long fast. David set his steamed vegetables to the side and picked at the tofu. My mom stared at her place mat.

"What you are doing here?" she asked, after I had taken thirty-three bites. "Might you enlighten me?"

"I'm not sure," my father replied without hesitation.

"Not sure?"

"I'm not sure. I might be asked to leave."

"For a job? An appointment with Social Services for a psychiatric evaluation? Tell me."

"You know."

My mom chewed, but I wasn't sure she had any food in her mouth.

"I do? How could I possibly know?"

"It's the same as before."

"Oh that. That little reason. What was it? Hmm. It was so small I hardly remember. Could you, might you, tell me again?"

My father wouldn't look at her.

"I want to hear it, because, frankly, last time you told me, when you were living in your tent, that . . . that was more like a nightmare. I was too shocked to remember any details. I vaguely remember something about God. Is that correct?"

My father took another bite of food, although smaller. His eyes were firmly locked on the salt and pepper shakers.

"Unbelievable," my mom said, after a century of silence. "Absolutely unbelievable. Who . . . who exactly the hell are you? Why are you even here?"

"I'm not sure."

"Not sure who you are or not sure why you're here?"

"Neither. Not yet."

"The last few months . . . that wasn't enough time?"

"No."

"Of course not." She set down her fork and placed her napkin next to her plate. "Well, look, Mr. I Don't Know Who I Am, just give me a couple days' notice before you take off this time. Before you leave. I want to be prepared to pick up the pieces again. Or am I asking too much?" She looked upward and clasped her hands in prayer. "Am I, O Great Almighty?"

"Don't be blasphemous in front of David and Samuel."

My mother saw that she had finally gotten under his skin.

"Then answer my question."

My dad tapped his fork against his plate. David glanced at me and raised his eyebrows.

"Yes, yes. If God lets me know, I'll let you know."

My mom pressed her lips together. Then she stood and went into the kitchen. We listened as she scraped her food into the trash, dropped her plate in the sink, strode across the floor, and slammed her bedroom door. Then she immediately opened her door, came marching back out to the table, and glared at my father.

"I'm doing this for Samuel. If he wasn't here I'd have changed the locks long ago. So do me a favor. Try to set an example. Try to pull your head out of your ass and set an example for your son. Because the next time you come back he might already be a man. And I don't think you want him remembering you like this."

"Or you," my father mumbled into his food.

My mother brightened into a strawberry. Then she did an about-face, stomped across the creaky floorboards, and slammed her door again.

※

That night my mom stayed in her room and read magazines. At one point, I brought her a cup of tea and she made me rub her aching shoulders. She said her spine was telling her the pressure was changing, that a storm was heading our way.

"I'm sorry about tonight. I shouldn't do that in front of you."

"I've seen worse," I said and made her smile.

Before bed, David, my father, and I watched *The A-Team*. At the end, just when The A-team had completed an elaborate mountain trap consisting of plywood, a radiator, a bag of old lightbulbs, tar, sixteen rabbits, four boxes of nails, and a cup of gunpowder poured from bullet casings, my dad changed the channel to Christian Pledge-a-Thon. An overweight white woman with gold hair, gold necklaces, gold rings, and gold hoop earrings was singing "Nobody Knows the Trouble I've Seen." When David and I started to complain, my dad switched back to *The A-Team*.

"I don't know which is worse," he said and went into the basement to read his Bible.

✠

At bedtime, David and I brushed our teeth together. I was done in ten seconds flat. David was an old lumberjack with his floss, sliding it lazily back and forth along the base of each tooth.

"That was crazy tonight," I said. "At dinner. I'm glad you were there."

He held the floss with his tongue. "Good. I'm glad someone was happy."

"I didn't say I was happy. I just said, I'm glad—"

"You know, there is such a thing as double meaning," he interrupted. "A sentence, a reference. It can mean two things at the same time."

"So, what was the double meaning? There was no double meaning to what you just said."

David glanced down at me. Then he gave me the middle finger and said, "There. This has only one meaning."

I hated David. I counted one second, two seconds, three seconds . . . David reached way in to the left side of his mouth, wrapping the floss around his molars.

"I told your grandma today that I forgave her."

"Really?"

"No. I'm lying."

"Really?"

"No. I'm lying again."

"What did she say?"

"She said, 'Fabulous.' "

"That's it?"

"That's it."

Then he turned to me and cocked his head. "Was it like this before? The fighting. With your parents?"

"Yes and no."

"I guess it's still better than living with Rhoald."

Then he reached out and twisted the alligator on my Izod shirt, pinching my nipple so hard that I yelped.

"Alligators bite," he said with a smirk. "If you want to just hang out, talk about your dad, I'll be awake for a while. No questions asked."

"Okay. Thanks."

"No problem."

Then David stepped out, switched off the bathroom light, and closed the door behind him, leaving me in the dark.

✗

The smell of the stockyards was in the air; a winter storm was bearing its way south from Wyoming, over the hundreds of cattle lined up in their pens, over the thousands of people sleeping in their ranch houses, and over the millions of prairie dogs on the plains, curled in their holes. I knew my mom was tossing in bed, trying to ignore the pain in her bones.

A snowstorm was heading directly toward Denver, the forecasters had been warning all evening. And now, in bed, I could almost hear the storm chugging along in the black sky. It would bulldoze over the flat parts of Colorado, leveling every bump with white powder, charging along until it reached downtown, where it would get tangled up in the high-rise buildings, remaining locked there until it shed enough snowflakes from its cloud fat to slip away.

When I woke up the next morning, the light from the window was thick and pasty. I got out of bed and my toes curled on the cold floorboards. A snowbank had completely swallowed the Wallacks' fence, huge drifts were pressed against the house like tiny ski slopes, and the clouds hung so low you could see every detail of their bellies.

The snowflakes were huge, bigger than squares of toilet paper, and when they landed they didn't melt, but stacked like pancakes. This meant that the snowflakes were piling up at my school, on the roads leading to my school, and on the buses that drove us to school. And . . . and . . . and most important, no one had come in my room to wake me up.

I ran from my room and flung open the door. My mother was standing in the bathroom, rubbing moisturizer onto her face.

"Is school canceled?"

She nodded.

"Honest?"

She nodded again.

"Honest, honest?"

She didn't nod this time.

"Honest, honest, honest?"

Her eyes narrowed.

"Can we take your car out and do donuts?"

My mom closed the bathroom door in my face. So I wandered into the kitchen and found my father standing over the stove. He was wearing his old flannel pajama bottoms and a SKI ASPEN T-shirt.

"Morning," he said, scrambling eggs in our cast-iron pan. A pot of oatmeal on the stove boiled like prehistoric tar pits. Eight strips of the bacon my mother kept in the back of the freezer for guests were now twisting and shrinking in a pan on the back burner. I knew that my dad would never touch pork, or eggs. He was cooking just for David and me.

"School's canceled."

"I know."

"I can stay home today."

"I know."

"With you."

"That's right."

My mom walked into the kitchen and my dad handed her a plate of scrambled eggs with buttered multigrain toast. She gazed at him blankly, her mind close to short-circuiting.

"Yours is coming up in a minute, little buddy," he said to me.

Then something happened, something I couldn't control. As my mom carried her plate into the dining room and my father poured himself another cup of coffee, a balloon started filling inside my chest.

"Do I smell meat? Real meat? Oh my God, I thought this day would never come!"

David pushed by, smacked me in the back of the head, and burst the balloon in my chest. Tears fell from my eyes and scattered on the floor like BB's.

"Thank God," David said, waving the smell of the sizzling bacon into his expanded nostrils. "Thank God. Thank God. My prayers have been answered."

⋇

After another silent meal, my mom announced that she was going to the nursing home to visit Grandma. She dressed in her biggest jacket and boots and kissed me good-bye on the forehead. She opened the door, pulled down her hat, stepped out into the blizzard, and closed the door after her. She was so small against the storm, as if the slightest gust could send her tumbling and rolling away with the other snowflakes.

Once my mom turned the block and we could no longer see her, my dad suggested we make a snowman. I said we should construct an ice sculpture, like the ones in Helsinki. My dad told me to think big, but start small. Then he told me to go get my cousin. David was in his room. He had "Breaking the Law" on repeat. I asked him if he wanted to help.

"Snowmen are gay."

So, my dad and I layered on our clothes so thick that we looked like astronauts. We laced boots, zipped up jackets, tied each other's scarves, bent our heads low, and stepped out into the storm. The snow came flying straight through the entryway, and by the time it hit the living room, it melted in midair. We stepped out onto the porch and braced ourselves. My dad closed the front door and there was nothing but snow silence.

"Maybe we should yell?"

"No," my father said. "Let the peacefulness be. It won't stay like this for long."

He took the first step into the storm and was immediately stuck knee high in a drift. He strained to lift his leg out of the snow, took another step, and sunk back in. I took a deep breath, pinched my nose, and plunged in behind him.

Since it was a thick, wet snow, we were able to roll the snow-balls without much packing or compressing. We pushed the first ball in circles until it doubled, tripled, and quadrupled. When we finished, the ball was almost half my size. My father told me to test its strength. I climbed on and started to jump up and down. My father told me to take it easy. I kept jumping, harder and harder, as if trying to reach the clouds on a trampoline. Suddenly, my foot slipped. I tried to regain my balance, but it was too late. My butt smacked hard against the ball and I tumbled into a snowbank. As I lay there, my head submerged under the snow, the only thing I heard was the muffled laughter of my father.

We used four different snowballs to make the body, rolling each one in the same way. We then placed one ball on top of another until the snowman was as big as Mr. Roosevelt. My father sculpted goofy ears on the snowman. I made a snow top hat. My dad used a carrot for a nose. When we were all finished, my father and I stepped back and examined our work.

"We make a helluva team," he said.

Then he walked over and carved a cross on the snowman's forehead with his index finger.

✠

Late in the afternoon it stopped snowing, and the fat albatross flakes became thin white specks of powder that somersaulted through the air. Our clothes steamed by the fireplace, and the bittersweet scent of burning sap filled the entire house.

My father made a cup of coffee and descended into the basement to read the Bible. David was still hibernating in his room and my mom hadn't returned, so I ate a bowl of granola by myself. I read the back of the granola box six times. I read the back of three other cereal boxes, the heating bill, and the telephone bill, and then reread the cereal boxes.

I went into my room and tossed my balsa-wood glider from one end to the other. I took out my Erector set and made a miniature skyscraper. I went into the living room, turned on the television, and flipped between the local news and *The Young and the Restless*. I called Jonathon, but no one answered. I called Jesse, but his mom said he was sleeping. I drank a glass of water and then tiptoed down into the basement. My father was sitting on a stool near the washing machine, reading from a new Bible, the bare bulb casting a teepee of light.

"I'm bored."

He smiled and said: "Bored is a state of mind."

I didn't know what this meant, but knew enough to know that if I asked what he meant, I would get a fifteen-minute explanation.

"What are you reading?"

"I was refreshing myself with the story of Nathan."

I found it interesting that he had to refresh himself with anything in the Bible.

I sat down on the cold cement floor.

"Read to me," I said.

He lifted his eyebrows and puffed his lips outward.

He flipped a single page back and forth. "Of course." His excitement grew quickly. "Here." He tapped the page. "I'll begin with what I was just reading. Ready? *The LORD sent Nathan to David. When he came to him, he said, "There were two men in a certain town, one rich and the other poor. The rich man had a very large number of sheep and cattle, but the poor man had nothing except one little ewe lamb he had bought. He raised it, and it grew up with him and his children. It shared his food, drank from his cup, and even slept in his arms. It was like a daughter to him. Now a traveler came to the rich man, but the rich man refrained from taking one of his own sheep or cattle to prepare a meal for the traveler who had come to him. Instead, he took the ewe lamb that belonged to the poor man and prepared it for the one who had come to him.' '"*

My dad checked to see if I was still listening. I hadn't looked anywhere except directly at his face. He continued slowly: *"David burned with anger against the man and said to Nathan, 'As surely as the LORD lives, the man who did this deserves to die! He must pay for that lamb four times over, because he did such a thing and had no pity.' "* My father took a deep breath here, as if to finish meant leaping over a hurdle in his own brain. *"Then Nathan said to David, 'You are the man!' "*

My father closed the Bible and set it on top of our dirty laundry bin. He rubbed his eyes and gazed emptily at the top of the reading lamp. A blush streaked his forehead and the tops of his cheeks. I was waiting for him to crack, for an earthquake to take place inside and split him in two.

The twilight sun was being filtered through several feet of snowy whiteness, casting a cool light onto my father's face. I could see the veins and arteries stretching from his temples to the corners of his eyes. My mother and I had once seen Rodin's *The Thinker* at the Denver Art Museum, an enormous sculpture of a man weighted with thoughts. And now, my father reminded me of *The Thinker,* not so much of the *The Thinker's* expression, but of the black meteoritic material the statue was made of.

"Dad?"

"Hmm."

"Are you Nathan?"

"No one in this country is listening."

He exhaled and rubbed his palms into his forehead.

The next morning I woke up early, before the sun was up. My first thought was that my father had packed his stuff and disappeared into the night. I leaped from the bed and went out into the hallway. He was sleeping on the couch. I kneeled and put my head on his chest. He was snoring lightly, his eyes bouncing under his eyelids.

I pressed my hands together and said thank you.

✕

School was canceled for the second day in a row, planes couldn't land or take off, and people were trapped in their cars. During the weather segment of *Good Morning America,* filmed all the way in New York City, they showed Denver snowplows stuck in drifts. Larry Green said it was the worst storm in ten years and that his weather team would provide us with school and road closings and emergency updates as they were made available. Then he said we should leave our television on and tuned to Channel 4, all day.

"It's a state emergency," I pleaded.

"Right," my mom said, turning off the television.

My father spent much of the morning reading his Bible, sitting quietly on the couch, his legs folded underneath him. As my mom shuffled around the house, tidying and cleaning, I would catch her stealing glimpses of him, her cheeks reddening, the lines in her forehead deepening, and her lips pursing.

David was stretched out on the living room carpet, reading a book about famous terrorists. He would examine a picture of a collapsed building or the burned shell of a car, read the following page of the book, flip back, and reexamine the picture. I helped my mom clean the stove and match socks.

Around lunchtime, my mom, dad, David, and I sat down to eat tofu tacos. My father and mother were both staring out the bay windows, not really looking at the falling snow or drifts piling higher and higher. A couple of times David looked at me, looked at my parents, rolled his eyes, and went back to eating. I was glad he was here.

Eventually, my father finished eating, pushed his plate to the side.

"That was delicious."

He leaned back in his chair, set his napkin on the table, and put his arms behind his head.

"Can I help out? Would you like me to wash the dishes?"

My mother was quiet for a minute, before replying, "Do you know what I really want? I want you to apologize to Samuel and me for what you have done. I want you to apologize for how you have screwed up our lives and generally made everyone miserable because of your selfishness."

"Wasn't last night enough of this?" my father asked.

My mom waited.

"No apology? Figures. You'll wash the dishes, you'll eat my food, and you'll enjoy the warmth of this house. But you won't agree to come back and have a family again. To really do your part. You'll wash the dishes. Of course, you'll wash the dishes. But the really important stuff, the stuff that makes us a family—"

"There's a part in the Bible where—"

"Oh, damn!" My mom pounded the table. "Damn. Damn. Damn."

I swallowed. David smirked. I wasn't sure my mom could stop.

"Damn. Damn." *Pound.* "Damn. Damn." *Pound.* "Damn. Damn. Damn."

My mom, holding back her tears, stood and picked up her plate, then mine, even though I wasn't finished.

"See this? See? You're making me into someone I don't want to be. Someone ugly and bitter. I'm over you, Mark. Over all this. I want you out of the house by this evening."

"I'll do better. I'll leave now."

He pushed out his chair, grabbed his jacket, and went to the front door. As he laced his boots, my mom stormed into the kitchen and threw the dishes in the sink. The crash was louder than if she had dropped them onto the floor. Then she fled into the basement, beginning to cry before she even made it to the bottom of the stairs.

My father finished dressing in seconds, flung open the front door, and vanished. I couldn't allow this to happen.

I grabbed my jacket and gloves and began putting on my boots.

"Here," David said, and buttoned my hat around my chin.

The road was ice-packed, and my feet slipped out from underneath me. The cold air entered my lungs and froze my stomach. The hairs on my neck prickled as a light wind blew a silk wall of crystals from one side of the road to the other.

From the back my father looked like an avocado; his green

winter jacket narrowing his shoulders, his waist wide at the pockets, and his curly hair stemming out from his high collar.

When I finally caught up, grabbing his jacket for support, my father didn't turn or look over. He just kept walking as if leaning into a hurricane.

"I don't want you to leave," I said, out of breath.

"Tell that to your mother."

Mr. Wallack was out with his snowblower, the snow arcing up and out of the big-wheeled machine like a white tsunami.

"There's nothing this way," I said. "Nothing but the gulch."

A snowplow was clearing Colorado Boulevard, the steel blade grinding against the asphalt. My father turned abruptly onto Jackson Street, where seven-inch drifts balanced on three-inch branches. Everything was weighted down and ready to snap.

"What is that?" my dad asked, stopping suddenly.

"The gulch?"

"No, that."

"It's a waterfall. It comes out of the tunnel."

My father walked faster, his arms swinging. I struggled to keep up, taking long, slippery steps. When we reached the gulch, my father turned off Jackson and stepped down through the thick snow toward the waterfall.

"It's amazing. Absolutely amazing."

There were millions of icicles, all piled up on one another, crawling downward, the big ones giving birth to smaller ones. The farther down the waterfall, the more icicles there were: clusters of short stubby ones; chunks of dull, narrow ones; and bundles of long, slender ones. The sides of the waterfall were like curtains, ruffles of ice bunched together in thick columns, extending from the top of the waterfall to the gulch below. And in the middle, the icicles gave way to bumpy sheets, a smooth serving tray of water that appeared to have frozen as it fell. A satisfied look came across my father's face.

"This proves everything I've been saying. In a matter of days this will all be gone. It's like us. We spend so much time arguing and fighting. But our existence on this planet is as random, as fragile, and as beautiful as these icicles."

He scrutinized every inch of the waterfall.

"Remember the book I was compiling on evil? I've come to realize that you don't need the Bible to understand what evil is. Evil is simply a being in itself. A human creation. A consequence of our choices."

He leaned down, pressed his face against the waterfall, closed his eyes, and shut me and the world out.

✠

"Dad?"

My father kept his face pressed against the icicles.

"Dad?" I repeated.

The world was silent, frozen and crusted. As if bitten by something, he pulled himself free and stumbled away from the waterfall.

"It's . . ."

"What?"

"Do you see it?"

He balled his fingers, tucked his lower lip under his teeth, and punched the waterfall with his bare fist.

"What are you doing?"

"Don't you see it?"

He punched again and again, each time harder. After the sixth or seventh time, blood appeared on the ice.

I wanted to leave him there. Here, in the cold, in the solid whiteness, I wanted to turn and go back home and forget. My mother, David, and I would sit by the fireplace and watch the snow continue to fall and block him from our minds.

"Stop! Please, Dad!"

"Damn it!" he shouted. "You're not looking."

I moved slowly next to him and peered into the frozen waterfall. There was a dark shadow buried deep in the back of the ice, something long and distorted.

"What is it?" he asked frantically.

"I don't know."

"Tell me! What is it?"

He punched again, throwing all his weight into the ice. Blood was dripping down his arms, sweat was forming on his neck and forehead, and the muscles under his eyes flinched rapidly. He wrapped his hands around my neck, thrusting my face into the icicles. I gasped, tears forming in my eyes. My dad had never grabbed me, never forced me to do anything.

"Look, damn it! Open your eyes!"

I fought the tears, took a deep breath, and squinted through the bloodied hole my father had created. There was something there. Something twisted and distorted. Then I recognized a long black ponytail and the quick twinkle of gold teeth.

"Oh my God," I whispered. "It's Geronimo."

My father started searching for rocks. He found a chunk of
cinder block buried near the edge of the gulch and trudged back
to the waterfall, and soon, icicles were exploding onto the snow,
onto my jacket, and onto my father's flushed face.

"Call 911," he said.

I ran through the snow as fast as I could, lifting my back foot
out, stepping forward, and sinking all the way back in. At the top
of the gulch, I had to stop. My lungs were on fire and my heart
was thudding against my ribs. I glanced over my shoulder and
saw my father still pounding the waterfall with the cinder block.

"Stop," I whispered. "Please. Stop."

I heard shuffling. I looked to my left, then to my right. I saw
two shadows. Inside Geronimo's tin house were the two Rottweilers, watching me, their eyes jewels set in black fur. I backed
away.

I turned and ran, jumping through the thick snow, my leg muscles swelling with pins and shards of glass. When I was a good distance, I looked back. The Rottweilers hadn't moved.

I headed toward Double Donuts, where the nearest pay phone was. I had to catch my breath and brush away the snow from the phone before I could dial. When I got an operator, I explained that my father and I had found a man frozen in a waterfall. She told me that prank 911 calls could get me two years in prison.

"I swear on my own grave," I said, and told her exactly where Geronimo was.

She sighed. "Go back and wait. Someone will be there soon."

The siren from the firehouse started wailing, the sound reverberating through the deserted buildings. Hoping to avoid the Rottweilers, I cut through a lot behind Rick's Audio and slipped under a hole in the chain-link fence, ripping part of my jacket. I walked behind a row of bushes, grabbing the thin branches for support, and held in my stomach in order to squeeze past a NO TRESPASSING sign. When I emerged from behind the bushes and onto the top lip of the tunnel, I could see my father down below. He had broken open most of the waterfall and dragged Geronimo into a circle of snow.

"Jesus said, *'Our friend Lazarus has fallen asleep; but I am going there to wake him up.'*"

I dropped onto the bottom of the tunnel and almost slipped on the ice. Now that I was closer, I could see giant purple spots on Geronimo's torso and chunks of ice stuck in his mouth.

"*And they came not for Jesus' sake only, but that they might see Lazarus also, whom he had raised from the dead.*"

My father leaned back and lifted his arms toward the sky, over Geronimo's body.

"*Come out!*"

The wind was no longer blowing. The rumbling of the approaching fire engine vanished. The water running out of the tunnel and under the frozen waterfall ceased. My father had managed to stop time.

I leaned against the cement back of the tunnel for support.

"Prove to me!" my dad screamed, his voice echoing through the gulch. "Prove to me that You are there! Bring this man from where you have taken him! If I am your son! If I am your true son! *Father, into your hands I commit my spirit!* Take away the evil done here, the negligence, and bring this man back!"

My father closed his eyes and reached upward, waiting, waiting, waiting.

Then, gradually, the water in the gulch started to flow again, the wind swept away loose snowflakes, and the fire engine turned down Jackson Street, rumbling toward us. The sun continued to shine, a sliver of the moon appeared, and the sky cleared.

But Geronimo lay there, dead, a thin smile on his face.

✗

After the medical workers wrapped Geronimo and took him away in an ambulance, Police Sergeant Benjamin asked me all sorts of questions. I thought my interrogation would be like on television, where the police raised their eyebrows at the end of every statement. But Sergeant Benjamin seemed to believe everything I said, even if I changed important details.

After my interrogation, I searched everywhere for my dad; between the buzzing engines, among the groups of police and firemen, and back by the tunnel. When I asked two of the firemen if they had seen my father, they both shook their heads with pity, as if I'd been born without arms. They called my mom, and after talking to her, she came and led me home, biting her bottom lip and staring straight ahead.

✗

That night, as I lay in bed, memories of the day danced in my head.

My mom came in and sat at the end of my bed. In the dim light, the way she smiled, there was no doubt that she was Grandma's daughter.

"You know there's nothing to say."

I nodded.

"There's nothing like this in the parenting books."

"I know."

"All words become trite." She stroked my hand. "I love you, Samuel. I love you more than anything or anyone in my life."

And with that, she kissed my cheek and left.

Around midnight, I went down to the basement and knocked on David's door. As he rubbed his eyes, I asked if I could lie in bed next to him. David nodded, tore open a Kit Kat, handed me half, and said the best way to fix my problem was to talk until I couldn't talk anymore.

So I sat there, on the end of his bed, telling David everything, from the moment my dad left after lunch to when the firemen arrived. I told David that I didn't know who my dad was anymore, what he wanted from me, and if I should even try and find him. And the whole time, David listened quietly, raising his eyebrows here and nodding there.

By the time I finished, it was two o'clock in the morning. David didn't give me advice or tell me that everything would be all right. Instead, he said I could sleep in bed with him as long as I didn't snore or act gay. I nodded and we got under the sheets together, me on the right and he on the left.

The next day at school, during lunch recess, we had to stay in and watch nature movies because they hadn't cleared the snowy grounds behind the school yet. After being stuck at home, everyone had cabin fever. Cheeze Doodles and spitballs flew through the auditorium while gazelles and hyenas loped around on the projection screen.

During the movie, I told Jonathon and Jesse about Geronimo. I purposely left out the part where my dad tried to revive him.

Halfway through the movie, Mr. Roosevelt came in and announced that those of us on the honor roll could go into the gymnasium. They read a list of names including Jonathon's, Jesse's, and mine, and all the dorks were herded out of the auditorium. I was hit by a Cheeze Doodle and called Gerard the Tard, but I didn't care. While these losers were stuck in the stinky auditorium watching a stupid movie, Jonathon, Jesse, and I would be playing full-court basketball.

Inside the gym, Jesse grabbed the Dr. J signature basketball, which the cooler kids always got first. Mr. Man didn't lay down any rules; instead, he read the *Rocky Mountain News* while Jonathon, Jesse, and I shot from half-court, ran up and down the sidelines, and dribbled wherever we wanted. For the first time, no one complained about our behavior, and no one tried to take our ball. Most of the other honor roll kids sat around trading Dungeons & Dragons character cards or practicing for band.

When the bell rang, Jonathon, Jesse, and I were the last to leave the gym. Jesse went the opposite way from Jonathon and me, toward woodshop class. He waved and we waved and he yelled that we sucked in basketball.

As Jonathon and I walked down the hall, Jonathon whispered, "We got it. This time it'll work."

I didn't shake my head or nod. I just tried to read his eyes.

"Why don't you just stop?"

"Why don't *you* just stop?" he replied.

"I talked to them. The Mexicans. They're not that bad. They don't want to fight anymore."

Jonathon tensed. "Where's your self-respect? Huh? Talking to Mexicans. Of course they don't want to fight anymore. They know we're gonna get them and they're scared. Scaredy-scared."

"You don't need to get them," I whispered. "You don't. You forgive them and they forgive you. That's it. Then it's over."

"Forgive," Jonathon growled. Then he grabbed my shirt and pulled me close. "I'll forgive them. But I won't forgive you. How about that?"

"What's wrong with you?" I looked down at his hands. "Let go."

Jonathon loosened his grip. I was dizzy from his temper. The bell rang.

"You want something from me?" he asked. "Come on, then."

"Come on?"

"Right here."

"What is this?"

In the past, when Jonathon and I had fought, it had been quick. There had been no space leading up to the punches. But now as he stood in front of me, ready to drop his backpack and swing away, I realized that this would be the kind of fight that ended everything.

"I have to fight you so that you'll make peace with the Mexicans?"

"Yes."

"That's the stupidest—"

"If you fight me, I'll leave the Mexicans alone."

"Jonathon?" The words stuck and snagged as they came out: "I'm not going to fight you."

"Because you're scared."

"I'm not."

Then Jonathon snapped his teeth, just like the Rottweilers used to do with me.

"They're evil. You'll see."

"They're not evil."

"You won't be saying that when they're doing to you what they did to Jesse and me."

"I know what they did to you. And it wasn't even the Mexicans at our school. It was other Mexicans. Mexicans from North Denver."

"Other Mexicans? What's wrong with you? Mexicans are Mexicans."

Then he pulled away, and without another word, began walking down the hall. As he turned the corner, he gave me the middle finger.

✕

After school I waited for David by the bus. Although we'd been told ten times over the PA system that snowballs would not be tolerated, the minute the last bell rang the sky was filled with white projectiles. Mr. Roosevelt kept busting kids, knocking the snow from their hands, grabbing them by their collars, and dragging them into the building for after-school detention, but there were simply too many offenders. After ten minutes or so, Mr. Roosevelt simply gave up, lit a cigarette, and monitored the chaos with a scowl.

I stayed close to the bus, melting into the yellow metal panels. I had no energy to make a snowball, much less get involved in a full-scale battle.

Just as Roger started the bus and announced that he was about to leave, Paco emerged from the snowballs, untouched. He told me that David had gone to the gulch to go sledding with some of the other Mexicans.

"He wanted me to let you know."

"But we're supposed to go to the nursing home."

Paco shrugged. "He didn't say anything about that."

I thanked him and started to board the bus. Just as I got to the top step, Paco said, "Hey, you talk to your friends?"

I stopped. I turned. I wish he hadn't asked.

"I tried," I said.

He waited.

"I don't know. They won't listen."

"Why not?"

I didn't know how to reply. I stared. He stared. Roger closed the door.

✕

I was sitting on the edge of Grandma's bed. She was sitting next to me. We were both looking out the window, at the peeling pillars in front of her window, at the snow-covered courtyard.

"The days are getting shorter," she said. "But the sun feels brighter."

She had lost a lot of weight and her pale skin hung farther off her face, but her smile was permanent.

"Every day is a blessing."

My grandma slowly pushed herself to her feet, walked over to the windowsill, and adjusted a vase of sunflowers. The light coming through the glass illuminated the thousands of yellow veins in the petals. Jennifer came by, peeked in, and set a tray of covered food by the door. When she left, I could hear the inside thighs of her jeans swishing against each other.

"I'm starting to hate this world," I said.

My grandma returned, sat down next to me, and pulled my head toward her bony chest.

✕

The mountains of snow had cut the normal speed of Denver in half. Only a few airplanes were able to take off, so the sky was almost empty of white stripes. I had to walk in the middle of the street because the sidewalks were pyramids of snow.

Every tree, car, house, telephone line, satellite dish, wood fence, flower bed, building, office, store, bank, blade of grass, and anthill was covered in two feet of snow. The buses rumbled along, the chains on their tires rattling through the slush. The sky was endless blue because even the clouds knew that if they came too close they would instantly turn into giant snowballs.

And yet everything was melting. Icicles dripped, oily asphalt began to warm patches through the sandy snow, glaciers slipped from rooftops, and frozen puddles began to bubble and crack. Huge icebergs flowed along the enormous rivers on the sides of the streets, clogging sewer drains, stacking up behind car tires, damming the water into chilly reservoirs that stretched far out into the road. The sun cut through the overloaded tree branches, chasing away the coldest cold and commanding authority over the temperature.

There was the crunching, popping, twisting, snapping, bursting, slipping, thudding of a world unburying itself. The white would gradually disappear, and all the hidden bushes, trash cans, driveways, garden gnomes, doormats, sprinkler heads, doghouses, porch swings, firewood, birdhouses, storage sheds, lawn chairs, and flagpoles would emerge.

Two cars passed by, traveling in opposite directions, splashing a wave of wet snow. An enormous man wearing a black snowsuit ground a shovel along a sidewalk, lifting a cushion of snow and tossing it over his shoulder.

"Whew," he said with each scoop.

A lady with short white hair and knee-high orange boots stood on the corner of Iliff and Cedar, throwing pumpernickel crumbs to sparrows, whose brown color was the same as that of the sand dumped onto the roads for traction. Two five-year-old boys, Michelin men in their overstuffed coats, waited patiently inside a Toyota Tercel while their mother scraped ice from the window shield. Three boys pushed a Ford Bronco out of a snowy rut, cheering when the 4x4 was finally free.

A snowplow deposited another load onto a mountain of snow in the middle of the JCPenney parking lot. The mountain was bigger than Space Mountain, bigger than Mount Everest, bigger than the entire volcano of Hawaii.

As the snowplow drove away, I ran over and ascended, grabbing and clawing my way to the top. My feet slipped, my gloves wouldn't dig, and I fell three times, my cheeks smacking against the cold chunks of ice and snow. When I finally reached the top, when I finally made it to the very highest point, I sat down, unbuttoned my jacket, and sucked gallons of cold air into my hot lungs.

From here I could see the tips of the pine trees in my front yard, the crusted shell of Collegiate Shopping Mall, the roof of Jonathon's house, the ventilation ducts of the nursing home, the frozen torsos of the Rocky Mountains, Dairy Queen, Double Donuts, Happy Mountain Chinese restaurant, Wrangler Liquors, Kate's Boutique, Bill's Gun and Pawn, Mile-High Fried Chicken, Simply Suds Cleaners, Big Todd's Auto, and the hole in the fence that was the back entrance to the gulch.

And after fifteen minutes, I descended back to the JCPenney parking lot, feeling perfectly at peace.

✗

On the way to the gulch, I stopped at Double Donuts and bought a bag of donut holes for a quarter. They had left the donut holes near the ovens so they were still warm. I ate most of them in seconds flat, but saved three for later.

When I crawled under the fence overlooking the gulch, taking extra-special care not to get snow in my donut bag, I emerged to see more people in the gulch than I had ever seen in my entire life. The hill next to the tunnel was covered in kids. Paco and dozens of Mexicans were sledding on pieces of cardboard, their jeans frozen solid. Lawrence Bimburger, Jeffrey Logales, and Roberto Tavares all had plastic discs that shot them out over the frozen pond and right to the edge of the waterfall. Saula Sobinski was sitting by Geronimo's pile of recyclables making a small snow castle. Michelle Beard and Scott Rogers were traveling a million miles an hour on a toboggan. David was carrying my Radio Flyer to the top of the hill, his jeans frozen white-blue pillars that stayed stiff with his every step. The two Rottweilers were still in Geronimo's tin house, lying on their bellies and calmly watching all the activity.

I trudged over to Tina Turner's Tabletop, sat down on the rusted bulldozer, and finished my three remaining donut holes. I counted forty kids, all different colors and shapes, screaming at different pitches, cheering in different HOOOSSS! or

YA-HAAAAASSS!, throwing snowballs at different heights, shaking snow out of their jackets in different ways, laughing by either snorting, cackling, shuddering, screeching, bellowing, or snickering. From this height, even the Mexicans looked different. The Mexican girls had different hair lengths, different snow boots, and different-colored earmuffs. Some sledded on their cardboard pieces on their bellies, others on their knees, and others on their sides. Some wore thick down jackets, while others wore only jean jackets and shivered whenever they stood still.

David and Paco were both sitting on my Radio Flyer. One of the Mexican girls raised her hand in the air like a gun, and made a fake firing sound. David and Paco began to dig feverishly into the snow, and the sled picked up speed.

"Hey," Jonathon said, suddenly appearing next to me.

He was alone, and judging from the redness in his cheeks, he had been outside for a while.

"Hey," I said. Then I looked around. "Where's Jesse?"

"I don't know. He didn't come."

We sat there for a minute, watching everyone without saying anything.

"I'm sorry about today," he said, finally. "You're like my best friend. You don't want to fight. Some things you just can't change. You don't want to fight. Okay."

He stood.

"Where're you going?"

"This doesn't feel like my gulch anymore."

"Why? Because of the Mexicans?"

He smiled, nodding out over the gulch. Following his eyes, I noticed, at the top of the other side of the hill, a group of Mexicans huddled around something.

"I gotta go."

"What is that?"

"You're my brother," Jonathon said, reaching out and giving me a quick hug. "I'll see you."

As Jonathon headed toward the torn fence, panic, fear, and sadness surged through me.

"What is that?"

There were so many Mexicans now, all gathering around. More and more. Gravitating.

"Jonathon!"

The crowd of Mexicans became bigger and bigger and angrier. I couldn't control my panic.

"Jonathon!"

I leaped from the bulldozer and ran as fast as I could from Tina Turner's Tabletop, across the gulch, past Geronimo's recyclables, past the Rottweilers, past Scott Rogers, Michelle Beard, Jeffrey Logales, Lawrence Bimburger, Roberto Tavares.

My legs were lead, my muscles lava, my lungs too small for all the oxygen I needed. The sleds had packed the snow, making it slippery. I kept falling.

When I finally made it to the top of the hill, I shoved my way through the Mexicans, and found what they were all looking at. It was Jonathon's three-foot-tall stuffed Elmer Fudd, with the cardboard sign still hanging on a string around its neck.

SHHHH. I'M HUNTING MEXICANS.

I grabbed the Elmer Fudd.

A few of the Mexicans shouted.

I turned and ran and ran.

"Shhhh, I'm hunting Mexicans."

I headed straight for the tunnel. The cardboard sign kept hitting me. Elmer Fudd's legs dragged through the snow.

As I got closer to the tunnel I fell, and Elmer Fudd rolled away. I pushed myself to my feet, grabbed his hand, and kept running. But my feet wouldn't hold. I fell again and rolled right into the waterfall.

I sputtered and kicked my way back onto the ground. I should have left Elmer Fudd there. I should have gotten back to my feet and run and . . .

But there were two Mexicans, a boy and a girl, both about Paco's age, making out right at the entrance of the tunnel, only a few feet from where Elmer Fudd now lay. Their lips were sealed together, their tight jeans interlocked.

I grabbed Elmer Fudd's hand and ran into the tunnel. I could hear the sizzling and popping. But still I ran. I ran as far as I could from the Mexican couple that I had never seen, never met, never talked to.

And the farther I got into the tunnel, the darker it became. Darker and darker until I was just running into nothing.

"*Phezzz-zit,*" Elmer Fudd said. "*Zzzzz-pop!*"

I threw Elmer Fudd as hard as I could, and since it was so dark, I couldn't tell how far he went. There was no sound of him hitting the ground.

"*Shhhh, I'm hunting Mexicans.*"

"*Zzzzz-pop-pop-pop.*"

I turned and tried to double-back as fast as I could.

But it was too late.

"*ZZZZZZZZZHHHHBBBAAAA!*"

The glass cracked, the nails came spinning in millions of different directions; Elmer Fudd became a fireball.

Behind me was the flame and in front of me the light. I was caught between the two.

I saw my father. On his knees.

And then I was knocked down as Armageddon came screaming past.

And in the End

✗

When Revelations was read to me, I was sure that the end of the world would be full of lava and winged horsemen.

"Damn it, Samuel. Listen to me. Listen to your mother. Hold on to my voice."

But it is nothing like that.

"They won't let me put a Kit Kat in your feeding tube."

People do not need to be saved.

"I have a new quarter for you."

People are already saved.

"I wouldn't go with him, Samuel. I didn't go with him. I knew what Jonathon was doing. It wasn't me. Not this time. Forgive me. God, please forgive me. I should have stopped him. . . . "

Came the Beginning

✕

Please. Please," he whispers. "If you can hear me, please don't let this happen to my son. My one and only son."

Do not worry, I think.

"Please. God. Please."

Don't cry, I think.

"Anything. I will do anything. I promise. And I will never leave again. If you bring my son back to me just this once. If you can hear me. I will never leave. I will never . . ."

I open my eyes to a new light. One so refreshing and pure, I begin to choke. My skin is bandaged and it is difficult to breath. At the same time I can feel every inch of my body.

"Samuel!" he screams. He screams and screams. "Samuel!" Then he takes my hand, gripping it so hard it hurts.

Someone takes my other hand and I am being squeezed from both sides.

"*I say to you, whoever does not receive the kingdom of God like a child shall not enter it.*"

"I am here," I say.

"I am here," my mother says.

"I am here," my father says.

Acknowledgments

✕

Thanks to everyone at St. Martin's and especially my wonderful editor, Regina Scarpa, who never lost sight of the real Samuel. To Sara Crowe, one of the most perceptive and supportive agents a writer could ask for. To David Sharp for proofreading and then proofreading again and one more time for good measure. To my teachers: Matt Spampinato, Harry Schankar, Barb Caruso, Rex Burns, Frederic Tuten, Brian Kiteley, Mark Mirsky, Tom Jenks, and many, many others who took the time to guide me in one direction or another. To all my friends who slogged through sloppy, unedited drafts, thank you and I'm sorry. Loving thanks to my father, Carl, for a lifetime of encouragement, affection, and hundreds of other little things that comprise future novels as well as short stories. To Sunny for her sincere devotion and graciousness. To my aunt

Dolores, who shares, among many things, the sadness of a life lost early. And finally, to the two most important people in my life, Ellen and Kes, who've helped me understand what a family is all about.